The Flame Keeper

Healer Series Book Five

Sharilyn Skye

This book is a work of fiction. Names, characters, places, and incidents are the product of the author's imagination. Any resemblance to actual events or persons living or dead is coincidental.

Dark Horse Publishing

Morgantown, WV

Chapter 1

"Wait, Lara, stop," Grania said from behind me. "Where are you flying off to?"

"Aedan. Aedan is down there." I barely registered her interruption, nearly sliding down the hill.

"Okay, I'm not going to ask if you're sure because you look sure, but stop." She grabbed my arm, jerking me around to face her.

I glared at her arm. She dropped it. She was bound to me now, vampire to human, slave to master. The fact that I wasn't completely human was irrelevant.

"Sorry." She had the common sense to look contrite. "Look, you can't just waltz down there and rescue him."

"And why not?" Now that we were so close, I felt like that was exactly what I could do. Aedan was the Governor of the Eastern Region of Vampires, my neighbor, and my something else. I loved him. I think. It was complicated.

He had been abducted by unknown persons, and since then, all hell had broken loose. A lot of lives had been lost, and I was sick of shouldering the burden.

The locket filled with downy, almost blonde baby hair that had been given to me by a Goddess, and had helped me to find him, was driving me mad to get to him. I wanted this over.

I was a nurse, scratch that, a Faerie Healer, and I needed to get back to my own life and my own problems. Fighting to hold his place in polite vampire society was not one of them. Needing to find him had nothing to do with the fact I missed him and kind of, maybe, loved him, either. Nothing at all.

Right.

One of the burdens I inherited in Aedan's absence stood in front of me, six feet of pale blonde hair and ice-blue eyes, trying to glare at me and failing. Since I had saved her from madness in the absence of her Master and death at the hand of Mikolosi, Aedan's former second in command by binding her with my blood, she had a hard time glaring at me. She was my best friend, my sparring partner, and my magical coach.

I missed her, too. I missed everything about my life from a week ago, and I can't believe that I actually felt that way.

I was hoping that Aedan would just take her back or whatever they do, and things could return to normal. I needed a vacation. Spring in South Carolina was gorgeous, and I had a shiny new beach house to go hang out in. I didn't need this.

"How many men are down there? Are they armed? What's the layout? What is the most likely place to find Aedan?" she asked, dragging me back to my current reality.

Oh yeah, she was also Aedan's security adviser.

"Um." That was all I could manage.

"Exactly. Let's sit down and think about this a minute."

We sat. Being her current boss didn't make me smarter.

"First, we should take the SUV. It'll allow us a faster getaway and a more plausible excuse for being there. If there are guards posted, we'll say we took a wrong turn or something. On foot, we'll just look guilty. Also, if, um, when we find Aedan, he may be too weak to walk all the way back here."

"Makes sense. Okay, go on."

"Second, what if we do find him?" She lifted her eyes to mine, holding them in question.

"What do you mean?" I zeroed in on her, giving her my focus.

"What's your plan? Have I mentioned that he's likely to be highly pissed off and not at all himself? He's also liable to be hungry. Very hungry."

"You've mentioned it about a hundred times. I told you before, I'll take care of that." And I would. I would figure out a way.

"But, he may not," she started.

"Look, I hear what you're saying," I interrupted. "I know he might not be all that happy, but I'm sure he'll feel better with a little added intravenous fluid in him."

"But…"

"No buts. I don't want to hear about it. Look, I know it might be bad. I get that. I also get that there isn't a choice and that I have to do it anyway. I'll deal with it, whatever it is." I rubbed my temples, allowing my eyes to close in frustration.

She stared at me a moment before shutting her mouth and shaking her head.

"Well, you're not going alone."

"Well, You're not going with me."

"Yes," she countered, doing a better job glaring. "I am. You know I can't disobey a direct order, but you have to consider you might need help. I'll stay back, or something. When, I mean, if things get hairy, you can call for me, and I'll help. What if there are a dozen humans and you get caught. Come on, think about this."

She had a point, but I had a better one.

"How do you think he'll react to finding you there? You keep trying to tell me how unstable he might be. How do you think he'll react to you not being his anymore? Don't you think he might need a minute before he has to deal with that?" From the look on her face, I knew I had made a point.

"Look. I know, okay. I know that it's going to be bad. I know that it's going to be dangerous, and I know that I have to be careful. I do. I also know that you have to stay here for all the reasons that you listed. I can…handle Aedan if I have to. I can handle whatever is down there if I have to. I've got this, and it isn't like I think you don't; I just think that it will be safer with you here. For both of us. Maybe even for Aedan, too. If he comes after you, then I'm going to have to try to fight him. It puts us all in a bad spot. You need to trust me." I forced myself to be calm and to focus. I wanted to just walk away from her, but I couldn't; she would follow right behind me. I needed her to see it my way.

"Things have changed," she whispered. "What happened to you in Talamh na Sithe?"

"Nothing happened," I lied. I wasn't telling anyone that story anytime soon. I didn't think it was in my best interest to reveal that a Goddess had taught me Goddess magic.

Probably best to keep that little tidbit to myself. It was bad enough as it was. "I went to learn how to rescue Aedan, and I learned. I'm going to go do that, whatever that means. Okay?"

"I guess it has to be." She touched my arm, then let her hand fall.

"Look, this will be good for us." I gripped her by her upper arms. "You and Aedan were too close, and it cost you. I'm going to go down there alone. I won't be long, and if I need you, I will call you through our bond. If you need me, you will call me. It will be okay, and we will both grow from this." I tried to reassure her. She needed to learn to be alone, even if it was just for a little while.

"Okay." She watched my face carefully. "Okay."

It was the last thing she said before I turned and continued to make my way down the hill to the farm beyond. I could have taken the SUV, but I thought I could be stealthier on foot. It's hard to sneak up on such a remote location when driving a big vehicle.

At the bottom of the hill was a line of short, fat pine trees. A river curved, running slowly. Muddy brown water glistened in the growing dark. It was not between the farm and me, more like it ran adjacent to the property, and its snakelike curves allowed for a clear path through. Beyond that was an old overgrown animal pasture with a broken fence surrounding it. I picked my way along the edge of the fence, using the darkness and fence posts for cover.

I remembered my dream about Aedan. We had talked in a white room while I held his hand. He told me that he was dying and that if I wanted to find him, I would need to dig deep. I had to believe that dream to be real, that somehow our subconscious had met in a dream state. I mean, I had spent the night on the moon with my mom when I thought I was dying too, so why not? Digging deep could mean a lot of things, actually digging, as in a hole, or digging within myself for strength, which I had done. I had strength in spades right now.

I paused behind a pine to survey the layout. A large, old farmhouse lay to my left. It looked like it had been added to numerous times until it was a sprawling mess. Paint chipped off the sides, and dim lights on the first floor leaked through old window panes. There was an equipment shed of some type to the right of the house that contained several newer model cars.

To the left of the house were several small outbuildings. No lights burned in any of the other structures. I watched for several minutes, trying to see if some guards or dogs might be a problem. I saw nothing. I edged along the field until I came to the first outbuilding. It looked like an old chicken coop. My VDS didn't react to it, and neither did the locket. After a quick peek inside that revealed only old boxes and trash, I moved on. I came to the next shed and found that it, too, was shoved full of junk and old furniture.

I froze where I was when a screen door slammed, and I heard voices on the porch of the farmhouse.

"I don't know why you are so twitchy, John. There ain't nobody out there. The sour smell of cigarette smoke floated through the night air.

"I'm twitchy because the Boss said there is a strike team coming this way."

"Man, there ain't no fucking strike team. That's just political bullshit. Ain't nobody knows where the old guy is. Nobody that's telling anyway, you need to relax, finish your smoke, go fuck your lady, or whatever it will take. Your bein' antsy ain't helping nobody."

"I just think there is something wrong tonight. Something doesn't feel right. We should just go cut that fucker's head off and be done with it."

"The boss says he's got another night's worth of blood in him. We'll be back home and in our own beds this time tomorrow, John. Now come back inside and stop worrying. We'll finish with dinner and then finish with him. I'll do your turn tonight. That old bastard isn't strong enough to fight even one of us. You stay here with your old lady. That'll make you feel better. I'll go and finish this shit up."

"I sure hope you're right; I'm done with all of this."

Chapter 2

The voices faded away, and the screen door slammed shut again. I leaned against the shed, trying to catch my breath. We were out of time; I had to find Aedan fast. Find him before their dinner was over, and they finished whatever it was they were doing to him, and it had to be Aedan they were talking about. No way it was anyone else.

Taking advantage of the fact that they were busy, I rushed through the next two outbuildings and found nothing. Behind the house, I checked out a spring house and a dilapidated greenhouse filled with nothing but weeds. I had almost made a complete circle around the house, and the only other building I could see was the equipment shed. I didn't want to check there yet, because it would bring me in view of the kitchen, and I didn't want to be seen unless it was a last resort. I stood, looking again. The structures were laid out in a basic circle if you counted the old pasture as a structure.

The house was in the center, and everything else was spread out at regular intervals around it. I had to be missing something. I looked again from building to building and noticed a place in the layout that was devoid of a structure. The other outbuildings formed almost a perfect ring with the exception of that blank area between me and the only other place I hadn't searched.

With nothing to cover my movements, I crouched low as to stay out of the sightline of the windows and half crawled, half walked to the empty section. At first, I didn't see anything at all. I felt like I was still missing something, and the locket around my neck was letting me know I was warmer, my VDS kicked in with a gentle hum, and I knew I was close. I moved in small circles and expanded out until I came across a well-worn path. The path was fresh. Tread marks went both to and from the house. I walked beside the path and away from the house.

I came to a set of doors built into the ground. It looked like an old tornado shelter, but in this region was probably just a root cellar. The doors were new steel, and the hardware on them was heavy duty. They were held closed by a thick logging chain and a large padlock. I had to dig deep. Maybe he didn't mean actually dig, just that he was underground. You can't expect dream conversations to be exact, right?

I heard the screen door bang shut again and knew they were coming. The blood in my veins turned to ice, and my stomach sank to my feet. Reaching down, I grabbed the lock in my hand and focused on the metal- it was of the earth. Everything is, in some way. I unmade it with a thought, just like the Goddess taught me. It came so easily, like breathing or my next heartbeat. With strength I didn't know I had, I flung the doors open and peered down into the dark. I couldn't see anything.

The moon was bright at my back, casting deep shadows inside the depths of the cellar. I started down the stairs. The pit smelled of death, decomposition, and long-dead earth. I thought then that I was too late.

I felt the person rushing up behind me. I could smell metal, oil, and gunpowder in the air. I drew the sword from behind my back and turned to face him. I don't know what I said or did, if anything. I was so sick and tired of being alone and in control of stuff that I had no business controlling. I tell myself that the sword did it. That the sword took over and cut that man in half. I say it wasn't me because I don't want to be a killer. Yet there I stood, hot blood running in rivulets down my face and a glowing sword in my hand while that man's body slid in two pieces to the ground. Something else to mourn, I guess. Another piece of myself lost.

A sense of urgency spurred me on. Whoever else was in that house would come soon. I turned back to the darkness of the cellar and saw movement. Just a hint of something near the far wall. I could see, now that the sword was drawn, I could see…something hanging from chains driven through a thick beam in the cellar's ceiling. I rushed down the stairs, dropping the sword.

What was left of Aedan hung naked, all wrong angles and sharp edges. I could not make out exact parts of him but knew with absolute certainty that it was indeed he that hung there. I looked for a way to cut him down, but the roof was eight or nine feet above me, and his feet were off the ground.

I scrambled around the room, looking for something to climb on. Boxes and boxes lined the walls. When I pulled one out, whatever was inside clinked and tinkled daintily. I pulled the top back and found hundreds, no, thousands of tiny vials filled with black liquid. Aedan's blood sang through my veins, and I knew. The vials were blood. Aedan's blood. All of the blood that should have been in his body. His blood and mine. Our bond. I twitched, turning from them.

Anger and frustration took me back to the hanging man, and I knelt growling low, using dirt from the ground and magic to weave a set of steps up to him. I ran my hands over his body, looking for a way to set him free.

"Aedan, oh my God, oh my God, Aedan. It's okay. Shit. It's going to be okay. Let's get you out of here. Holy smokes. Holy hell. It's okay. Goddess, help me." I didn't know what to say, so I just kept talking in a low sing-song voice, my southern accent deeper than I had heard it in many, many years. A sign of true distress, if ever there was one.

At the top of the set of stairs I made, my breast was even with his head, and I could look down on him. His hair hung lank and limp from his scalp; he did not raise his head. I thought, for a moment, that he was dead, but I could feel him. He was in there; I just needed to get him down. Reaching up, I grasped the chains in my hands, and a sharp pain went through me. Cold Iron. It had to be. I could feel my magic leaching away.

"Oh, no, oh no, no, you don't." I quickly wove gloves around my hands to protect myself and turned the chains to dust. Aedan dropped like a stone and sat hunched on the ground. He did not move. He was so still. Nothing about him moved. His hair fell around his… I guess it had to be his neck, but it looked like a bony spine. White vertebrae shone through the leather skin of his neck. He stayed there, and I felt him waiting.

I had only seen one other in this position, and I did not like it. Rushing back down the steps, I reached for him, and then he was gone. Just gone. No words, no nothing, just gone.

I sat on the steps and cried. I cried and sobbed and said a whole lot of bad words. Then in a rage, I got up and grabbed the sword. I smashed every box, every vial, everything in that room to dust. Then, using Grania's witch magic, I set it all on fire and calmly walked away, tear stains drying in the blood on my face.

I came to the first body, not twenty feet beyond the one I had laid at the cellar entrance, his dead eyes staring at the moon. His neck was ripped open and drained dry. He looked like a mummy lying there, a husk, and nothing more. The other bodies were dropped where they stood on the porch, a pistol in the hand of one and a rifle in the hands of the other. A woman lay in the doorway, wearing only a tee-shirt, her bare legs still in the house. All of them drained. I could feel him now. He was close, but moving away quickly, not towards the little inn, as I had feared, but away from the place and shadowing the interstate eastward. I sagged in my skin and let him go.

I dragged myself up the hill to get Grania. We needed to clean up the mess at the farm. I knew that. I could call her down here, I knew that too, but I needed a cup of coffee first. You can't bury bodies and destroy evidence when you are low on caffeine. The room had one of those little two cup jobs that hotels think is big enough, and right now, it would have to be.

Grania hadn't bothered locking the door; I guess she didn't think it would help had Aedan came this way looking for her. I shut it behind me and leaned against it.

"He's gone," I said, shaking my head.

"What? Like, gone dead? Gone, how?" Grania rushed from the bathroom, her face was wet and her hair in a ponytail. She looked me over for injuries and, finding none, visibly relaxed.

"Not dead, just gone. There are five dead people down there; I don't recognize any of them. I need your help getting it cleaned up." I moved from the door and went over to the little coffee pot. All I wanted was a shower and a cup of coffee. I didn't have time for the shower, but I stood a few minutes, waiting for the coffee to brew, then took it and Grania and walked down the hill.

Chapter 3

Grania whistled low when we came to the bodies on the porch. "Aedan doesn't usually kill like this. He hasn't for a long time, but better them than you, I guess." She slowly scanned the mess Aedan left in his wake, eyes taking in everything.

"He didn't stop to talk or anything. He was…wrong when I got him down." My stomach clenched tight as I stared at the bodies laid out in the pale light of a full moon. It had risen high above the trees already. It hadn't taken me long to free Aedan, maybe an hour and a half total time. It wasn't even midnight. It was going to be a cold night up in the West Virginia mountains. Frost was forming like tiny snowflakes on the surface of the grass. We needed to get moving before the ground froze altogether.

"He's super pissed." She continued to stare at the bodies for longer than was necessary.

"I mean, I guess I would be too, but the last thing we need is five bodies that so obviously look like they have been attacked by a vampire. Well, four, one of them was the sword's fault."

"Um, what?" she asked; I admitted nothing.

We dragged the bodies together in a sad pile, starting with the ones on the porch and ending with the one by the entrance to the root cellar.

When Grania saw that one, she gave me some serious side eye but said nothing. The inside of the cellar had been burned clean. The metal roof and iron beam remained, along with the chains, but the fire had burned so hot that there were no remnants of the boxes or glass vials of blood. I ignored what was left of the chains, and we touched nothing but the bodies. The fire had scrubbed the place clean.

Tossing the guns on top of them, we rested when the last man was piled with the others.

"Now what?" I pushed my hair out of my face, wishing I had a bottle of water. A shower, some jeans, another bottle of water, and a pot of coffee. My list was growing.

"Well, we can't burn them. Fire doesn't destroy everything and will char the ground. We can't take them with us because, ew gross, and getting pulled over the way you drive is too real a risk." She cocked her head at the pile of destruction.

I punched her on the arm and waited for her to finish. "We need to bury them, but deep and we don't have the time or tools to do it by hand. I say we use magic." She nodded her head once in punctuation. That was her final answer.

"I'm in," I agreed, wanting this over. "You lead."

She knelt on the ground, placing her hands on the frozen grass. She didn't say anything, no chants or spells like she often did. She just stayed with her hands in constant contact with the earth, her face breaking into a sheen of sweat. I walked opposite her, having some idea what she was doing; even before I could get settled, the ground began to churn. I added my power to hers, and together we asked the earth to open and accept those bodies deep into the heart of it.

The ground shifted. Slowly, the pile of bodies and weapons disappeared. The ground churned for a long time after the last body slid under the surface. Finally, the earth stilled. It looked undisturbed. Frosted grass glistened in the moonlight, and there was no sign that anything had ever lain there. I pushed power down into the earth, thanking her for helping us, she took, and I gave until power began to come back up through my hands. In my mind's eye, I could see the bodies. They were so deep, deeper than any machine or human would ever look. I broke the connection when balance was achieved.

Grania stood, staring down at me, and I knew my skin was glowing. I could feel it. Taking deep breaths and rolling my shoulders, I stood, pushing that little bit of extra power back into the earth through my feet. My skin faded to its normal glimmer.

"So, what about the cars?" I asked, looking over at them.

She blinked, staring at me just a beat too long before scouring her surroundings, then following my gaze to where they were parked in the equipment shed.

"Let's leave them. The less we do, the better. Any evidence of a vampire attack has been removed. Whatever blood stains or DNA that remains is not ours, and you took care of Aedan's, let's keep it simple. Without bodies, they have only a mystery. One we know will never be solved. Even if there are others involved in what happened here, they will keep their mouths shut. Now that Aedan is free, the shit will hit the fan for them anyway. Once it comes out that he is alive, I imagine there will be lots of flights booked. Not that it will help them. He will never let this go."

"I just wonder what they wanted with all of his blood," I said more to myself than anything.

"What?" Grania asked. I hadn't taken the time to fill her in, but I did now. I told her about what I found in the cellar, leaving out how I freed him.

"That's troubling," she said when I was done. "There are tons of applications for blood like his. No wonder he was pissed. Once the dust settles, we need to look into it."

"Yeah, wait until Aedan gets home and sees his house. I'm kind of glad he took off. Let Alisondro fill him in, so we don't have to. Talk about pissed."

"Then, there's me."

"Then there's you," I followed. "Now that he's free and I'm off the hook, I'm thinking about taking a week or so off." I laughed; it came out of nowhere and felt so good. I couldn't remember the last time I had laughed. I let it wind itself down. "We'll deal with it. It will all be okay. I believe that."

"I applaud your enthusiasm." She cracked a smile herself, her shoulders visibly relaxing.

We left the farm and walked back up the hill. I was glad for the cold night and the frozen ground. We wouldn't leave any tracks in the dirt, and as the night grew, the frost would cover our footprints on the grass. I finally felt the chill; I hadn't worn a coat or been cold until after it was over. I started shaking as we rounded the top of the hill and couldn't stop. I shook so hard my teeth rattled.

Grania opened the door to our little room, and I started stripping before she closed it behind me. Away from me, the dress I made from my aura and intent to wear to the Spring Conclave of vampires what seemed like months ago faded until it was gone. Huh, I hadn't counted on that.

Grania stopped, staring. She had been doing that a lot lately, and I couldn't blame her. I would stare too. As she said, things had changed, but for all she knew, Aramea had made that dress. I let it go, calling out for her to round up some coffee while I cleaned up.

Turning the water on sear-all-thought-from-your-mind-hot, I stepped in, allowing the fog from the heat to carry me away. The great thing about hotels is that they have an amazing capacity for hot water. I washed everything, conditioned my hair, and stood with hot water pelting me, never cooling. I gave up before it did, my fingers pruned and stiff. The smell of coffee coming from the other room pulled me from the shower, even though the water was still hot.

Grania waited on the edge of the bed. A carafe of hot coffee sat on the dresser. She had the TV on, watching something. I didn't even know what day of the week it was, let alone what was on TV anymore. Funny that. When I worked as a full-time nurse, I never knew what day it was either. I guess some things had changed and some things hadn't.

I poured a cup of coffee then went back into the bathroom to get dressed. I wanted to put on my pajamas and go to sleep, but I would rather sleep in my own bed, so I kept moving.

Cleaning up the farm had taken several hours; it would be a tight run to make it home before dawn. I felt better as I dressed in jeans and a soft long-sleeved tee shirt. The magic washing out of my hair made me feel more like myself; it hung damp and curled at my waist. I would get it cut soon, I promised. I couldn't remember the last time I had eaten. I guess it was right before we left Westminster, but that was over a day ago. I needed to do better at taking care of myself.

Finishing the coffee and pouring more, I sank on the bed beside my best friend.

"You think you can make it if we leave now? I'll drive. The windows are tinted, and we brought a blanket. I just want to get home."

"Yeah, that's fine. We shouldn't stay anyway. If someone comes to the farm to check on things, we need to not be here. I'm just worried you will be too tired." She smiled over at me, patting my knee.

"Nah, I'm good. This coffee you stole from the lobby will get me there."

She laughed, rising to gather her things. "How did you know?"

"I'm like Sherlock Holmes," I answered, getting up and gathering my bags.

We pulled out of the hotel at about three-thirty in the morning. We wouldn't make it back before dawn, but I didn't care. I felt like a weight had been lifted from my shoulders. Even though I worried about Aedan, and I worried a lot, he was free, and I could breathe again. At least for the moment.

I stopped at a McDonald's off of I-68 to grab a Big Mac. I didn't know how starved I was until I smelled it. I ordered two. I ate them and drank a large sweet tea while Grania leaned back in the passenger seat beside me.

I had once heard a story from the Neonatal Intensive Care Unit about a baby that had severe symptoms of drug withdraw, but the mom swore up and down that she did not do any type of drugs. Her drug tests were all negative, and the stumped NICU attending had finally traced the root of the kid's addiction back to McDonald's sweet tea. There is a ton of sugar and caffeine in it, which was fine by me. Maybe it wasn't suitable for growing babies, but for full-grown Fae? Amazing.

My driving wasn't an issue this time because what I hadn't known was that eastern West Virginia is considered a bedroom community of both Baltimore and The District. Traffic slowed to a crawl by six, and it took me over four hours to drive home, not including the stop. We pulled in the drive at a little after eight. I opened the garage door and parked the Envoy inside. Grania was out in the backseat, and there she could stay.

Inside, the air was crisp, and the lights were off. The house felt empty, and a quick search revealed that it was. Paul and the others were safely in South Carolina, and Aedan was, well, not there, although I could tell he had been. I could smell the faint scent of him in my bedroom. The clothes I had bought for him were missing from my closet, and there was a wet towel hanging on my towel rack. It smelled like him. I held it to my nose and breathed him in, glorifying in the smell of blood, honey, and fall leaves. At least his scent had recovered. I was hoping the man would too. In time, I knew he would come around. A lot had happened.

He probably needed a minute.

I could understand that. I needed one, too.

In the kitchen, the plate filled with eggs, pancakes, and sausage stopped me short. Steam rose off everything, and a hot cup of coffee sat beside the plate. I walked through the house again, checking the basement as well, and found nothing. I shoved the food in my face anyway. It hadn't killed me yet. After filling my belly to bursting, I closed the door to my bedroom and slept well for the first time since I left Faerie, and the Goddess had let me nap by her lake.

Chapter 4

I awoke six hours later, rested and feeling good. Grania still slept in the garage, and I let her be. A lunch of lasagna and green beans waited for me on the table when I came back in from the garage. I hadn't heard a thing, no noise to indicate anything had moved inside. I needed to find the thing feeding me. Now that I had nothing else to do, that was my top priority. I shoved lasagna in my face and swallowed it practically whole. It was amazing. If I could find the pan, I was eating it.

I looked in the fridge and found a small pan. I piled it on my plate and heated it, calling Paul while I waited. He didn't answer. I left him a message telling him that we had found Aedan and set him free, but advising him that he might want to stay gone for a bit because his boss was pretty cranky. My phone did not ring, and I got no texts. I let it go.

He would need some time to digest what had happened to him. He had no phone, no house, no clothes other than what he had taken from my closet, and no people waiting for him upon his return. It might take a few days to get that together and maybe a few more to gather his thoughts.

I needed some time too. I had been in charge of his outfit for about a week, and it was too much. Way too much. How he had done it for as long as he had, I didn't know. I needed to sit in my house, ride my horses and drool a little. I needed to be me again.

When the lasagna was gone, I got up and began the methodical search of my home. Somewhere was a person or persons providing me with fantastic and magically appearing meals. I crept around unafraid, calling for him to show himself and feeling like an idiot for doing it. I was in the clinic when I found him. He was making his home in a little cubby under my stairs, despite the presence of empty bedrooms.

"Och, Lassie, sorry if Ah frightened ye. Ah was tryin' tae bay oot a yer way," he said when I caught him coming from the small door there.

"Um…what?" I am nothing, if not multilingual.

"Och, Aye. Ah am Aedan's cook, and I dinnae want to tae lae ye ta starve ta death." His Scottish accent was so thick I could only make out about every other word. I think he was trying to keep me from starving, but then again, he could have been poisoning me with excellent lasagna, I wasn't sure and didn't care. The food was to die for.

"His what?" I asked.

"His Cook. Cook. Ah am tha cook." He spoke very slowly, moving his mouth in uncomfortable ways to get the words out right.

"Oh. Why didn't you leave with the rest of the humans? It isn't safe here right now."

"Dinnae fash yerself aboot'at lass, Ah coodnae lae ye hare by yerself. Ya need me. Ya cannae be runnin' awe th' time an' nae carin' fur yerself. Yoo'll starve."

"Um. Ok…uh, Thanks?"

"Di'na thenk me, jist keep tha fridge fool er lae me yer mooney card and Ah'll keep ye fat. Yer ancestry demands it! Ye needs tae be fat when yer runnin' fra th' vampires."

And with that, he closed the door to under my stairs and left me standing there, mouth open and staring. He wasn't a vampire; I was sure of that. He didn't register as anything other than human. He was maybe five feet tall with brown hair and brown eyes that twinkled merrily when he spoke. I knocked on the door, but he didn't answer.

"Uh, you know there are lots of empty rooms, right?"

"Ah ken lass." His echoed voice sounded like he came from much further away than from under my stairs.

Okay then. I shook my head and went back upstairs. I went to my room and brought out several one hundred-dollar bills, laying them on the counter. He was an employee of Aedan's and not being paid right now, so if he was going to feed me, I was going to pay him. Problem solved. It was nice that it had been so simple. Finding the mystery food source was the easiest thing I had done in weeks.

I piddled around the house, putting laundry in the washer and watering plants before I went out to see to the horses. In the barn, all was well. I cleaned stalls and shut them in for the night. Galahad said nothing, just eyed me over his hay. Maybe he only talked when he needed to say something. Maybe tomorrow I would ride. Maybe tomorrow Aedan would call. My heart sank a little. I missed him.

Inside, Grania sat in the kitchen, sipping hot coffee, her hair wet from the shower.

"Did you know a man is living under my stairs in the clinic?" I asked, moving to pour myself another cup.

"The Cook?"

"So, you did know," I laughed.

"Well, not really, but I figured he was around here somewhere. Food always shows up when he is around.

He's an odd bird." She buried her nose in her cup, inhaling deeply.

"What's his story?"

"Oh, no. No, you don't. No stories." She shook her head violently back and forth, causing her white-blonde hair to sway.

We both laughed at that. She was right, too. His story was probably just as tragic and painful as the rest of ours. I would enjoy his coffee and his food until Aedan took him back. I would not ask his story. I would not. See, I can learn.

Aedan did not come that night, and I worried more and more. There were a lot of things he could be mad about. I wanted a chance to explain myself before he went from mad to done. I had done things I thought were right at the moment but probably weren't and made decisions that were not mine to make. I knew there would be consequences for my actions. I was okay with that. I just wanted to have a chance to help make it right. I had no way to know what was going on in his mind, though. Our bond was as broken as it had been the night I had almost died. None of my blood remained in his veins.

I went to bed early, asking Grania if she needed to feed before I went. She declined. I would have done it had she needed it, but I did not want to. She stayed up doing whatever they do in the wee hours of the night. She didn't seem to mind our separation, and for that, I was glad. I was going to find a way to make her more independent. Make her learn to be alone. Baby steps. She should have been fine when Aedan disappeared. At her age, there was no reason for her to be joined at the hip to him or me. She needed to grow up a little, and while I had access to her, I was going to help make that happen. Operation Best Friend was underway.

I awoke to find that Paul, Alisondro, Jason, Carter, Domingo, and Aisha, had returned. I didn't get out of bed until after dawn, but Paul was in the kitchen eating off a platter of…well, everything. I mean everything. The cash was gone, and in its place was food. Piles of it. I grabbed a plate and filled it twice, drinking enough coffee to drown a giant elephant. We sat in pensive silence.

"Aedan called me." He soaked up the last bit of egg with a biscuit, refusing to meet my eyes.

My heart sank. I had told myself his lack of communication with me was because he didn't have a phone. "He asked us to come back but to leave the rest at your beach house." He kept looking at his empty plate like it would tell him what to say next. "He just told us to come here. He knew about the fire. He asked a lot of questions I couldn't answer," he finished, still not moving to look at me.

"Where is he?" I got up, placing both our dishes in the dishwasher, and covered what was left on the platter before placing it in the fridge. I tried to sound casual and probably failed.

"Downtown," was all he said. "Something is wrong with him." He looked at me then, his brow creased with unease.

"I don't doubt it. Did he say anything else?"

"He said he would be around when he 'gets the answers he is seeking.' He was very formal."

"Isn't he always?" I asked with a half chuckle.

"Maybe. I've been around a while; he was off. Way off."

"I'm sure he just needs time."

"I hope that's all it is, Lara. I really do." He looked at me a moment longer, then got up and walked away.

It was early, probably the earliest I had been up in a while. Morning sun shone through the windows, lending cheer to the house that I didn't feel. I went to the living room and turned on the TV.

Aedan's face filled the screen.

"So, the fire at your House, can you tell me about it?"

I couldn't hear anything else, my vision narrowed, and all I could see or hear was him. Aedan was doing an interview on a station out of D.C. He looked good, healthy even. Maybe there was a sharpness to his face that hadn't been there before, a definite thinness to the angle of his suit. Or maybe I was reading too much into it. His eyes were a few shades paler than their standard aged whiskey color, and all of his usual media flirtation was missing. He did not laugh and joke with the reporter this time. He had cut his hair. All of it. It was styled in a fade, a little longer on the top, almost shaved on the sides. He looked like a military General, aged and stern. His hair made the features on his face stand out and gave him even more of a presence than usual. I liked it.

Goddess, but he was beautiful. My breath caught in my throat, and my heart sped up. I tried to listen to what he was saying, but all I could see was his face. Nothing else mattered. My stomach flipped. I had overeaten; I should have stopped after the second plate. I felt like I was going to vomit and tasted the sour rise of it in the back of my throat.

I kept changing the channel until I found a national network that had picked up the entire interview. I listened to every word and watched every nuance, trying to guess what he was feeling.

"So, obviously, the rumors of your death are untrue." The reporter leaned into Aedan, lowering her voice in seriousness.

"Obviously." He sat still as a stone; nothing about him moved. I had not seen him act so much like what he was on such a public stage.

"What happened, Governor?" she asked, catching his more somber mood. She had interviewed him before, back when they first came out. She would notice the difference in his demeanor.

"I am not completely sure of everything that has happened. I know this; I was unavoidably detained out of town," he added at her apparent confusion. "I was unavailable by phone or email. I left suddenly. My representative made a statement in my absence, but that did not quell the rumors or the disturbance that spread through the community. The behavior of my People during this time is most vexing and will be dealt with." The way he said it sent goosebumps up my arms, and I'm guessing the reporter had a similar reaction, judging by her face.

"Do you care to explain that remark?" she asked.

"I care that my house was burned down in what was assuredly an act of arson and that nothing has been done to find the individuals responsible. I care that my representative was so browbeaten by my supposed colleagues that she had to not only defend my House and herself at the Spring Conclave but also had to go to great lengths to secure the safety of the city and the stability of the community beyond. I care that she did this largely unaided and grossly overpowered when she should not have had to. I care that my People did not stand with my House in my absence and instead chose to attempt to usurp my position."

"You sound angry." She leaned back, steepling her fingers. Her face grave.

"Of course, I am angry. We came out of the shadows to forge legitimate bonds with the local community, and there are those that threatened this legitimacy. This cannot be allowed to stand. There are bills in both houses of Congress that seek to limit our rights, this type of behavior can be used as fuel against us. It will be dealt with."

"In what manner?" she asked, trying too hard to look relaxed.

"In the way that is ours, alone. There are no facilities that hold our criminals. They are dealt with permanently, and that is all I will say. We have lived among you since the beginning of time and were barely rumored to exist. Our laws and traditions are why this was possible. We will continue to live by those laws, and the laws put forward when we came out of the shadows."

"I see. What is your argument for not limiting vampire rights, and doesn't this incident prove they should be limited?"

"In actuality, it proves the opposite. If vampire rights are limited, there are those that will return to the shadows and not uphold the laws they have been sworn to. The current way of governing them would become more difficult. The cat, as they say, is out of the bag.

"All People in power have such issues. Members of Congress are on the television fighting daily with this one or that one. Many individuals who run for political office fail, and many succeed; few have the same exact idea of how the government should run. If our president chooses to shut down the government, he can, and those workers suffer for it. This is no different.

"There are factions within our community that do not agree with the laws put forth for us and are sowing seeds of discord. It is no different than human political groups. However, if the laws we live by as a People have been broken, then those persons must be dealt with. I have a plan to address this dissonance among us.

"My plan is to centralize and strengthen my position and to deal with those who would prefer to bring back the old ways. I will continue to move forward. My People will continue to move forward. It is the only way left to us now." His eyes bled just a fraction paler. I doubted the average person would notice, but I did. His control was slipping.

"You sound convinced that you are the best leader for the vampires," she asked.

"Yes, and this incident proved it. In my absence, conditions deteriorated. I not only need to remain their leader, but I also need to strengthen my role. I have existing relationships with those in leadership around the globe, human and otherwise. I have worked to strengthen the rights of supernaturals, and I will continue to do so."

"Can you comment about the night of the Spring Meeting? There was a big commotion, and there are a lot of stories circulating about what happened. We have video since you weren't there." She cut Aedan a quick glance, seeing if her comment had struck center mass. It had.

Aedan stilled in a way that he seldom does in front of humans. The video began to play behind them on the screen. My insides rolled so hard I thought I was going to vomit. Aedan turned to watch.

Someone had been in the hallway after the fight. The footage was grainy. Shot from a cell phone camera, most likely, using no lighting. It was footage of me from the back. If you didn't know who I was, you might not be able to place a name with the face. To anyone that knew me, it would be obvious.

I was surrounded by moving darkness. It bumped and swirled like a dark and slow-moving river. I knew it was the cats, and I thanked the Goddess that you could not see them in the footage. The last bit of dark fuzzy shape reached out to me and rubbed my legs. I could see the outline of Noah's giant head against the gray of my dress; it would look to most watching like a deep shadow. Human brains were just not programmed to see this. They would see a shadow and nothing more, but I saw Noah. So, would any other Supernatural seeing this. He bumped my legs, and his fangs flashed white when he had nipped at my fingers. I turned, leaning down to him, and the pale of my profile lit up on the video for just an instant before the camera lost it. I placed a kiss on the cat's nose. The darkness purred low and wild, an unmistakable purr of a cat.

This was huge. Not that anyone would recognize what Noah was. Maybe. Me, though, oh yeah. I would be recognizable. I released the breath I hadn't known I was holding. Trying to process what this might mean.

Aedan's face had stilled, and his eyes bled a shade paler still.

"I am not sure what you are asking me to comment on. That is footage of my representative leaving the meeting room." He leaned back into his seat, relaxing his muscles visibly.

"What is she doing, and what was in that darkness? What kind of creature is that?"

"As I was not there, I cannot say what she is doing, and I see nothing but a shadow. There is no way to see if anything was in the darkness. My representative appeared to have dropped something in her rush to leave. The footage is without any detail." He dismissed it with a wave of his hand, regaining his composure. Most would not have noticed that he lost it at all.

"Who is she? Who was your representative that night?" Her eyes narrowed as she closed in on what she desperately wanted to know.

"Ah, now that is personal business. Not all of my associates enjoy being associated with me." He barked a short but real laugh that took the reporter off guard, causing her head to turn sharply to him.

"I see, Governor. Are you going to rebuild in Westminster or here in the District?" she asked.

"First, I am going to clean up the mess my absence has created, and then I will address the issue of rebuilding. Thank you, that is all the time I have now." He smiled at her, but it didn't reach his eyes.

The interview cut to commercial, and I sat thinking hard. He was masterful. He always was, but I guessed that this interview was more about his 'People' and less about anything else. He was firing a warning shot to them.

I did not doubt that many of those folks out there were worried about it. I wondered about Mikolosi. He deserved what he got. I also wondered about myself. What would this video mean to me? Aedan had called me an associate. He played it off the best he could, but there could still be trouble.

I hadn't meant anything when I kissed Noah, but there are others out there who might not see it that way. I didn't think Aedan would care, but what about all those others? Politics. I hated it. I flipped channels and listened to the speculation about the video for a while.

Some news anchors agreed with Aedan about the darkness being nothing, and others did not. All of them speculated about my identity. I figured it was only a matter of time until they found me out. I would need to come up with a story. I hoped Aedan was back by then so he could help. He could spin a damn good tale.

Chapter 5

My house was quiet all day, no one came to the clinic, and no one called. It felt like the eerie, yellow calm before a hurricane. Having grown up in a hurricane-prone area, I recognized it for what it was. I called and left Noah a message, even though I'm sure he was aware of what was going on. He didn't call me back.

My cell ringing jarred me from a deep nap I hadn't known I needed. I answered with a grunt because that's all I had at the moment.

"You keep very interesting company, Hennessey," Agent Johnson said, all bright and chipper as if being awake wasn't her enemy.

"I've been hearing that a lot lately," I mumbled, pulling myself up into a sitting position.

"Sheriff Collins," she said, the excited edge in her voice waking me up finally.

"What about him?"

"Definitely Ben Devers the dead guy. Also definitely related to a long string of trouble that goes way way back. I looked into that group of folks and those names you gave me. Devers, the not-so-dead guy, is related on his father's side and his mother's side to two very influential Watchers that go back to the original founders of this country. They took very different paths, though. On mom's, side you have Thomas Jefferson, who, according to a source helping me with this, was true to the original manifesto of the group in that they watched and recorded but didn't get involved. Now on dad's side, well, that's a whole other story. One of Devers's great grandfathers, maybe with another great in there, was a man named Samuel Parris. Now Samuel is an interesting fella. A Puritan minister who basically fueled the Salem Witch Trials from the pulpit. He had, not only a cousin but also his own daughter burned at the stake for witchcraft," she stopped, taking a breath.

"Now, none of these girls were actually witches. History is clear on that. Documents suggest that Parris fueled these trials to get rid of girls and women from rival families as he tried to increase his influence in Salem. He is a well-documented member of the Brotherhood of Watchers, but his line is obviously a big fan of not only getting involved, but of twisting the truth to meet their own ends. Very intriguing research, Hennessey, very intriguing indeed. Turns out Collins is on many government watch lists. His radicalism is becoming well known and is one of the reasons he never stays in one place long. Currently, he is off the grid. No one seems to know where."

"Well, that helps. It does. It also explains an awful lot," I said, getting up to grab a cup of coffee. "Let me know if he turns up, though."

"I will, and good job on getting your vampire home. Nice tale he spun on TV. I'm glad that all worked out and sorry I couldn't jump in and help more, but that situation was complicated for the bureau in a lot of ways. I do have one more thing, though. That farm you texted me about, the one where you found Aedan, has been in the Devers family since the first families moved into West Virginia and staked their claims on the land there. I'll let you know if I find anything else." She hung up without another word.

Aedan had been taken by Aiyana to that farm, he was certain of that, and she basically admitted it. Seeing as how there is no such thing as a coincidence, that meant she was working with Collins or, more likely, he was working for her.

Why would a vampire team up with a Watcher, especially an extremist like him? Maybe it was a case of the enemy of my enemy is my friend, who can say. We would need to keep sharp, though. With all the Fae coming into the area, there could be more problems now from a man like Collins.

I left a note then went out for a few hours to pick up horse feed and run the few errands I needed to before returning home. I pulled into the drive not long before dark. The others were up and watching reruns of Aedan's interview. They said nothing as I walked in. Dinner was laid in the kitchen, and I ate in silence. Grania joined me, waiting for me to finish.

"I talked to him today," she said as I pushed my plate away.

"It seems everyone has. Well, except me. I'm starting to get a complex. What's going on with him?" I asked, my heart sinking.

"He just wanted to check on you. And me. He's not mad. He's...messed up. He's worried that he doesn't have it together enough to see you. He's so pissed at how everything went down. I mean, not at what you did," she added when I locked my eyes to hers. "I mean, he's mad that it wasn't me or Mik or someone else who came to get him. He's mad Mik didn't try to foster me and that he walked away from his responsibilities. He thinks we have involved you too much in our issues and that it should've been one of us. He's all over the place. He's riding the edge of control, not out of it, but not in it either." She leaned against the wall, arms crossed.

"Is he mad about, um, you? And me?" I asked.

"No." She started crying then. She hugged herself and rocked back and forth. "No," she said with finality, sniffling and trying to control her sobs. "He said," she stopped, catching her breath. "He said he loved me and that I was his daughter in the only ways that mattered and always would be. He said any father would want his child to be safe, Lara. He is grateful because he thought he would come home to find me gone. He cried. He cried into the phone and then hung up without saying anything else. He won't take my calls now.

"I'm such an ass. All those things I said and did after you bound me, I am so sorry. Goddess, I am a dolt. I didn't even know the man could cry." Tears pooled in her eyes, threatening to fall. I never thought she could cry either. Not after everything she had been through.

I smiled at her, reaching to put my hand on her knee. "It's okay, Grania. I get it. I do. Your situation is not ideal, and that's why we are going to fix it. Maybe I didn't do the right thing, but I didn't do the wrong thing either. I believe that. I'm glad you're here and that we are still together. It's all going to be okay." I offered her a smile, her eyes brightened, and she returned it.

"What do you mean we are going to fix it?" she asked.

"Don't worry about that. Now I have this list of things for you to do tonight if you don't mind. I'd like to send you and Paul out for some stuff. It's very important, I added at her quick look. I need to get some more sleep; I've been pushing it and need to catch up." I smiled inwardly. I would send Grania all over hell and half of Baltimore. She could return the Suburban and get a few things I wanted from downtown.

It would keep her busy. She would be away from me, and she would be doing something positive. I didn't need a damn thing, but I would make her a list anyway. Then I would make her another. She would be okay. The list would focus her, I had asked her to do it, and Paul would bring her back if she started getting twitchy. Baby steps. I would stretch her bond so often that she wouldn't notice when it was cut.

With Paul and Grania gone, I went in search of the others only to find they had left, too. All three vehicles were missing from the driveway. I tried Noah again, and upon getting no answer, I decided to do as I said I was going to and get some sleep.

I heard them come in, laughing and trying to shush each other. My door creaked open, and I could feel Grania peek in before moving on down the hall to where Paul was staying. I rolled over and went back to sleep, enjoying the feeling of having the bed to myself. I dreamed nothing.

I awoke at dawn and went to shower and get ready. I hadn't been up at this time since I was working as a nurse at the hospital up the road. It was nice and weird at the same time, like going from a crowded club into the quiet of your car. The silence was deafening. The locket with the baby hair that the Goddess had given me to find him hung on the necklace tree on my vanity. I took it, opening it up and touching the soft hair within.

I wondered what was keeping him away. If what he said was true, and he wasn't mad about Grania, and he wasn't mad about the other stuff, then why wasn't he here with me? I didn't understand. I turned the shower on the ninth level of hell hot and plunged in, trying not to think about it.

Chapter 6

The clinic was busy. After a light breakfast and an entire French press full of coffee that Mr. Cook had set out, I found myself in the basement looking to tidy up and organize when my first client rolled in. Jenny, Paul's sister and Jess's wife, was pregnant with her sixth baby. She was starting to show at only about ten weeks along. She was also complaining of morning sickness that lasted morning, noon, evening, midnight, and morning again.

In typical fashion for these people, she was not seeing a doctor. She said she was taking prenatal vitamins and had easy deliveries and didn't need to see a damn doctor. We argued, and as usual, I lost, also as usual. I started an IV on her and gave her some fluid and Zofran from the stash of drugs I had on hand.

I placed my hands on her belly and looked into it with my eyes that see and found everything looked as it probably should. She was having a boy, at least it felt to me that way. It's kinda hard to tell at this particular stage of alien life formation, but I got the feeling in my gut and trusted it. Another boy. Making her current total to four boys and two girls. While they had switched from man defense to zone many babies ago, I still shuddered. Four boys running around might be the end of poor Jess. I didn't think I could do anything else for her, and the medicine seemed to work, so I stopped worrying about it. She lay on one of my chaise lounges, nibbling saltines while I sat at my desk and ate her payment to me. Chocolate pie.

I had a fork and the pie and watched steaming Vevo on my new TV. The clinic had gotten an upgrade after three vampires, and one shapeshifter destroyed it the night Daniel had attacked me. I lived. All's well that ends well, I guess. I leaned back, enjoying the silence of the house.

The silence didn't last. By noon I had seen four patients, nothing big, just general stuff. I called in a few prescriptions and did one small healing using my magic. By four, I treated a total of ten. It was my busiest day ever. I didn't know half of the people I saw, but they knew me or of me and had ties to the community.

I tried to do very little magic on the people I did not know. I used traditional medicine as much as I could. When I needed more, I tried to sneak it in on them. Like, oh, here's a bite of cheese with some magic healing inside. Eat this, and you'll feel better. I would need to talk to Domingo, Aedan's high-priced vampire lawyer, and see about getting some kind of confidentiality form made up. The video made me nervous, and the nervousness made me paranoid. I charged money for the services I provided, trying to keep things official, except for Jenny. Pie was the only thing I would ever accept from her.

I was getting ready to go outside and see to the horses when loud crashing and screams came from the silence upstairs. Before I could even stand, I had a face full of six-foot tall, white-blonde-haired, very freaked out vampire.

"I'm bleeding," Grania yelled and jumped from foot to foot in complete terror. I spun her around, running my hands over her looking for her injuries. I couldn't find anything.

"What happened? I heard the noise. Did you fall? Where are you hurt?" I asked, using my calm voice to try and bring her anxiety down a notch.

"I. Am. Bleeding," she said, eyes rounded in terror, fixing on my face.

"Grania, calm down. I don't see anything; maybe it's already healed." I grabbed her shoulders and willed her to calm down.

"I am bleeding. From Down There."

"From where?" Then it hit me. "Oh, my God. You are bleeding from your vagina?"

"Yes. Something is wrong." Her eyes paled in abject terror. If mine could pale, they would have too. Instead, I'm sure they were impossibly wide.

I pulled her to my little bed, and we sat down together.

"Grania. Have you ever had a period before?" I calmed myself as much as I could. She could feel me through our bond; I didn't want to scare her more.

A Period? What are you asking?" She took a big deep breath, trying to focus.

"Menstruation. Your monthly cycle. Your phase of the moon or whatever they called it a thousand years ago. Aunt Flow? That thing I buy tampons for that you heckle me about?" I stared at her, concerned.

"I do not get a Period." She used air quotes around the word. "I am a vampire," she finished weakly. "You must look at me. I woke up this morning with fluid and blood coming out of me. It is everywhere. Paul's bed is ruined.

"Where is Paul?" I asked, already knowing the answer.

"He went to the store; he said he would be right back." I just bet he did. Chicken shit. I just hoped he picked up a box of tampons or something while he was there.

"Ok, come on." Pulling her up and into the bathroom, I made her sit on the toilet pants down. She peed. I almost fainted; my peripheral vision became gray. She began to freak out, again, the truth of what was going on hitting her. "Wipe," I ordered.

She wiped and stood; we turned to look at the toilet. It was stained with dark red clots and bits of black tissue. We stared at it way longer than anyone should ever stare at something like that.

We stumbled back into the clinic, sitting side by side on the bed.

"So." I couldn't think of anything better to say. Having never had kids or been an actual pediatric nurse, this discussion was going to be an epic failure.

"So." She replied. "Are you sure that is what this is? Shouldn't you, like, look or something?" she begged. At that moment, I knew she would rather be bleeding to death from some other horrible thing than getting her period. I was almost hoping the same thing. I laid my head on her shoulder and placed my hand on her muscular flat belly. I looked into her uterus. I had never tried this before and didn't know what I was looking at on a vampire, but everything looked, uh, normal? Nothing felt or looked sick that I could see. I moved my hand.

"You never had a period, ever?" I asked.

"I, uh. No. I don't think so. I think that is something one remembers."

"Usually, yes." I refused to think about what that meant.

Aedan and Grania had made peace with their past. It was not up to me to dredge it up. Plus, the age of first periods had lowered over the centuries. I would go with that. I sighed, placing my head in my hands.

"What does this mean?" she whispered, looking at me for answers I didn't have.

"I don't know. I really don't." I put my head in my hands and scrubbed my face hard.

"I'm scared," she said, turning to me. Her hands fidgeted, twisting on each other.

"Me too. I mean. Have you, you know, peed or anything since the, uh, thing happened?" Cold sweat dripped down my back. There were ramifications to her answer that I didn't want to think about. Not today. Not tomorrow. Not ever.

"No. Vampires do not pee. Or poop. Or anything. The liquids we take in nourish us and are utilized completely. There is no waste. They plump our skin, our cells, our hair, our nails, everything. They provide nourishment. We can cry and occasionally sweat them out, but that is all. Our bodies are not living," she explained, sounding calmer.

"I don't believe that. You are living. It's just different." And I believed that. I did. Vampires were not animated corpses. I've had one vampire under my hands, and I felt his heartbeat. He was definitely a living creature. Of some sort anyway.

"I mean okay, whatever, but I peed."

"Yeah, you did."

"I have to pee again. This is horrible." She got up, laughing, and went back into the bathroom. You got any, um, lady stuff in here?" I heard drawers opening and closing. "Aha! Got it." There was a lot of swearing and knocking around, muffled curses and complaints before she finally emerged, pale and triumphant.

"What does this mean?" she asked again.

"I honestly don't know; come lay down." She did as she was told. I put her on one of my exam tables and did a full nursing assessment, stethoscope, and all. Lungs clear, heart regular, positive bowel sounds. Wait, positive what? I listened again.

I didn't think that should be a thing.

"Are you hungry?" I asked with as much nonchalance as I could.

"I drank from Paul last night." She looked at me; her eyes had returned to their white-blue husky color.

"Ok, and that all went, you know, normal?"

"Well, duh." She said, sounding more like herself.

"Are you breathing on purpose? Heartbeat?" I asked.

She stilled. Holding her breath. She took a breath. She held her breath. She took a breath.

"I. I. I'm breathing."

Her eyes paled, and I could see her begin to panic again.

"No, no. It's okay," I lied. "You're probably just thinking about it. I'll ask Paul what happens at dawn. No big deal." I laid my hands on her, touching here and there. I used my power to see inside of her. I needed to know.

Her blood pumped through her veins, looking very little like Aedan's. It didn't look anything like mine either. I could see the vampire cells, or whatever they were, floating around in there, and I relaxed a shade. I had seen her blood before when I was healing Paul from the Vampire Infectious Disease Aedan had given him. It didn't look much different, but much is relative. I hadn't healed Grania completely. She was still a vampire. The question was, what kind?

Another question hit me hard and fast. If my blood had done this to Grania, what had it done to Aedan? If my blood had given Grania's magic back to her, had it done the same for him? Fear knifed through my heart. He never said, but that didn't mean anything. He played his cards close to the chest, and if I had given him back his magic, he might not want others to know. He was already powerful beyond any vampire and possibly any faerie in existence.

Maybe it wasn't my blood but was the binding instead. I couldn't know, but it gave me pause. Why wouldn't he have told me? So many questions. I put another brick back on the wall.

Sighing, I removed my hands from my hybrid bestie. They shook. I put them behind my back so she couldn't see.

"You are still a vampire. I honestly don't know what kind, though. I don't know. Your blood has changed from the last time I looked at it, but you're still you. I took a scalpel from its package and sliced her arm. She yelped, pulling it to her and glaring at me.

"No fair. No medical tools when fighting." She mean mugged me, brow knit together in a scowl.

"Move your hand." She took her hand off the cut. Relieved, we watched it heal together. She was not human, according to my healing sight. Quick healing was intact, blood lust present, vampiric reflexes, check. We would figure the rest out as we went.

Chapter 7

Grania went upstairs to wait for Paul, and I went to the barn to try and find my sanity. I seemed to have lost it somewhere. I spent time with the horses. I talked to Galahad, and he listened but kept his pie hole closed on the matter of Grania and everything else. Maybe he didn't know either. I just talked and talked while I brushed and fed them. Tomorrow I vowed to ride. I needed to get out and get back to normal. The weather was warmer and more like spring. Flowers were beginning to bloom, not from my magic, but from the magic of the ground they came from. Daffodils, lilies, and tulip heads peeped up, and the grass was greening. The trees had not yet begun to bud, but that was only weeks away. The weather was wild this time of year, snow one day and sun the next, but tomorrow was supposed to be warm, so I would take Galahad and ride.

As I walked back toward my house, I saw a woman standing at the edge of my backyard. She was dressed in a dull gray dress that came to just below her knees. Her hair was long, brown with natural highlights, and pulled back into a ponytail. I stilled where I stood. New people made me nervous. I had been attacked, beaten, munched on, and generally abused a bit too much lately to be open and trusting with strangers. I stopped and waited, watching her. She approached with slow movements, keeping her eyes on my face. She was cautious, as well. Not afraid but wary. I went to meet her.

"Healer," she said, bowing her head but keeping eye contact. She was a pretty woman of indeterminate age. Her eyes were mismatched, one green and one brown. I had a sinking suspicion she was from Talamh na Sithe. Not because she radiated power, she did not, but I could feel a low level of it thrumming off of her.

"My name is Lara. What can I do for you?" I watched her for sudden movements and dropped my shields enough to feel magical build-ups.

"I would like you to look at me," she said. Her accent was thick; English a language way down on the list of dialects she was fluent in. I hesitated just a moment.

I had let strangers into my clinic all day, but one quiet Faerie woman gave me pause. I had told Aramea that my clinic was open to all those that came to me. So, I tamped down my worry and walked her to the basement door.

"You healed our land," she said once we were inside. "It is growing again. One of my husbands saw you that day. He said you were with the Goddess and that you have great power. Our Queen does not want us to come to this place, but I felt that I must. I waited until I could learn your language; I could wait no more," she finished, facing me in the dim light of the clinic. I walked over to the wall and turned the lights up.

"You learned English in a few days?" I asked. I didn't know what else to say. Most of my mind was still processing that one statement.

"According to my husbands, time passes differently there." She stood still and patient in my clinic. Waiting. It didn't pass that much differently, I thought, knowing it would take me a lifetime to learn her language. I had taken French in both high school and college and could barely remember a word of it.

"Have a seat." I walked over to my desk, indicating the chair next to it, where I often talked to patients before working on them. I sat, waiting for her to continue. She looked up at the door leading out, took a deep breath, and moved to sit across from me. Maybe she was afraid. If her husband saw me, then that meant he was one of the warriors present when the Goddess and I had ridden back to Aramea.

That alone must have been a sight to see. Then after riding a ghost horse up to the furious Queen, I had knelt and pushed a crap ton of power into the land, cycling it through me to clean out the poison that the Goddess had allowed to fester. I can't even imagine what that had looked like. All Aramea's warrior dudes had dismounted and knelt to me. She had not been happy. I wonder what her displeasure looked like to them, too. Oh, wait. I had seen that. My Grandmother was often not happy with me, and Aedan's repairman had probably put a new wine cellar in his house with the money I paid him after those visits. Aramea was Queen of what was left of Faerie, or so I surmised based on the fact that everyone kept calling her 'Queen.'

"Aramea has forbidden you to come?" I asked, growing angry at the thought. I told her that I would help my People if they came to me. I wondered at her motivations in forbidding it.

"She has suggested strongly that we do not come," she answered, glancing again at the door.

"I don't care what my Grandmother says. I told her before, and I tell you now that you are welcome. I will not hurt you, and if I can help, I will," I said, looking her in the eye and willing her to believe me.

"You are different than I expected," she said, smiling for the first time. Her smile made her face stunning. Her mismatched eyes sparkled with it.

"I get that a lot. What can I do for you?" I smiled, too. Sometimes, smiles are contagious.

"My babies die in my womb."

The smile dropped from my face.

"Oh my," I said before I could stop myself. It was OB-GYN day at the Lara Hennessey BSN, RN, Faerie Healer, Clinic.

"How many pregnancies have you had?" I asked.

"Countless. I cannot say. I used to count, but I stopped."

"That many?"

"Yes."

"What happens, I hate to ask, but it's important." I lowered my voice in sympathy.

"I cannot carry them past the fourth month. My body expels them, and they do not survive," she said, looking down. "My husbands do not hold it against me. I have carried all their children, and none survive, so it must be my fault," she said, dropping her eyes.

"First of all, it's no one's fault. Not yours. Not theirs. No ones. Okay? Let's get that out of the way. Second, I know for a fact that there are very few Faerie children, if any, born anymore. Is your particular problem common?" The Goddess said that she had ruined the land and let the bodies of her People spoil. I wondered if this is what she meant.

"Some cannot conceive at all. Others cannot carry. There are no children born to us. I am among the last."

"Did you know my mother?" I asked. "Aramea said she was one of the last too," I said, hungry for information about her.

"I did. We are friends and contemporaries. Not in power but in time. Age, I believe, is the word." She smiled at me again.

"She gave her mother fits, as do you, I hear. I pray to the Goddess that you continue to do so. Aramea has not been a good or kind Queen, though of late, she has tried harder to be so. Your name is known to us. It is spoken like a secret on a dark night."

"I see. Well, I'm not anything special, but I will help you where I can." I didn't trust my Grandmother, and I trusted her less and less the more I found out about her.

"I have no American money, but I have jewels." She looked worried again. I didn't care about the money, not at all. I had enough so that I wouldn't need to worry, but I also didn't want to set a precedent with an entire population of people that I worked for free.

"I will trade my services if you tell me about my mother, any stories you have about her. Will that work?" I asked, watching her smile back at me.

"You have a deal," she said, grinning, and for the first time, I caught a glimpse of the girl she probably had been before she held so many lifeless babies. Her face was lovely with her mismatched eyes and large heart-shaped lips. She had downplayed her appearance, probably on purpose. She was gorgeous; I could see it when she smiled.

"Let me take a peek at you, and then we will talk." I led her to my exam table and waited for her to get comfortable. I doubt she had ever seen a doctor. Knowing others like them, they might not even have one. She probably muddled through as best she could.

Maybe they had some kind of healer among them, a midwife, or something along those lines. She looked pale and was probably anemic. If the land had not been well, likely, their food was not nutrient-rich. Maybe healing the land would take care of the other problems in time. I placed my hands on her belly and looked inside with my sight. The vision of her popped into my head immediately. As many times as it happened, it still took me by surprise.

Her uterus was a scarred mess, and she had abnormal growths burrowed in the lining of it. Her cervix was misshapen and also bore the evidence of too many deliveries. I thought about what needed fixing, what a healthy uterus should look like, and tried to make hers look the same. Her ovaries were healthy, and her Fallopian tubes were open, so that was something. Grania mentioned that Faeries were fertile throughout their lifespan as long as the Goddess 'blessed' them.

Pregnancy was often seen in ancient times as a blessing from the Gods. Being unable to become pregnant was viewed as the opposite, either caused by the devil or because the Gods didn't favor you. In reality, there are so many reasons a woman can't conceive, and most of them are fixable with modern medical care.

It didn't take much effort. Heat spread through my hands, and I heard her sharp intake of breath beyond my closed eyes. She relaxed under my touch as my hands warmed her body. I tightened her uterus and removed the growths by simply unmaking them in my mind the way I had been taught by Aedan's mother, Dani, aka The Great Goddess Danu. Her cervix took a little work since it is a layered and complicated little sucker. In the end, I had her uterus looking as pristine as it once had been, possibly better. I couldn't guarantee she would become pregnant or carry a pregnancy to term if she did, but I gave her a better shot.

"All done," I said, pulling back from her, smiling at the look of wonder on her face. "I can't promise you a baby, but I can give you a better chance. Okay?"

"Okay? You. You. I felt what you did. I have no words. I know no words." She sat up, flipping her legs over the table, her eyes bright with unshed tears.

I walked to the shelf by my desk and scrounged up a bottle of vitamins.

"Take these. Take one every day. Please. It might help. There could be a lot of reasons for the, uh, amount of female problems y'all seem to have, and these might help with a few of those. At least until the land is fully recovered and new crops are grown." I felt my southern accent deepen, which was my tell that I was feeling something strongly. Or drunk.

I'm not sure what it was about this woman that moved me. She knew my mother, maybe. I don't know. Maybe it was her palpable joy at what I had done. I was moved, regardless of the reason.

"Your mother is fearless," she said, smiling at me through some memory. "Airmed, my friends call me Ari, my mother calls me Daughter, and you may call me nothing. That is how she introduced herself to us the first time. I think we were aged five or so, we don't measure the years in the way humans do, but she was a tiny thing. We all were in actuality, but she is the youngest of The Eight."

"The Eight?" I asked, my eyebrows knitting together.

"The last female children to be born to the land. As a group, we became known as The Eight. We lived and trained together until we were given to our chosen mates, my name is Keelin, and I am the oldest."

"You were given away?" My heart stuttered in my chest at the thought.

"Yes, four mates were chosen for us by The Queen, and we were given to them in hopes of having more children and keeping us from further decline," she said, looking defensive. "It has not been a bad life, not for most of us. Ravena's problems were solved, and only Ari ran from it, but she loves her mates. All of them. Looking at you and knowing what you are, I know why she left. Aramea would have taken you and twisted you or worse. She hates any threat to her power, and you are surely that. You share a piece of all your fathers. I can see them in you."

"That's not how it works, Keelin," I laughed. I had known my father. The only thing I shared with him was my feet and my nose; the rest was all mom.

"The Goddess weaves great magic; weaving four into one would not be a difficult task for her." Her eyes were bright as they looked me over. "You have Laith's hair and eyes, Lann's lips and cheekbones, Saige's cute nose and face shape, and Seal, well, Seal, I do not see so much, but I sense him in you. You are the perfect mix of all four of them. You look very little like your mother. Ari was smart to take you and run."

"My mother left Talamh na Sithe a long time ago; I'm only thirty-four," I whisper.

"Time passes differently; that is all I can say. I know what I see, Healer. One day they will love to meet you. They have missed Ari and Seal horribly and have not been happy since they left."

"My Grandmother said that she left because she fell in love with a part-human man and didn't want to share," I said, watching her face.

Tossing her head back, Keelin laughed. "That was their story, yes, but their friends know the truth even if they did not tell us. She loved them all. Yes, she left with Seal; I don't know why she chose him over one of the others except that he is possibly the deadliest of them all. Aramea is a harsh ruler, and she would have taken you. Ari would no longer have been useful to her once you were born, and what the Queen deems useless does not usually live long. She left to protect herself, her mates, and you. It was the only thing she could do. I see that now in one short meeting with you." She smiled sadly, touching my hair. "You are the last Fae child to be born, Lara. Imagine what your grandmother would have done to you over time." She rose to leave, and I rose with her, stunned.

Showing her to the door, I stopped, "Let me know how it goes, and please let the others know I am willing to see them. Thank you for telling me about my mom."

She smiled again, then turned and walked away.

I shut the door to the growing night and went to clean my exam table. On it lay a small black bag. It made a soft rolling sound when I picked it up. I turned the bag over, dumping the contents into my palm. Ten perfect diamonds stared back at me.

I knew diamonds. I liked diamonds. Unless there was some weird Faerie stone resembling them, I was looking at what was perfect three or four-carat stones; their color and clarity would be the envy of the finest jewelry stores on the planet. I ran out the door and into my backyard, trying to catch her. I yelled her name, but she was gone, leaving me with about a million dollars' worth of diamonds in my hand.

I stood stunned. Guilty. Maybe they weren't worth anything there; I had no way of knowing. I did know that I was going to ride my ass back to Faerie one of these days to give them back to her. In the meantime, to a safe deposit box, they would go. Suddenly tired, I shoved them in my pocket and went inside.

Chapter 8

I felt the buzz of my Vampire Detection Syndrome as I walked back to the house. It was nice feeling it again, I thought. Things had been too quiet and lonely without that low-level hum in my brain. It was kind of nice having Paul, Grania, and Alisondro around.

I walked into the living room from the garage to find Aedan, Domingo, Alisondro, and Jason sitting facing one another. I froze, taking him in. He looked bigger somehow. His six-foot-four-inch frame loomed over the others. He had his legs apart and elbows on his knees in that classic guy pose.

His head rested on his hands but flew up when I came through the door. God help me; I made it to him in three strides, planting myself on the floor in front of him so I could see his face. I placed my hands on his knees; his eyes were many shades too pale when they met mine.

"Aedan." His name came out hushed. "Oh, my God. Are you okay? Listen, I'm sorry. I'm sorry about everything. I know I probably screwed it all up, but please know I did try. Please don't be mad." I felt tears threaten and hated myself for it. His eyes snapped up to find Alisondro, who returned his stunned look, shrugging his shoulders.

"Leave us," he said. They left.

I waited for him to say something. Anything, but he just sat there, staring at me. I didn't know what to say either. Everything I thought about saying if I had the chance flew out the window and was replaced with white noise. I rose to sit next to him on the couch.

"Lara," he started, stopping at the sound of my name on his lips. He rarely used it. I was always one of his nicknames, never just Lara. It stopped me cold. "You. You were amazing. You did what no other offered to, what no other could. I am...humbled by you and in your debt. There is no anger. Only awe," he finished, still not looking at me. He hadn't looked at me since I sat next to him. He didn't sound all that awed.

"Then where have you been? Why haven't you called me? Texted? Something?" I shrugged, staring at the side of his face, quietly glorifying in the scent of blood, honey, and fall leaves. It was his signature scent, and it went to the core of me like a lightning bolt, tightening things down low. I wanted to touch him, but his body language shut me down.

"I am…struggling. I do not trust myself with you. I do not trust myself with anyone, but I need to get my People together. I have obtained rooms in the city. I need to be there. I need to straighten things out with them." Usually, Aedan spoke with confidence and eloquence. Tonight, his words were stunted and choppy. They didn't flow right. Paul was correct. Something was very wrong.

"You can stay here. You are all welcome," I whispered, keeping my eyes glued to him.

"And I thank you for that, but that is not possible right now. I need to regain control of the city's vampires; I cannot do that from here. I need to be at the heart of Baltimore and the District. Many things are happening very quickly. I am sorry." He looked at me for the first time. His face twisted with emotion I couldn't name, and judging by the look of it, I didn't want to feel either. A knife went through my heart at the sight of it.

After everything, and I do mean everything I had gone through to bring him back, this was not at all what I expected. I pulled my emotions in, tightening my control over them, and stiffened my spine.

"I see," I said, rising and walking away from him. I needed coffee, and I needed food.

In the kitchen, I found my new French press filled and steaming. The aroma of hazelnut seeped from the lid. I poured a cup, not missing the fact that Aedan had not followed me. I picked the steak off the top of the salad sitting on the counter before deciding I wasn't hungry anymore.

I turned to walk into my bedroom when Aedan appeared in front of me. He didn't walk in; he didn't slip in; he was just there. I could see him fighting himself. His eyes, usually the color of aged whiskey, were a pale shade of yellow, indicating that he was near the edge of his control. The lighter they bled, the closer he was to losing it. There were not many shades left in his color palate.

"My House was supposed to fight for you. To protect you," he growled in my ear, sending a chill down my spine. "They did not. Instead, you protected them and fought for them. You stood for me when no one else would. You believed in me, but even more, you kept them safe, against all odds and all challenges. You came for me when no one else offered to look. You saved me from my final death. You saved my daughter and made her better than she was before. You sacrificed yourself to the flames of a burning house to save those whose names you did not know. You did what you should never have had to. You walked into a meeting of the worst possible creatures, and you kept my House intact. You were chillingly efficient in dealing with them. I know because I saw the video. The REAL video from that night. A video that no one else will ever see, but I SAW you. You were Glorious. You were Terrible. You were Beautiful.

"I saw the crown you did not wear. You are a Queen. Your identity will come out because of that night, there is no doubt. It is just a matter of time, and none of this even begins to cover what must have happened in Talamh na Sithe, for I know you went there too. I have not heard that tale yet, or what troubles you faced there. You did everything for me, and I can do nothing in return." His anger was palpable. It mixed with power and rolled off him, so thick it was suffocating, making it difficult to breathe. I couldn't take my eyes off his, and he had held them in laser sharp focus with his own.

"Aedan, I don't want anything," I started, but he was gone. Not in the house, not in the yard, not driving away. Gone. I sank against the wall, and I cried. I let it all out. The pain, the frustration, the anger from the last week or so came flowing down my cheeks. I sat on the floor in my kitchen until I was completely cried out. Getting up, I stumbled into my room and fell into my bed, not even bothering to take off my clothes.

Chapter 9

The next morning, I rode. I took Galahad to Union Mills recreational area. I loved it there and knew the trails by heart. The terrain is rough and rocky; there are streams to cross and a small meadow to gallop in. I rode until sweat dripped off of him, and I was limp with content. It took many hours. He did not complain. In fact, he said nothing until we were crossing the last meadow that leads back to the trailer.

"I talked to Coi," he said, using Aedan's given name.

"Fucking everyone has talked to Aedan, Galahad, everyone but me." I huffed, sinking onto the horse.

"He is having a super hard time of it."

"I mean, I get that, but why stay away? Why not be around people who care about him?" I asked, swinging my legs and playing with the Guardian's mane.

"He is afraid he is going to lose control and start hurting people." He lowered his head and grabbed at a hunk of weeds, chewing. "Think about it," he continued, "he has been mister large and in charge and all of a sudden that was taken from him. He was tortured. They did things to him, and he couldn't stop them. He doesn't think you are safe with him," he finished, snatching at another weed as we walked back so he could cool off in the warm spring sun.

"Oh, for fuck's sake," I said.

"You are saying that word a lot," he complained.

"Because I am mad, Gally. I mean, God, he can talk to everyone else, but he can't come and talk to me for more than a second. We can't work this out together? I mean, what the Fu..."

"Don't say it," he interrupted. "There is a thing that soldiers get, what is it called? When they come back from a war, and they aren't quite right?"

"PTSD? Are you saying Aedan has Post Traumatic Stress Disorder?" I asked, incredulous at the idea that someone as old as Aedan could have that after only a week away, regardless of what had happened while he was gone.

"Think about it. He was taken from that field by someone powerful enough to neutralize him and move him to a place hours away. He is, by far, the most powerful creature, except maybe you, that this world has seen in a long time, but yet they took him anyway.

"Then they exploited his one weakness, found his kryptonite and made him powerless, and THEN they tortured him. Which if I were a head shrinker, then I would assume that brought up memories of his original situation all those years ago.

"Then he comes home, and everything is gone. Everything. He has lived for a long time with complete control over his life, and now that life is gone. Everything is a mess. On top of that, there is you. He loves you; he swore to Tuffy and then to me to protect you, but you flipped the script and saved his ass. He's kind of an old-fashioned dude, and he's having a hard time with everything that happened to you. He's pissed and afraid that he won't find his control again. Sounds like PTSD to me," he finished as he crested the hill to the parking lot.

"I mean, I guess. I get it. He needs time. That's fine," I said, but in the back of my mind, a plan was forming. A dangerous plan. I loved Aedan. I admitted it.

I wasn't going to let this come between us like we had my kidnapping what seemed like a hundred years ago. We both had taken a step back after that, and it cost us. He had pulled away, and I had run away. Literally. I went to South Carolina, slept with another man, bought a house, and everything. It almost ruined any chance we had of being together, and I wasn't going to let that happen again.

I wanted him. I wanted him more than anything I had ever wanted before in my life, and I wasn't going to take no for an answer. I got that he needed to get control of himself, and no one wanted a repeat of Aedan circa two thousand years ago. I wasn't going to let that happen.

My plan solidified.

"What are you thinking?" Galahad said as I jumped off, distracted now, putting the pieces together.

"Nothing. Nothing at all," I said.

"When a woman says nothing, it means everything."

"Don't worry about it, Galahad. I've got a plan."

He groaned while I threw a cooler over him. He loaded himself onto the trailer, and I shut and locked the door behind him. "Tell me what you are planning," He yelled at me.

"I've got this," I said, getting in the truck and shutting the door on the Guardian's curses. Turns out he can say the F word a lot too.

On the way home, I got a text from Aedan's number. He must have gotten a new phone. All it said was, 'I will see you soon, and we will talk more.' I didn't answer; I was planning and scheming. Aedan needed to find control, and I needed to lose it, needed to blow off some steam, and find a way to ease the hard pit of tension in my gut.

I wasn't the one who was supposed to have all the answers. I was the one who drank wine out of the bottle and got into trouble with my quick mouth and easy sarcasm. I did not have the tools to deal with these issues.

Not to mention sex. Oh, yes. Sex. Now, that was something I knew how to do. I was loaded, chambered, and ready to fire. I hadn't felt like this in a long time. My heartbeat ran ten beats above average these days; my breathing was always too fast. I needed an outlet. I was tense and coiled. The plan formed details. Oh, did the plan form details.

"I have a busy day planned; come at midnight. We need to talk." I texted Aedan back. "Why are you up at noon?"

"Tonight will not work; I am not yet ready to talk more about this," he answered immediately. "I have not been sleeping well," He added.

"It's Urgent, Aedan," I responded, using his name and his chivalry against him. I knew if I said it was urgent that he would come. He couldn't resist. He didn't answer until I was almost home, and then all he said was, "Okay."

I pulled the horse off the trailer, putting him away, and dropped the trailer by the barn. Then, I pulled off in my truck to go shopping.

I hit the liquor store down the road and picked up some wine for Aedan and vodka for me. We would work this out, drunk or sober; he wasn't leaving until we did.

I had hours before midnight, and I needed to set the stage, so I slipped down to Baltimore and into Emily's. Emily's is the hottest vamp clothier on the east coast and possibly the entire country. I had never been there but owned an outfit, or two Aedan bought me for one occasion or another. The place was amazing. It dripped with expensive taste and chandeliers. The decor was white and gold, and it smelled like money. I mean, it actually smelled like money.

When I walked in wearing dirty jeans, an old shirt, and cowgirl boots, the clerk was not amused, but the boots were clean on the bottom and didn't mar her white carpet.

I picked out a few outfits I stumbled across before I found the one thing I came for. When I handed the clerk my diamond card, she became very friendly. Whether it was the name on the card or the black diamond in the center, her helpfulness increased tenfold. She showed me a few accessories to add to the outfits I had picked before leading me to the back, where clothes were kept separated by color- as in House color.

Aedan's House had its own section filled with cute outfits, nothing dripping with sex appeal. All were black, gray, or white-based, with red as an accent, and most were reasonably conservative. None of them were solid red. Huh. No solid red. I snapped up several more outfits as the clerk eyed me sideways in speculation.

She took my card, and I had to practice looking bored at the total. After scrawling my name on the receipt, I climbed back in my big one-ton Chevy diesel and drove home.

Grania was awake and nearly frantic when I walked in the door. I had forgotten to leave a note.

"Where the hell have you been?" she asked, causing me to do the slow turn of death toward her. "I mean, I'm just asking; I was worried." She ducked her head and averted her eyes.

"I went to Emily's. Help me get the bags."

"You went to Emily's?" she squealed. "Without me? I've always wanted to take you there." Disappointment flitted across her face, making me feel bad.

"I'm sorry, G. It was spur of the moment. I needed some retail therapy. We'll go again. That place is smoking." I rearranged bags on my arms so that she could grab them.

"Hell, you already bought everything." She snatched a few out of my hands and stalked away from me to the bedroom. Operation Best Friend was going according to plan. She had been defiant and salty. Almost back to normal. I was going to fix her and us at the same time. It was going to be great. Then we could go to Emily's. As friends.

She sorted through my bags, pulling out each outfit, eyed it, then hung it up.

"I'm impressed; I didn't realize you had good taste in clothes. Did Jackie help you?" She smirked. I smacked her with a bag.

"I'm not sure. They were kind of snarky about the way I was dressed, but when she saw my credit card, she became more helpful." I laughed. Grania took in my outfit, and for the first time, she laughed too.

"I bet they were snarky," she chuckled. No one but you would dare to walk into that place dressed in dirty cowgirl chic. They should have known who you are based on that alone," she howled with laughter, dropping to the bed. "Your reputation precedes you on that front." She lay on her back and kicked her legs up, just like a typical teen. It was adorable, just like old times.

"Yeah, well. I didn't know." I cracked a grin at her, grabbing the last bag with tonight's outfit in it. I hung it up in the bathroom, where she couldn't see it. I didn't want her trying to talk me out of my plan or, worse yet, ratting me out to someone else.

"Where's Paul?" I asked.

"He ran out to pick up some laundry detergent and a few other things while I waited for you to get back.

"Okay, hey, I need you to run a few errands for me tonight. I'll give you a list." I turned away so she couldn't see the evil grin that crept across my face.

"Ugh, not another list. The other night took forever," she groaned, throwing her head back so that her blonde ponytail grazed her back. She popped her gum, her fangs flashing in the light.

"It's super important. I have some stuff I need you to put in my safe deposit box at the bank; I hate to leave it lying around, and the clinic is so busy I need to make sure to get enough sleep at night." There was a bank downtown that catered to vampires. They didn't open until eleven p.m., and I had been keeping human hours on purpose so that Grania would feel me in the house but not see me. I had also been sending her on errands to get her away from me with the ultimate goal of making her independent. I sent

Paul with her to keep watch, but phase three involved sending her out alone. He wouldn't live forever, and she needed to start living without a crutch. Tonight, though, I would have him take her to dinner then run my few errands.

"Ugh, okay," she said, popping her gum faster.

"Also, I want you and Paul to check out the new restaurant in Fell's Point and let me know if it's any good."

"You're telling me to go on a date? For you? What are you up to?" she said, eyes suddenly sharp.

"I'm not up to anything. Aedan is coming to talk tonight." I met her eyes, waiting for her to freak out.

"I don't think that's a good idea. I know you want to talk to him, but he's dangerous right now.

"Grania, he's always dangerous. It's just more obvious right now." I shoved my hands in my pockets and looked away from her before I sat on the other side of the bed.

She took a deep breath, holding it, then let it out.

"You can take care of yourself. Maybe you can help him. If he doesn't get it together soon, there will be problems. Now that he's back, the others have dropped their challenges, but if he appears to be unstable, they may reissue them. Maybe talking it through with you will help him," she finished, picking at my bedspread.

"I'm hopeful," I said, not letting on that I wasn't planning on talking to him at all.

My plan for Aedan was simple. I knew from the time we had spent together over the last few months that he presented himself to me as a gentleman. I knew what he was capable of, but I also knew just how meticulous he was at cultivating a specific image with me. I was also very aware of the image he presented to the world. Whether it is a conscious effort on his part or who he has become, I was banking that he would not want to show me the worst of himself. I was also banking on the fact that he had left the worst of himself behind a long time ago.

This feeling of being out of control was a blip in the normal for him. I was placing my faith, and possibly my safety, in that belief. Control is like a sword, the edge is fine and straight, and the tip is sharp and pointed. Both can cause cuts in different ways and different degrees. The only way to be in control of the sword is to have a firm grip on the handle; that is the safe side of the thing. I believed I had a firm grip on this problem, and I could help Aedan get off the sharp edge he was walking.

Also, in the time that we had known each other, I had tried to get him into bed. More than once. I had teased, begged, and tempted. I knew he wanted me. I could feel it through the bond we used to share and see it in the way his eyes paled when he looked at me. I was going to use all of this against him. I was going to push him, and by push him, I mean shove him hard. I was going to hit every trigger he had, and the gun would either go off, or the safety would engage. One or the other would happen, and honestly, I didn't care which way this went.

I wouldn't let him hurt me, but either way, I would get what I wanted tonight. I loved Aedan. He loved me. We had never shared this, but I knew it to be true. A Goddess had told me, and Goddess forbid I not listen. I had promised to bring her boy home, and tonight I was going to make that happen the only way I knew how. My way.

Chapter 10

Cook had placed a dinner of fried chicken, mashed potatoes, gravy, and green bean casserole on the counter in the kitchen. Grania and I sat in silence as I shoveled food down my throat by the forkful. She sipped from one of my new bottles of wine and watched me from the corner of her eyes.

"That looks good." I could hear her stomach growl; hell, people in the town over could probably hear it.

"Um, take a bite?" I said, arching my eyebrow at her.

"I can't eat." Her shoulders drooped, and she sipped from her bottle of wine.

"I hear your belly growling. I'm not so sure about that. I'm not sure about anything when it comes to you. What happens when you try?"

"I haven't tried in a long time, but it just comes right back up. It doesn't even sit in there. It's immediate."

"Take a bite," I said, curious. I had heard her bowel sounds when I listened to her belly with my stethoscope. I knew what that meant. I just needed to see it.

Grabbing a small spoon of mashed potatoes, she swallowed them tentatively and waited. Nothing happened. She took another bite. Nothing again.

Then it was game on.

That's how Paul found us, shoving food into our faces as fast as we could get it in there. He almost fainted, and his face paled to the point where the line between skin and lips was absent. He stood staring until we finished, not daring to interrupt. With a loud belch, I pulled away from the table filled with the joy of food and friendship.

It was apparent I had done something to her. I never heard Aedan's stomach growl or noticed that he was hungry, not like Grania. It had to be the way I bound her. I pushed a lot of my power into her as she fed off me that night. I had changed her. She was happy and healthy, so I refused to worry about what else might have happened. It was done.

I talked to Paul about the need for them to leave tonight, and he agreed. He worried but agreed. It was nice that they both trusted me to deal with it. That, or they knew something had to be done regardless. I shooed them away with a list and instructions on when to leave and what to do when they got back so that I could shower and take a nap. I had been up since seven, and if I was meeting Aedan at midnight, I would need some rest. I mixed a Grey Goose and lemonade, taking it into the shower with me. I undressed and turned the water on you-aren't-really-going-to-like-this-hot and dove in. I scrubbed, using all Aedan's brands of products in massive amounts. I washed, conditioned, shaved, and exfoliated with everything I had picked up during my stop between the liquor store and Emily's. I slipped a gauzy gown over my head and lay down, setting my alarm for eleven. I wouldn't need much time to get ready.

I awoke refreshed five hours later, thinking naps should always last so long, then went out to the garage and flipped the main breaker, causing the power to go out. Moving through the house, I placed and lit candles in every room. In the bedroom, I flipped open a book, turning it over on the bed, and arranged the pillows to look like I had been reading. In the bathroom, I lit more candles. They glimmered and reflected off the mirror, highlighting the wildness of my hair. It looked beautiful. It was curly from sleeping on it wet; the red highlights in the auburn glittered and shone. I carefully applied minimal makeup, light powder, and blush. I coated my lashes in mascara and used a matte nude color on my lips. It was perfect. Simple. Beautiful.

I went to the kitchen and opened my favorite bottle of wine, and took it and a glass into the bedroom, placing it by the bed on the nightstand. Back in the kitchen, I made myself another vodka and lemonade, downing it. I made another and took it back with me to the bathroom, where I slipped out of the nightgown and into a transparent silk robe the color of candlelight that I bought at Emily's. It shimmered in the glow of the candles, just as I knew it would.

My nipples were already hard under the translucent fabric, and my heartbeat sped up even more. I was nervous. Not that he would hurt me. I was just nervous and excited.

I sipped my drink and waited, letting the warmth of the vodka spread through me like a low fire burning. I didn't have to wait long. I felt the buzz of my Vampire Detection Syndrome build, and my heart sped up another epic notch.

"Lara? You have a power outage?" I heard his voice from the kitchen, hesitant and low. The poor man didn't know when he'd been set up. Darkness and candlelight were trigger number one. Electricity shot through me, and my heart pounded in my chest.

"Yeah, It's been out a while. Hopefully, it will be on before too much longer. I'm in here." I said, waiting in the bathroom. I heard him come in.

"I'll be right out; I just woke up. I was reading and fell asleep, sorry."

"I should not stay," he said. The growl in his voice was almost a question. "We can talk another time when things are better." I heard him sit on the edge of the bed anyway. The sound of him scenting the air deeply reached me through the closed door; I grinned to myself. Trigger number two, check.

"Do you remember what happened the last time we didn't talk? I don't want a repeat of that. Just give me a few minutes. I need to talk, even if you don't."

Justin had happened the last time he pushed me away; he wouldn't forget that. He wouldn't want a repeat of that either.

"Of course, I remember," he hissed. Trigger number three activated.

Opening the door, I saw him. He sat with his back to me, hunched over, his forehead rested in his hands. My breathing quickened, and my stomach tightened at the sight of him. He looked beaten; exhaustion rode the lines of his body. Walking to stand by him, I placed my hand on his shoulder, saying nothing. I waited for him to look up. Instead, he stood, moving to leave.

"I cannot talk tonight. I thought that I could, but I cannot," he said, still not seeing me.

"That's okay because I don't want to talk either, Aedan. Just you. Just me," I whispered, willing him to look at me. My words caught his attention, and he looked then. Holding his eyes, I took the robe and slipped it off my shoulders, letting it puddle at my feet, and stood naked before him. Trigger four. His eyes were lighter than I had ever seen them. He had gotten worse, not better, since coming home.

The gun went off with a bang.

One second, I was standing on my own two feet, and the next, I was pinned to the bed on my back, my knees spread wide apart and the hard length of him pressed against me through his clothes. He held my arms taut over my head; I didn't try to pull away. I just gave in and trusted him, relaxing against his body so that every line touched his.

Aedan's face was buried in my neck, but he did not bite. I turned my head, giving him access to it. He growled low, and every particle of him shook. The smooth side of his fangs pressed their entire length against the hollow of my throat, and I could feel him warring with himself. I waited, completely relaxed. No fear. None. I wanted this. Either way, I got it. The easy way or the hard way, I needed it. I arched against him, pushing him harder. His growl deepened.

"Anamcara." He stretched each syllable out, his voice low and dangerous. "You wicked, wicked, dangerous little Faerie."

"You should punish me," I whispered. My body shuddered against him, so full of need that even I could smell it. He stilled. His free hand roamed my naked skin in soft touches and gentle strokes, bringing me off the bed. I moaned in my throat, but still, he did not take me with his fangs.

He looked up at me then, his eyes the color of fine, aged whiskey. "You are masterful," he said, a slow grin spreading across his face.

"I don't know what you're talking about," I whispered so low he had to listen to hear and smiled back, meeting his eyes.

He released me and rose from the bed. My breath caught in my throat, and I almost cried out, thinking he was going to go, but instead, he stood and started taking off his clothes, his eyes never leaving my face. They roamed every line and angle of it, looking for any fear, any doubt, and finding none, he let his clothes fall to the ground.

I rolled onto my side to watch. He was exquisite. The lines of his body were harder than I remembered, more muscular. A thin line of hair went from his chest to the waistband of his pants. His muscles rippled when he moved, the candlelight catching their definition. He lowered his pants, and the hard length of him bounced back, hitting his stomach. He eased himself onto the bed, facing me. The length of his skin pressed to mine made my breathing come faster.

"You undo me," he said, wrapping his hands in my hair and brushing his lips with mine. "I did not need proof that God is female. I already knew this, but you have proven it to be true once again."

"Aedan." My voice came out cracked and filled with need.

"Silence, Liomsa. You will receive your punishment with grace." He wrapped me up and turned me onto my back, placing himself between my thighs, kissing me deep and hard but not out of control. His whiskey-colored eyes drank me in.

He softened the kiss, pulling away to nip down my chin. He did not use his fangs. In fact, the feel of them disappeared from his kiss as they retracted completely. He kissed down my neck and across my collarbone before taking one of my nipples into his mouth, rolling it with his tongue, causing me to whimper. I couldn't move, couldn't respond. I was flooded with desire, my heart hammering against its cage. He moved to the other nipple, and I sank my hands into his hair, trying to pull him back to my lips.

He had barely touched me, and I was ready to come. Goosebumps rose on my skin, and I shivered uncontrollably as he pulled at my other nipple. His fingers brushed the spot between my legs, already slick and ready. I bucked against him, begging him to finish what I started.

"Please." I couldn't get the rest out; I couldn't take it. I had waited so long, had been put off so many times.

His power rippled over me at the word, bringing me to the edge. My hands roamed his body, kneading his shoulders and neck, trying to pull him up to me. I bit my lip hard to keep from crying out again and tasted blood. He paused and inhaled the scent of it before coming back to my mouth and sucking the blood from my lip. My hands roamed his back and down to his hips. I could feel the head of him, just there. I tilted my hips, trying to take him into me, but he was delaying. This was my punishment for being so wicked. He would make me wait just a little longer. He stared into my eyes, his bleeding just a fraction paler, and watched my reaction as he slid into me. I tried to hold his gaze but couldn't. I arched against him and threw my head back, giving him access to my neck. I wanted all of him in me.

When he was sheathed deep inside me and my flesh open to accommodate him, he began to move. With each thrust of his hips, he destroyed me. He took my control, ripping it away from me, and gave back more pleasure than I had ever felt before.

His power flowed without apology or restraint over my skin as he drove himself deeper and deeper into me. His lips found mine, crushing them. He did not make a quick punishment of it. Instead, he worked me until muscles strained and sweat rolled from both of us. I came, clawing at his back and begging for him to stop, telling him that I couldn't take it, but he did not stop.

With slow and deliberate strokes, he tore my soul apart. My own power that had been wrapped up tightly and put behind closed doors for tonight ripped out of me and met his warm for cool. It wove around us in threads of silver and gold. His tempo built, and I could feel him swell inside of me. Digging my hands into the flesh of his hips, I urged him on.

Sweat dripped off his sides and onto me. Everywhere I kissed him, the salty taste met my lips. He brought his mouth to my neck, and in one final deep thrust, he struck the big vein there and drank while he came. He pulsed inside of me in time to his swallows, filling me with himself as he gave what I needed and took what he wanted.

Not expecting it, I came again. It flowed through me, taking all thoughts and my sanity with it as it went. He collapsed onto me. Wrapping my arms around his back, I held him there. Both our hearts pounded, one against the other. Candles flickered, and the room was awash in the smell of blood, honey, fall leaves, and amazing sex. My legs shook so hard I didn't think I could stand if I wanted to.

I did not.

His head rested, nestled in the hollow of my neck, and he lay there still, unmoving. I felt wetness that had nothing to do with blood, and I worried about him. He had been through so much. My body slowly calmed, and all my vital signs came back from skyrocket status.

"I love you, Aedan. I didn't understand it then, not really, but I've loved you since almost the beginning." I rested my hand on the back of his head, cradling him to me.

He went still, still in the way only a vampire can. His breathing stopped, and his heart quit pounding against my chest, just for a minute. He pulled away, bringing his eyes to mine. He studied me for what felt like an eternity. Thoughts flitted across his face and were gone before I could understand them.

"I will never willingly let you go, Liomsa Go Deo, understand this." His eyes glittered by the light of the candles, faceted and brilliant like diamonds. They mirrored mine, whiskey to green. The look on his face was feral, but his eyes were whiskey-colored and not yellow. "You undo me, Lara. I love you. I have loved you since the moment I saw you. My one regret during my captivity was that I never told you this. I am telling you now. I love you as I have never loved anyone." He rose from me, just enough to take the glass of wine from my nightstand. He brought it to my lips and then his. We both drank deeply, passing it back and forth.

I reached away from him to put the glass back, and he pulled me to my knees, entering me from behind, shocking me with the quickness of it. He pushed in hard and held it, allowing my surprise to pass and my body to adjust. Then he showed me no mercy. He alternated quick thrusts with slow ones, hitting a spot that I had heard about in magazines, but never actually thought existed.

He pulled me to him, running his hands down the length of my body, and toyed with the bit of flesh at the heart of it all, I shuddered against him, and he stopped, making me wait. He bit along my shoulder into the nape of my neck, sinking his fangs in but not drinking. He held me in place, piercing me from both ends, keeping me right on edge. He retracted his fangs and pushed me back down onto the bed, pressing me into the mattress.

He rode me for what seemed like an eternity, bringing me up and making me wait, bringing me up and making me wait. Then he began thrusting deeper, hitting that spot again and again. I felt it start to break. Some deep, hard, terrible, amazing thing I had never experienced before shattered up and out of me. I didn't even notice as he bit the other side of my neck, drinking again. I was trying to breathe and trying to not die from the intensity of it all. I never had. Ever. Felt anything like it. His pleasure dripped out of me and ran down my legs. I fell onto the bed, smiling at the thought that I had been fucked to sleep and was instantly out.

I felt him rise and blow out the candles before covering us both with my quilt. He lay on his side, pulling me to him. Once more, he entered me like he couldn't resist just one more time. I whimpered from the soreness there but did not complain further. On our sides, we made love again, softly. Gently. He kissed down my back but did not drink. He came with a soft moan and a shudder of his breath. The feel of him pulsing inside me pushed me over, and I joined him one more time. We both fell asleep, spent, with him still resting inside of me.

Sometime during the night, Grania and Paul came home and flipped the breaker back on. I heard the smoke detectors beep and the soft hum of their voices. Grania opened the door and saw us there. I could feel her pause.

"I smell blood," she whispered. "Maybe I should check on them."

"That's not all you smell, dear, now mind your own business and come take advantage of me," Paul laughed. I grinned against the arms, holding me tight, and snuggled in deeper.

"I'm not going to willingly let you go either, Aedan," I whispered through the soft sound of his breathing. "If you thought that, you underestimated me. You're mine, and I'm not sure if that's a good thing or a bad thing for you," I finished. He sighed contentedly in his sleep, and I knew at that moment that I was lost to him.

Had he wanted, he could crush me. Never before had I felt like this; never before had I allowed myself to be vulnerable. I prided myself on having control over my emotions.

What I thought earlier about control when I set all this up, well, it went both ways. My God, it went both ways. There is no safe side of the sword, no easy way, and no holding back. Holding the sword in your hands does not protect you from the pain the blade causes. I had never been so scared in my life. Facing down a room full of angry supernaturals had been less terrifying than holding the warm, slick body of this one man.

I hadn't known. I hadn't known there was this thing deep inside me that, if I let it, would catch fire and willingly, gleefully destroy anything that tried to come between us. What had I done?

Chapter 11

I awoke not long after the sunrise, boneless and languid. The soreness between my legs a pleasant reminder of last night. I had spread out on my side of the bed and Aedan his. He lay facing me, eyes closed. I kissed the tip of his nose and got up to make coffee and take a hot bath.

In the kitchen, the French press was already full of hot, dark roast. A glass of orange juice and a tray of pastries, muffins, and fruit were laid out for me. Cook either knew my schedule when I didn't or had a way of keeping everything fresh, I didn't know. I downed the juice, grabbed one of everything, and took the entire French press into the bathroom, where I ran the water as hot as it would go, adding bath salts to the mix.

Turning to brush my teeth, I froze. The Goddess's locket was gone. On the counter lay a single, long, red feather. Picking it up, I ran my fingers over the vane. I had never seen anything like it or a bird that might sport such a feather. I laid it back down and turned to my toothbrush.

Sighing with pleasure, I eased into the bath and turned the jets on full. Soreness eased out of my muscles, and my mind cleared as I sipped coffee, the heat from it easing the soreness in my throat from a long night of God only knows what kind of noises had come out of it.

I was well and truly afraid. Aedan had made me feel things I spent my whole life avoiding. I was good at it. I had a doctoral degree in avoiding intimacy. Sex was one thing, but I had never experienced anything like last night. I wasn't sure if it was Aedan's magic, his feeding, or actual emotion that made me feel the way I had, but it scared me. I frowned, sipping my coffee as my heart sped up, and I worried about how best to handle it.

The door opened, and Aedan stepped through, naked and fabulous. He looked around; his brows creased until he spotted me. Sensing my thoughts, he sat on the side of the tub.

"You're awake early," I said, not meeting his eyes.

"I have changed my schedule. Events of late remind me that a firmer hand is needed upon my affairs. I require almost no sleep. Are you okay? Did I hurt you last night?" he asked, looking around my bathroom.

He spotted the feather. Rising, he walked to it in slow motion, picking it up and holding it like it might break. "Where did you get this Mo Chroi?"

"It was here this morning. I, uh, I borrowed a locket from someone. It helped me find you. This morning it was gone, and the feather was there. Does it mean something?"

"To me, yes. It used to mean everything. We will talk about this later. Why can I feel your fear, Anamcara? It woke me from my sleep."

"I'm sorry. I. I don't know what to say, Aedan. I was thinking about, well, everything. Last night was intense. It scares me. I'm sorry." I looked at him then, I had been avoiding it, but I finally caved to the need.

He leaned against my vanity, holding the feather. He was still watching me. His eyes were their normal whiskey color, and I was glad for that. My plan had worked.

He was beautiful; the sunlight leaked in the window, striking the highlights on his new short haircut. White scars laced his body. I had never studied him in the daylight or noticed them before. Fine white lines crisscrossed his core and laced the tops of both his thighs. In the mirror behind him, I could see more scars, some thin white lines, and some thickened cords. I knew what they meant; I had them too, only his made mine look insignificant. He was covered in them.

"You're beautiful," I whispered. "You are so beautiful. God. It's so intense," I finished, looking away from him.

"Was it my feeding?" he asked, very carefully, watching my face.

"No. No, Aedan. It wasn't that. I understand that it is a package deal and could care less." I waved that thought away, not caring. I had known what being in a relationship with him would mean. I had thought long and hard about that part. I just hadn't expected the emotional stuff.

"It's everything else. I've never done this before. Is this real? Is it us, or is it some side effect of vampire magic causing me to feel this way?" I asked, tracing the white lines of scars down his body with my eyes.

Seeing me notice, he took one step and scooped me out of the water like I weighed nothing and carried me soaking wet to the bed, depositing me gently.

"It is real. It is the most real thing I have ever felt. I assure you it is no magic. If you are afraid, then you must feel it again. That is the only way to overcome fear."

He slid down my body, placing his lips on the soft bit of tissue between my legs, seducing it to firmness. I moaned, gripping the sheets. The soreness went away under the tenderness of his tongue, and I came up off the bed, gripping his hair in my hands. He tore a moan from my throat. Using his hand, he pushed me back onto the bed, then hooked his arms under my thighs.

There was no part of me that his tongue didn't find. He entered me with it, flicked me with it, and caressed me with it. He would bring me right to the edge, then find another damn spot to torment. One hand ran lazily down my sides, bringing goosebumps where it touched. He kept it up until I could think of nothing but him and what he was doing. Warmth rolled across me, and I knew I had reached the point where he couldn't take it back.

It started in my spine and flared out, I came off the bed, and only his strength kept me from moving away from him. My orgasm tore across both of us, and at that moment, he struck the vein in the groove of my thigh and drank, pushing me to another level. His power danced across my skin, and I knew I was going to die from this, it wasn't survivable, but it was exquisite.

It was terrifying.

It was a good way to die.

He licked the neat holes his fangs had caused, sending raw shivers through me, then slid up my body. I lay spent. He pulled me to him and nestled me under his chin.

"Anamcara," he said into my hair.

When I could think again, I wrapped my arms around him and held him tight. He had said once that he wanted to show me how things could be between us. I know now why he had waited. Why he had waited for me to love him.

If I had felt anything close to this a few months ago, I would have packed my things and ran as far away as I could. Instead, I breathed in the scent of him and forced myself to relax. This was love; no one dies from that. It would be okay.

I lifted my mouth to his neck, licking along the corded muscle there. He pulled away, watching my face.

"May I?" I asked, meeting his yellow eyes with my green.

"You need never ask," he said, cradling my head to his neck. Using my tongue and a small amount of power, I opened the vein there and planted my mouth on it, taking him into me.

He tasted amazing, like chocolate and fine wine; hints of oak flooded my tongue. I felt our bond snap into place and gloried in its return. I had missed him more than anything I had ever known. I took only a few sips before pulling away. The wound closed as I watched.

He made love to me again. All the tenderness that had been missing the night before when it was about need flowed from him. I could feel his thoughts. We weren't all that different. He was afraid, too. He was in love, too. We would fight this new fear together.

I let my feelings flow between us. Fire danced across our skin in silver-blue and orange hues, hot to cool. In science class, we learned that the hottest flames burn a silver-blue and the cooler ones an orange-red. I had always thought Aedan's magic was cold to my hot, but that isn't the case. As he made love to me, showing me with movements and thoughts how he felt, I knew that he was the core of the flame that burned the hottest.

After all, he was the Flame Keeper.

Chapter 12

Later we sat together in the kitchen, side by side, and talked. Well, I shoveled forkfuls of omelet into my face and downed coffee in large gulps while he talked.

"I am angry about one thing," he said, eyeing the way I ate my breakfast. "You stole my Brunaidh."

"I stole your what?" I asked with a mouthful of cheesy eggs.

"My Broonie. My Brownie." He grinned a wicked fangless grin at me.

"I don't even like brownies. It's contaminated chocolate," I huffed, swallowing a mouthful of coffee.

"Not that kind of brownie. You stole my cook. I will never get him back with the way you eat."

I punched his arm and glared at him, raising my fork against him in mock attack.

"He does so love a good appetite." His eyes twinkled as he spoke.

"What is he?" I asked. "No way he is human."

"As I said, he is Brunaidh. They are a lesser Fae. They enjoy taking care of people. They feed them and do housework; I bet there is not one dust bunny to be found here." He smiled, sipping his French press coffee. "He never bought me a French press," he sniffed.

"Well, you aren't a faerie princess," I teased. "I don't know, though. He just showed up after the fire and refused to leave with the others," I said, wincing at the word fire.

"That is their way. He has been with me for many years. He showed up one day and started taking care of my People. He does not claim me, and I do not claim him. He serves at his pleasure and not the pleasure of anyone else."

"Uh, sorry?" Not sorry, I thought, grinning at him and popping a thick piece of bacon into my mouth.

"Stay with me in the city," he said, turning to me and waiting. "It will take some time to rebuild, and I need to handle affairs there." His eyes glimmered in the light of my kitchen; it was so weird seeing him up this early. Normal and weird. He fit so perfectly into my life.

"I have the clinic, Aedan. It's been busy. I can't leave it," I said, resting my hands on his legs.

"Come afterward, as you can; I know you are busy. I just do not want to miss you. Many things are happening quickly, and I would like to have you by my side," he paused, sensing my unease, but giving me time to work through it.

Taking a big breath in, "Okay. When I can. It will be nice. Like a getaway," I laughed. "What about Grania?" I fiddled with my hair, feeling nervous.

"We have not had a chance to talk about her. Or anything else. I am sorry for that; I was not myself when I returned home. I am grateful. I am honored by everything you have done for me. You are amazing. The others told me what they knew and what they did not know, Noah filled in, and what he did not know, I saw on video. The manager of that particular hotel and I have an arrangement. He records the Conclaves we have there in secret so that I can review them later. I have used it to root out problems in the past. You were brilliant. There are many irritated vampires right now who had thought to have a shot at you; you are a natural maker of contracts. But then you are Fae, I suppose." He smiled then; I think he smiled more in the last twelve hours than in the entirety of our relationship.

"I am not angry about Grania. I am not. I have done her many a disservice. Perhaps you can accomplish what I never did. I am not saying it is not a loss; it is a huge loss, but she is my daughter, always, and you saved her from death. You gave her magic back to her. She lives as none of the rest of us do. I will not ask how; I do not wish to know, but I am grateful.

"I am angry over Mikolosi. I am angry over the others of my kind, but I have no anger toward you." I could feel then that he did not. He wasn't mad at me, although he was plenty mad at the circumstances.

"Okay," I said, taking a deep breath and smiling. A weight I hadn't known, I felt lifted.

"Tell me of Talamh na Sithe."

And so I did. He didn't interrupt as I told the story from start to finish and left nothing out. Nothing except the fact that The Goddess was his mother. She had not wanted that known, and that was her business to tell. I told him of the lake, and he sat up, alert to every detail. I told him everything. It came tumbling out. I told him about healing the land and Aramea, the hunt for him, and how badly it went.

We talked about the white room, and I was stunned that he had shared my dream. We talked for hours. Afterward, I was limp with emotion. All the anxiety and pain that Aedan's absence caused flowed out of me and into the air between us. None of it mattered anymore. I released the breath I had held for over a week. His shoulders eased as we talked, and I could see his resolve strengthen. Resolve for what I didn't know, but whatever it was was in big, giant trouble.

We took a shower. He smirked at all of his products, lining the shelf but said nothing. I punched him anyway. I luxuriated in the feel of his hands as he washed me head to toe. No one had ever done that before, and it was incredible.

I returned the favor, and once clean, he dressed in the clothes I bought for him. It wasn't even noon yet. He made calls while I got ready, calling Guy first to have a crew start working on house plans. He then made appointments with countless people and media programs.

I was finishing drying my hair when he came around the corner, leaning against the door jamb to watch. I flipped my hair upright, turning off the dryer.

"I am going to Fangs tonight," he said, the bells of Ireland in his voice muted.

"Then I'm going, too," I said, smoothing my lipstick.

"No, you are not. I will go alone. You will not risk yourself."

"I'm going. I'm not letting you get anywhere near that conniving bitch by yourself. I think she's behind all this anyway," I said, anger making my hair float around my face. I tamped it down. "She was a royal asshole during your…absence."

"You know, Lara, we both have big reputations," he said, grinning widely.

"Big reputations?" I asked.

"You and I would be a big conversation." He sniffed, looking away.

"Oh. My. God. Are you quoting T. Swift? Are you a Swifty?" My mouth gaped open, and I was rendered speechless.

"I know not of what you speak," he said, grinning again at me. "My reputation precedes me, and I have some big enemies," he finished, the bells of Ireland deeper and twinkling in his voice.

"Oh. My. God. You are a Swifty. Well, here's the truth from my red lips: I'm going tonight. Where in town are you staying?" I asked, turning to face him before I fell over laughing. The oldest, most powerful vampire in the world was a Swifty. Mic drop. I was done.

"You and I are staying at the Four Seasons on the Harbor, in the presidential suite. The others are on their way or already there, by this point," he said, watching me carefully. "You are taking this well. Better than I hoped."

I laughed; I mean belly laughed. I laughed so hard I ruined my mascara.

"After everything else? In for a penny in for a pound," I said, kissing the tip of his nose. "Off you go, I have work to do. I patted his backside and herded him into the bedroom. I went to the closet, pulling out his sword and the packet of money and credit cards that Domingo had given me, handing them back to Aedan.

"Those are yours," he said, crossing his arms and refusing to take them.

"I don't need your money or your sword." I glared at him.

"The sword is yours now," he said, raising one eyebrow at me and daring me to argue. I was not intimidated in the least.

"No. It's not. I'm no sword fighter. Take it. Please."

He took the sword, holding it in his hand. It glowed a faint blue at his touch and shuddered, changing back into a longsword. Its intricate layered Damascus steel shimmered in the faint glow of the blade. Celtic engravings and script etched themselves into the side. We watched transfixed as it was remade once more. Aedan's eyes darted to mine and held them. I shrugged.

"Magic Faerie crap, I guess." I stared at the sword again. It looked better with Aedan holding it anyway.

"The cards and the money are yours, Mo Chroi, use them. I have more money than a hundred people could spend in a lifetime, possibly more. It will please me," he added at my look. I caved and took the envelope. Relationships sucked.

"What time do you want me to come downtown?" I asked, my voice cracking with emotion.

"We will head to the club around midnight. I want it to be in full swing upon our arrival."

"Okay." Leaning up to reach him, I brushed my lips across his. "It's a date." I moved away. I could feel his confusion. He had no idea what to do with me. I loved it.

Chuckling, I walked away. When I came back to the bathroom later, the red feather was gone. I had forgotten to ask about it.

Chapter 13

The clinic was again busy. A steady stream of patients came and went starting almost as soon as Aedan left. They were simple things, flu, severe colds, some GI bugs, but nothing serious. I fixed a broken arm on a twelve-year-old hereditary vampire boy whose parents had brought him from their home in southern Virginia. It was tournament season for some sport, and they didn't want him to miss a game. Parents.

Cook brought my lunch downstairs, and Grania came and helped out later in the afternoon, cleaning tables and instruments while I tended to the people. She gave me sidelong glances and grins, barely containing herself. The pinpricks on my neck would be invisible to anyone who did not intimately know them.

"Dish," she said, during the one quiet moment of the day later in the afternoon. "I mean, whew, I could feel it. So hot. Shields, girl, shields."

A slow grin spread across my face. The best part of my workday had once been talking to my best work friend, Ella, about our respective sex lives. I missed that kind of friendship. No holding out. No judgment. No rules.

"Ew, gross, but there was no shielding that, sister. It. Was. Amazing. Glorious. Terrifying." I might have squealed.

She jumped up and down like a little kid singing, "Mommy and Daddy Did it."

I punched her.

"So, it was great?" she asked. "No disappointment?"

"What? Disappointment? Oh my God, no. I thought I was going to die. I think I might have died a little between round one and round two this morning and definitely after round two last night. I was face planted and out." I nodded my head in emphasis of my definite short-term death.

"This morning?" she asked, flicking her eyes again sideways at me.

"He was up super early. Said he is changing his schedule."

"Interesting. So. It was good. I see he filled his belly. What else?" she asked, an evil grin lighting her face and eyes twinkling with orneriness. She bounced her head, sending her ponytail flying.

"I told him I loved him. I groaned. Why did I do that?"

"Because you do, you dolt, it's going to be okay. Better than okay." She flashed me a knowing grin and patted my arm.

"Do you care if we all hang out in the city for a few days? I mean, you can stay here, but…" I let that trail off, knowing she couldn't. She was bound to me now. I was trying hard to break that, but it would take time. "He has rooms at the Four Seasons. We're going to Fangs tonight."

"Fangs? Is that wise?" she asked.

"He's going anyway. I'm not letting him go alone. That bitch needs her day of reckoning, and I don't want her claws anywhere near him. Fool me once shame on you, fool me twice…" I said, fiddling with the hem of my jeans, knowing she hadn't ever fooled me. I knew from the look on her snarky, conniving, jealous bitch face that she was trouble.

"Have you heard?" she asked, facing me full-on. "Have you heard what's been going on down there?"

"Honestly, no. I've been preoccupied, I guess. All I know is what I saw in the interview the other day."

"He's cleaning house," she said, more subdued. "He's been picking off Aiyana's People and terrorizing the city's vampires, at least the ones he has an issue with. He isn't making it obvious, but it's obvious to anyone in the know," she finished. "The leaders of several other Houses have simply disappeared." She gave me a pointed look.

"Eh. They were assholes. Maybe he needs to clean house." Her head snapped back in shock at that.

"I mean, really, you put all these egomaniacs into the public spotlight, give them some semblance of power and then try ruling them by laws designed for humans. What can possibly go wrong? It's the worst of humanity, power grabbing, hubris, and megalomania rolled up into a powerful group of people that can barely get along. It was bound to happen. Maybe the power structure should have been different from the beginning," I said. Her mouth gaped open, and she stared at me for the space of many heartbeats.

"I. Wow. Did you know that my dad said almost the same exact words to me?" she asked, straightening.

"No, but it makes sense. There were bound to be issues with y'all politically. Maybe he spread the power base too wide." I got up, moving to put things away. It was heading toward evening, and I wanted to get my chores done and start packing.

"You guys are going to be good together. I can see that. It's going to take a strong man to keep you in line," she said. I looked at her, and her face was deadpan, then she broke into laughter at the sight of my expression.

"I'm scared. It all scares me. I mean. I don't even know how to do a relationship. I never even had one with my husband. We were just kids."

"You are already doing it. You are doing a great job." She smiled at me, a real smile. "Now, let's tune you up and get you into fighting shape."

"Uuuuuuugh," I replied. She smacked me into the wall and was gone. Taking a deep breath, I centered myself and felt for her. Through my binding, I should have known immediately where she was, but I could not sense her at all. It made me nervous, just for a second. I noticed the absence of her in my head for the first time since I used magic to save her from going insane. Her shields were excellent. Better than I had known and much better than mine. I needed to practice.

A faint poof of air and a light tap on the shoulder was all the warning I got when she came at me the second time. I reached out with my magic and found her crouched low behind some furniture in the corner. I waited, I would make her come for me, and the next time, I'd be ready.

I felt her move, and when I focused on her with my other sight, I actually saw her move. Binding to me had given her more abilities, we didn't understand why, but it had.

She came rushing at me, and I blocked her with a side kick, sending her stepping back. She brought her hands up and tried to strike me, and I blocked her again. We jabbed with our hands, feinting and blocking. Neither better than the other, she took me down with a leg sweep, but I countered, wrapping my own legs around hers as I fell, bringing her down with me. We sprang back to our feet, breathing hard and grinning. She hit me with a right hook, and I got her with an uppercut. We bounced on the balls of our feet. She tried a left jab, but I was too fast for her. Aedan's blood had made me amazing. Hell yeah. Boyfriend perk number one. Oh, wait. Definitely perk number two.

I lost focus thinking about perk number one, and she flattened me, sitting on my chest, laughing. Flashing her long fangs in delight.

"You're getting better. Don't think about sex when you fight, though," she chuckled. She hopped up and grabbed my arm, pulling me roughly to my feet. I ducked my head and felt my cheeks redden.

"What time do you want to go?" she asked.

"When does Emily's open?" I asked.

She squealed in delight, clapping her hands, and bolted up the stairs. "I'm packing fast."

Outside, I did chores and brushed horses, filled waters, and threw out hay. I did not miss the smirk on my black stallion's face as I went about caring for him. I dared him to say something. He declined.

Men.

I showered off the sweat from sparing and the sickness of others before I packed. I grabbed my luggage and stared at my closet blankly. I had bought a ton of clothes, but nothing struck me. I packed the robe I wore last night, underwear, toiletries, jeans, and a few shirts. I threw in two of the new outfits I bought from Emily's, the jewelry Aedan had given me, and that's about all. I had no idea how long we would be down there, and it's not like I wouldn't be home during the day anyway.

I dressed in sleek black pants with a matching jacket that had a red silk belt just under the breasts. The jacket flared a little and made the outfit more feminine. I pulled my hair up in a messy twist and clasped a black silk choker around my neck; it had a single red jewel in the middle that dangled into the hollow of my neck. I left my ears bare and applied only mascara and a hint of red lip stain. It was elegant, understated, but very fetching. I couldn't walk into the Four Seasons in muddy boots, and I was guessing Emily would toss me out herself if I pulled that stunt again.

Chapter 14

We took two cars; Paul went ahead to get checked in while we shopped. Emily's was busy. Humans and a few scattered vampires browsed the racks of clothing. The sales clerk who had helped me was at the register. Grania and I walked in, and heads turned. The place smelled of wild orange, spice, and hefty bank accounts.

"Grania, darling, who is your friend?" A tall, gorgeous, dark-skinned woman approached us. She had to be six feet two, as she was even taller than Grania. A long dark gray dress with modest slits up the sides graced her whip-thin body, and she moved with grace only dancers and vampires perfect. I was betting she was both. Her dark, creamy skin was nearly black and pulled the light and every eye to her. Her head was shaved bald, and her dark, expressive eyes roamed my face like she was trying to place me and could not.

"Emily, this is Lara. Hennessey." She added my last name when Emily cocked her head sideways.

"Mistress." Emily bowed low at the waist. "It's a pleasure to finally meet you. I have heard so much."

"Don't believe everything you hear," I said with no small amount of snark.

"Darling, I would love to believe everything I hear because if it's true, then you are my kind of woman. She laughed, rising from her bow to tower over me. Aedan said she was a designer in her human life, not just her vampire one, but she had to have also been a model. Her features were model perfect.

"I am grateful the Governor finally found someone worth shopping for. He has been in to pick out the style of dress for his House but never shopped until he met you." She gave me a wink. Jacquelyn at the counter just stared.

"Hey, yeah, sorry about dragging mud in here the other day, kind of a hazard of the suburbs." I smiled in return.

"You can drag whatever you want in here, any time you wish to drag it. What are you ladies looking for tonight, something special?" She asked, never taking her eyes off us.

"Something that will make a statement. In red."

"All red?" Emily asked, looking at Grania for confirmation, one eyebrow raised in a perfect arch.

"It's kind of her thing," Grania laughed at a joke I didn't get.

"Oh, darling, you will give him a run for his money," Emily laughed, her eyes twinkling in merriment.

"She already does. We don't need it to get worse." Grania smirked at me.

"Whatever. Red? You got any?" I asked, ignoring my friend as she waggled her eyebrows at me.

"Normally, I do not design in solid colors," she said, giving me a meaningful look that landed about five feet over my shoulder and somewhere to the left. "I had heard through the grapevine that you enjoy solids and designed a piece just for you on the off chance that you should ever come in. Let me show you."

She walked us to the back, where the clothes were separated by House color. She left us waiting while she went deeper into the store, coming out with a garment bag held high. Handing it to me, she herded me into a dressing room.

"I went by the size he bought your black high low dress in; I hope it fits," she said from outside the door.

Pulling the bag off, I stared in wonder at the outfit before me. It was ruby red. A fitted jumpsuit that zipped from the back with an A-line skirt overlay starting at the hips and dropping straight to the floor. It had a scoop neckline and cap sleeves. From the back, it looked like a cocktail dress, and from the front, it looked like what it was designed to be- a woman's power suit. It was perfection. I couldn't get it on fast enough. I opened the door to the dressing room, turning my back. "Care to zip me?"

"I would be honored. It is even better than I imagined." She traced the line of my neck as she zipped the dress, turning me so she could see the full effect.

Grania's mouth dropped.

Emily's eyes soaked up the light turning impossibly black.

"I'll take it," I said, not even caring about the price tag.

"Grania, you need to get something too. Daddy's paying." I laughed, throwing my head back as the women stared with something akin to bewilderment on their faces. Aedan gets that look too, and I can never understand why.

"That poor, poor man," Emily sighed with a half-smile.

"Makes you almost feel bad for him, doesn't it?" Grania sighed.

"Almost, yes." They laughed together and went in search of more outfits while I changed.

I hung the garment bag at the counter. I heard Grania and Emily still laughing and went back to join them.

Grania was wearing a metallic silver jumpsuit with emerald green accents and eyeing herself in the mirror.

"What's with the green?" I asked.

"That is the color of your House," Emily said from behind me.

I went still.

"My what?"

"Your House. I took the liberty of making a line just for you.

"I don't have a House," I argued, backing away from the both of them.

"Don't you?" Grania challenged. "You have me. Paul. Cook. That's a House. Everyone knows about us, Lara. Mikolosi can't keep a secret," she added, smiling. I backed away from both of them. "It's okay. Kinda cool, actually," she finished.

"Uh-uh. No. No House. I'm not a vampire."

"Doesn't matter," Emily said, handing me an emerald green blouse made of the softest material I had ever felt in my life. Fear swept through me.

"You've made a name for yourself. You are a strong woman. Never fear that. Own it, instead." Emily pushed the shirt at me, smiling. "Girl Power," she added, walking away to get another outfit for Grania.

I glared at Grania, and she glared back. I was proud of her and maybe myself. I could wear the shirt. No one had to know what it meant. I browsed around and picked up a few more things. Grania bought several outfits as well, emerald and ruby. I wanted to kill her. When we checked out, I handed Aedan's American Vampire Association black card bearing both our names to Jacquelyn. The total was outrageous.

Aedan should be very pleased.

"Where are you going when you wear my outfit," Emily asked us at the door. "I want to be there."

"Fangs," Grania answered before I could. "Tonight. You should come; it will be interesting." They exchanged a look.

"It might be dangerous," I said.

"I wouldn't miss it for the world." Emily closed to the door behind us, the soft bell on it tinkling.

The noise and lights of the Gallery at Harborplace were almost calming, and I soaked it in as we walked through the exclusive mall and back to my truck. It was a short drive to Four Seasons, and we rode in comfortable silence through the streets of the city.

"That was fun. Thanks for going," I said as we pulled up to the hotel, waiting on the valet.

"I'm glad we could finally go." She got out, deep in thought. I didn't ask her or press the issue, but I could tell something was bothering her.

Inside, a concierge met us. "Miss Hennessey?" he asked almost as soon as we stepped inside.

"Yes?"

"I will show you to your room." He took my bags and walked toward the elevator, snapping his fingers for another man to follow.

I hesitated for a minute, staring. The lobby was done in cream and silver. A massive crystal chandelier hung from the ceiling, and the lighting was dim in a good way. Windows opened out to the inner harbor, and lights danced across the surface of the water. An infinity pool stretched out so that you couldn't see where it ended, and the harbor began. It was a stunning view.

I had never stayed in a place this nice, I tried not to stare, but it was hard. Everywhere I looked, there was something beautiful. My mom would always say, 'act like you've been there before' when taking me to some fancy restaurant. I walked across the opulent lobby, trying to act like I did it every day.

He told the other bellboy to grab Grania's things, and they went a different way across the grand expanse of the floor.

Guiding me onto the elevator, he pressed the button marked with a P. There were only two buttons, P and L. Aedan had his own elevator.

When the door opened on the top floor, he carried my things in, setting them down, and left without taking the twenty I tried to hand him. Aedan must have taken care of it already.

I stood gaping. The suite was bigger than my house. Marble floors with warm area rugs scattered across them led to a full kitchen and open concept living room. Windows lined the far wall; I walked to them, looking down. The Harbor spread out before me in all its urban beauty. Lights from the malls and restaurants glittered on the small waves. Water taxis sat moored and dark. A set of stairs led up, but I ignored them, choosing instead to follow the sound of Bach coming from the other side of them. Another room stretched out, a low fire burning in the fireplace at the end.

Aedan, wearing black martial arts pants and nothing else, held his sword and moved through forms. I could only stare at his beauty. Muscles flowed across his back and arms as he moved; a faint sheen of sweat glistened on his chest. His face was peaceful and focused. He moved with predatory grace. It was absolute. No one, and I mean no one, would not know what he was at that moment. Power breathed across his skin, touching me where I stood.

"Hi," I said. It came out in a gasp. He brought the sword up to his forehead, his other arm straight to his side, and in formal acknowledgment. Then he strode to me like a cat, no bones and all sinew. I couldn't breathe.

"Hello, yourself." He smiled down at me, taking me in. His eyes lingering on the jewel at my neck."

"You've made a friend," he said, fingering it.

"Maybe. I like her," I said, taking one finger and running over his chest. "You look… amazing isn't a strong enough word, but that's all I've got."

He kissed my forehead. "Come," he said, pulling me along after him. We went into the kitchen, and he grabbed two glasses and poured a deep red wine into them. Notes of oak, honey, and chocolate hit my nose. The wine tasted like Aedan's blood. His blood made my senses sharper; every sensation around me was highlighted and surrounded by exclamation points. It was incredible. The wine smelled great. So did Aedan. I sipped the wine, letting myself feel everything. I closed my eyes, taking it all in. My head lulled to the side. I took a deep breath in and held it, letting sensation roll through me.

"Anamcara. You tear down my reason," he said the name like a prayer. I thought only southerners could drag a word out like that.

"I'm sorry; it's new and kind of hard to shut it down." I gave him a sheepish grin. "Grania said I need to shield better."

"Never apologize," he said, shaking his head and reaching for a roll of papers on the countertop. He had his own emotions shut down tight. He must be worried I wouldn't like what he had to show me.

He rolled the papers out, and I saw plans. Specifically, house plans. "I do not know what you said to Guy, but he was so convinced you would find me that he had these drawn up, even though no one asked."

"Oh," I said, looking through the papers. The first page was just architect mumbo jumbo that made no sense to me at all, but the next page was an artist's drawing of how the finished house would look.

It was an old Charleston-style home. Wide stairs ran up the center in a delicate curve to a porch that wrapped around the entire structure. A large double door graced the top of the stairs, and columns ran from the first to the third stories. All three floors had wraparound porches and large French doors at various intervals that would allow occupants to enjoy the porch. There were large dormers on the gabled roof with Juliet balconies on them. It was stunning. Colossal and stunning.

"What do you think?" he asked, his tone light, but there was a current of doubt that he couldn't hide.

"It's stunning." I flipped the next page and saw drawings of the finished interior, flipping through until I found the one for the third floor. It had more square footage than the upstairs of my house and was done in grays and reds. The overall size of the house doubled what had burned down. "Wow. He does amazing work. It doesn't look like your style, though," I said.

"It looks like our style; it is old world meets new." His eyes never left my face, and he must not have liked what he saw. He rolled the plans up and sat them back down, then walked to the wall of windows overlooking the water. He grabbed the shirt off the back of the couch, pulling it over his head as he went.

"Aedan," I said, walking to him. I love the house. It's absolutely amazing. I'm just... No one has ever done any of this for me. It scares me. I don't understand it, okay? No one has ever cared enough to want me happy or worry about what I think."

He crushed his lips to mine, shutting me up with his tongue. He let down his shielding, and I could feel his thoughts through our shared blood. They were overwhelming. It turned out that he was just as afraid as I was, just as overwhelmed, and just as nervous about screwing it all up. He slammed his shield up, breaking the kiss. "Only you. I want only you," he said, daring me to argue with one look. I did not.

Grabbing my bags, he took them upstairs, leaving behind the faint scent of his fear.

I leaned against the glass, looking out across the water, trying to get the jumble of my thoughts together. Was it too much, too fast? Or not enough, fast enough? I couldn't decide.

Finally, I walked up the stairs after him. In the bedroom that dwarfed my own, I went to the suitcase he had placed on the bed and began digging through it. I hung tonight's outfit up and pulled my hair down. He had left the bathroom door open, and I went in, watching him shower out of the corner of my eye.

"Aedan, I love the house. I do. I can't wait to see it finished," I said as I pulled out my makeup.

"Will you live with me there?" He asked.

"Yes and No," I paused, taking a big breath. "I won't give up my house, but I would love for us to share both places. Sometimes we may need a change anyway. Plus, if I do something super annoying or you forget to put your socks in the hamper, and we need a minute of alone time, I think it's good to have that option." I was so going to screw this up. I could feel it. I had been in a real relationship for five minutes and had already blown it.

"That sounds reasonable," he said, surprising me. I ran light oil through my hair before separating it into sections and ironing it straight with my flatiron. Aedan spent a long time in the shower, watching me through the glass. I took a minute to pair my phone to the Bluetooth stereo and started my favorite playlist. That got Aedan out and moving. He toweled off, kissed my nose, and left me to get ready. It took a while, but the effort was worth it. When my hair was done, it lay poker straight, sleek, and shiny past the curve of my hips, the waves it usually had made it look shorter, and its length was proof I was past due for a trim.

I lined my upper eyes in black and applied heavy mascara, a light dusting of powder, and red lip stain. Slipping the jumpsuit off the hanger, I stepped into it, contorting myself until I got the zipper up. I dug around in the bottom of the bag and pulled out nude-colored platform heels, and slipped them on.

I checked the mirror and found everything in place. I spritzed some coconut body spray over myself and called me done. I wore no jewelry; there was no need. The outfit was statement enough.

I went out into the bedroom and found it empty, the bed turned down, and the lights dimmed. Walking to the stairs, I saw Aedan, dressed like a million bucks, in a suit that probably cost just that. He stood by the window looking out at the water below, holding a snifter of some dark-colored liquor in his hand. I saw him look up at me in the window and do a double take. I started down, and he met me at the bottom.

"You have never looked more lovely," he said, taking my hand. "You take my speech and my breath."

"It's a good thing you don't need to breathe then." I winked at him. "You're the spiffy one. You are beyond gorgeous." I let my eyes travel the length of him.

His suit was perfectly tailored and made the strong lines of his body stand out. The shortness of his new haircut drew you to his eyes. The length of his hair had taken away from his face, and with it short like you see just how stunning he is to look at. Talk about speechless.

He wore no red except for the ruby ring on his right ring finger.

"Are you sure you wish to go?" he asked.

"I am absolutely going," I said, quirking an eyebrow at him. He could try to stop me. It might be a fun fight.

"I am going to make some very strong points tonight, Anamcara. Blood will be shed."

"Look, Aedan, I'm okay with that. I'm as pissed off as you are about what happened. Maybe more so. Those assholes fucked with us while you were gone, and they deserve what's coming. I'm in. I don't know who all was involved with taking you, but I know that there are plenty of folks that deserve a little karma. I'll stay out of the way. This is your ship to straighten out, but I'm going to be there as a show of support, and if Mikolosi or that little black-haired tramp so much as look sideways at me, they are going down."

"Goddess, do I love you," he laughed, brushing his lips to mine and put his forehead on my hair, taking in my scent with one deep breath.

Chapter 15

We met Grania in the lobby. Paul, Domingo, Alisondro, Jason, Carter, and Aisha were there as well. Everyone was well dressed tonight; Aedan had a tailor working overtime somewhere. There were smiles and laughter all around as we walked out of the elevator. The others checked Aedan's face and relaxed at what they saw there. Grania and Aedan hugged for a very long time, and when they pulled apart, he kissed her hair.

"Grania, you look lovely. I see that you shared in Lara's shopping spree."

"Yes, Father, thanks so much for the dress." She twirled once, and the skirt of her black, pleated baby doll dress flared around her. The pleats were red, which was cute, like a vampire cheerleader. Go Team Aedan. Her hair was in a high ponytail that fell down her back and bobbled when she moved. She wore emerald earrings. I could've killed her. She winked at me when she saw me notice them.

"You are welcome," he said, taking my hand.

"Lara, you look beautiful." Alisondro bent to kiss my hand, so I hugged him instead. He went all stiff and stern before he hugged me back, smiling into my hair. Aedan watched with a look of amazement on his face like he didn't know what to make of it.

"I told you he was alive," I said.

"I told you he wouldn't be mad," he countered. We both laughed.

The mood was light as we made our way outside to where a long black stretch limo waited. It was not a rental. It had personalized plates that read AVA One. Kind of like Air Force One. What had I gotten myself into?

In the limo, Aedan poured everyone a glass of the expensive champagne they sing about in rap songs and raised his glass in a toast.

"To new beginnings," he started, pausing to look at each of us. "To rebuilding our Family and to Loyalty. I am Ever so grateful to be here." He leaned over and kissed me with just a brush of his lips.

We all sipped our champagne as he continued, "Tonight is about statements. There are nine of us, only nine, where once there were one hundred. And, yes, I will need to add to my numbers and make my House larger, but you will always be the core of it. You are the family that will be at the center of our new House. I thank you for your loyalty, and I thank you for your support. I thank you for supporting Lara and for helping to avoid a war you could not win. Yet war is coming, regardless. I have made a grave mistake, thinking that I can rule others of our kind with tolerance and democracy. That thought allowed you to be targeted, and it allowed me to become weak. I have kept the scope of my power largely hidden because the others already fear me, but I no longer care for their fear.

"Tonight, I am going to make them fear me more. I am going to destroy any and all who dared betray me or raise a hand against my House. In short, things are going to change, and I am happy to have you all be a part of it. I intend to build a world that we could all traverse safely, our identities known, our heritage, and our legacy's no longer a secret. Still, some continue to want to do things the old ways, and that must end.

"Where diplomacy works, we will use it, but where it fails, we will use strength. I ask that you enjoy your night, but pay attention as things may happen quickly. Grania, I make you my second." He nodded once, and it was done.

"But," she interrupted.

"It matters not. What you are about to say matters not. You are strong. Stronger than you know, and you are loyal, regardless that our bond is not current. I am your maker. You are my daughter in truth, and should I fall, my House is yours by right. It was a mistake not grooming you to be a Master. I was too protective, and I have no doubt that Lara will remedy that."

"Father. I don't know what to say." Grania had gone still, her eyes filled with unshed tears.

"Do not thank me, that is for sure." We all laughed at that. Grania sat just a little bit straighter.

The limo pulled under the awning of Fangs, and the doorman rushed to open the door. Aedan stepped out first, reaching in to give me his arm. Paul handed Grania out, and the rest followed behind. Aedan and I walked through the doors. Once again, the bass took over the rhythm of my heart. As a group, we walked in, Grania on Aedan's right and me on his left. We didn't hold hands this time.

Every head, every eye, every conscience turned to us as we walked in. The only reason the music didn't stop was that the DJ was downstairs and couldn't see us. I kissed Aedan's cheek and headed for the bar.

"Charles, Aedan would like his favorite wine, and I'll take a…"

"Grey Goose and Soda with a twist. I got it," he said, glancing around the bar but keeping his eyes from mine. I laid a twenty on the counter, took our drinks, and walked away, trying not to notice the way he watched me as I went. Grania and Paul had walked down the long line of the balcony to the bar at the other end, and the others had fanned out among the crowd. We were not dancing tonight.

Aedan waited by the edge of the stairs. I handed him his drink. Together we stood, looking over the dance floor like it was our kingdom. He loosened the restraints on his power, and it leaked out of him in a small but steady stream. I never had great control over mine to start with, and together they mixed, his hot to my cool, making the air around us uncomfortable to others. It felt like heaven to me.

"There is a man here. He is an older, handsome fellow who goes by the name of Alex. He has a daughter in college and sells his blood to help pay her expenses. If he is here tonight, will you check his health? He was the last human I drank from before I found out about the VID; I worry about his health." He didn't look over at me as he spoke, instead choosing to keep his eyes on those around us.

"Of course," I said, taking my drink with me.

I walked the line of the upper level, checking out the dance floor below me and the booths behind. Aedan stood waiting, suffocating the place with his power. Surely word had reached Aiyana that we were here. No way it went unnoticed.

At the end of the booths without curtains, I found the man Aedan wanted me to. He sat by himself, texting on his phone. I lowered myself into the seat across from him, quiet until he was done.

"Alex?" I asked when he put his phone down.

"Yes? Can I help you? You don't look like you are after a paid meal," he said.

His eyes were kind and his color good, but there was a hint of sickness to him, just a tinge of underlying gray in the aura around him.

"My name is Lara, and I am a friend of the Governor of the Eastern Region. I believe you fed him not long ago, a few weeks, maybe?

"He is a good tipper." He smiled. Aedan was right. He was a handsome man.

"Well, you may have heard or not, but there is an infection going around that can be passed from vampire to human, even if the vampire himself doesn't know he has it.

Aedan is worried you may have been exposed and wants me to take a look at you," I said, meeting his eyes. The music was so loud it was hard to concentrate, especially when you are trying not to shout.

"I've heard of this disease, but I don't feel sick." He eyed me curiously from across the table.

"You may not until it's too late; I'd like to take a look at you. The disease has proven to be fatal so far. There is a small group of people working on a vaccine that has been successful in trials. I'd like to make sure you get it and that you are okay." I had been thinking long and hard about a lot of things.

I wasn't ready to come out as anything other than human, but I knew that the time was fast approaching when I wouldn't have a choice. Between the video taken the night of the conclave, the pressure on Aedan, and my promise to the Goddess to bring her people out into the world, I was going to have to throw myself under the bus. I just wasn't ready for that tonight.

"I am staying at the Four Seasons for a few days, or you can see me in my clinic in Westminster; either way, it is fine. Just let me take a look at you, please." I added.

"What about the others? Word is, this thing is spreading," he asked, fanning his palms out on the table, a wedding ring glinted in the soft light of the booth.

"I've heard that too. If you know anyone who is sick or could have been exposed and you trust to be discreet, bring them along. The trials we are conducting are limited for now. As I said, the results are positive, and Aedan thinks that the vaccine will be available very soon to everyone. I picked up his phone and put my name, number, and address in his contacts before walking away to join Aedan at the rail.

"Will he come to you?" Aedan asked, not looking my way.

"I hope so. He seemed nervous; he wouldn't commit."

"You did what you could, thank you." He reached for me, pulling me to him, fitting me under the curve of his arm.

I scanned the room and still saw nothing out of the ordinary. Dancers below us moved elbow to elbow, oblivious to anything going on around them. The patrons on our level had grown tired of staring and returned to their dates and drinks. I let my fingers trail along Aedan's arm as I pulled away from him and walked down the stairs. I was restless; I needed to move. Faces turned to me as I went.

I walked slowly around the edge of the dance floor, not knowing what I was looking for but knowing I was looking for something. More of my power leaked out, and I let it, suddenly in a bad mood that I didn't understand. Humans moved out of my way, and vampires eyed me nervously.

I glanced up at Aedan, surprised to see that Gregory Cavanaugh stood next to him, and Emily had joined Paul and Grania further down. I felt the bond between Aedan and me open, and he invited me in with a thought. I took advantage; I wanted to know why Cavanaugh was here and why they looked so chummy on the rail.

"Your Faerie looks positively murderous tonight, Sire. You, on the other hand, look healthy and entirely pleased with yourself, and I, for one, am glad to see it," Cavanaugh said to Aedan, who chuckled, knowing I could hear.

Sire? I asked Aedan silently, a part of me paying more attention to the conversation. I continued to walk, scanning for what, or who, maybe, I was not sure.

"Murderous? I was trying to come up with the exact term for her expression. I do believe you nailed it." I could feel the warm brush of his pride in my head as Aedan answered the man but ignored my question.

"Who is she prowling after? I didn't peg her as being quite so predatory."

"I am not quite sure, but I do hope she finds them. She was more than a little perturbed at some of our peers during my absence, and it might be fun to see her work some of that out," Aedan told the man. More power leaked out of me, and my hair raised a bit in a breeze that wasn't there.

"I presented the offer, just as you asked, my Lord, she is amazing, just as you said. Very diplomatically, she thanked me and told me my offer was kind but premature; she had every faith that you would return."

"She did not punch you?" Aedan's chuckle went deeper, and I stilled, not sure what was going on, but knowing he wanted me to know. I lost my train of thought for a bit and stopped along the wall.

"No, Sire, she was quite pleasant. There was no bloodshed."

"Well, that is good. She packs quite a wallop into that punch," Aedan answered, satisfaction filling his voice. "Don't get any ideas about her, Gregory."

"No, Sire, I don't believe that I am up to that yet," the other vampire said soberly. "Word is, Aiyana threatened her that very night after I presented my offer," Gregory continued. She told her that she would turn her into one of her whores and sell her to any that wanted to use her. They say Lara put her in her place as well, just not as kindly as she did with me. Aiyana went on a rage afterward and tore her home apart. Lara is quite impressive," Gregory said, making me wonder how he knew that. Aiyana had a snitch.

"That she is." I could feel Aedan still, and his power reached me, even here. I moved to continue my search.

"I suppose she is looking for Aiyana then," Aedan said, his tone more somber.

I moved under the balcony and lost sight of the men. I wove in and out of the people drinking, talking, and making out underneath it. A couple going too far for a public place moaned in the corner.

I kept walking until I noticed the dark curly hair of the man. His back was turned to me, but there was no mistaking who it was. Mikolosi held a blonde in his arms, her shirt was half off, and he was feeding roughly at her neck. Something inside of me swelled at the sight of him. I stalked forward and pulled him off the girl, using power to toss him into the center of the dance floor. Aedan snapped the link between us closed.

I think he was waiting for some cue, some sign, and it was immediately after that when the humans started to leave. They went out the door, not running but definitely moving with purpose. They went in singles and large groups. They chatted and didn't seem to notice that this was strange at all. It was as if they decided to go somewhere else. All at once. Right now.

I felt the pull of the compulsion, just niggling at the edges of my humanity. I recognized the magic by the gentle brush of it along my mind. Aedan compelled over a hundred humans to leave and not think a thing of it, like it was their idea, that maybe the vampire bar down the street had a better lady's night with two for one drink specials. They left, laughing and happy, including Alex. He nodded as he caught my eye from the rail above. He seemed to know he was being told and not asked to go. Maybe, like Paul, spending time with vampires had made him sharper than average. When they were gone, all that remained were vampires. They looked confused as they gazed around, trying to figure out what had just happened.

Aedan let out a pulse of the purest power I had ever felt from him, and the music thudded to a halt. He had said he was holding back; he wasn't kidding. His power was a tremor beneath my feet that no doubt could be measured by earthquake seismographs miles away. It shook the floor, and all movement stopped.

"Liomsa," he said. "You give me the best gifts." Aedan straightened at the rail, his eyes feral as he watched Mikolosi scramble to his feet.

I stopped walking to Mikolosi and headed to the stairs instead, saying nothing. I stalked to Aedan, waiting to see where he was going with this.

"Where is the Master of the House?" he asked, his voice booming above the heads of others. I could feel the pull of it, like a call. "She needs to stand for this. Aiyana, show yourself." Aedan's magic searched the space in long, silver tendrils.

I went to stand beside Gregory, leaving Aedan's right arm free should he need it. I looked down at the hundred or so vampires spread below me, their fearful faces fixed on Aedan. I felt almost bad for them. Almost. His power was suffocating. I pulled mine in and tamped it down. As angry as I was, this wasn't my fight.

"Ah, Aedan, you are here, so lovely to see you. My staff did not alert me." Aiyana strolled to us, acting like she was happy to see us. Aedan picked her up like she was a tissue and threw her over the balcony. She landed in a crumpled heap but recovered quickly, jumping to her feet.

"I challenge you for the rights to your House, Aiyana." Aedan jumped over the balcony, landing twenty feet below in a smooth crouch. Every creature in the room froze in only the way a vampire can. No one moved, no one breathed, and no one looked away.

"Governor," Aiyana purred. "We are friends, allies, former lovers, I do not wish to challenge you." She was back peddling now, her eyes stuck to his face, and refused to leave it as he approached her.

"You misunderstand; I am challenging you, Aiyana, right here, right now; we will end this. We were friends, or so I thought, we were lovers, at one point, but you drugged me and tried to usurp my power. You bound my last son, Daniel, and used him as a tool to try to take what is not yours. My Second waits at your side, even now, instead of standing loyal to his House. Accept the challenge and fight me, or die where you stand like a coward. You do not think you can win in a fair fight and used my grace against me. Trust me when I tell you, I have no weakness, and my grace with you has ended.

"You are breaking our laws, Aedan," she hissed at him, seeing this was not going to go her way.

No one moved to intercept him on his slow walk to her. Gregory came back from the bar and handed me a drink; I took it, saying nothing.

"I care not for those laws, just as you cared not when you tried to gain power using cowardice and betrayal. I put forth those laws to protect you from me, not me from you. I put forth those laws to protect humanity from us as a whole. I see my mistake. I have given you the impression that I am weak, given you all that impression. It ends tonight." He stopped in front of her, waiting for her answer.

Backed into the corner as she was, she did the only thing she could. She raised her hands and pulled power to her. I could feel it like electricity in the air, swirling and coalescing around her. She lobbed some kind of magical attack at Aedan, and while it did make him step back a half step, it killed the vampires standing behind him, turning them to ash in an instant. Mikolosi took a step forward; Grania jumped smoothly over the balcony and landed beside him like a cat. He stilled at the sight of her, wearing red and being all too sane for his liking. He stopped moving forward.

Using power, Aedan pulled Aiyana to him, taking away the use of her legs. When she was in front of him, he slapped her face. Aiyana looked up at me, and I raised my glass to her before taking a sip. She found strength then. She started fighting in earnest, pulling a sword and her power to her like a cloak.

Aedan's sword appeared from behind his back and glowed a soft silvery blue; gasps went up as the vampires around us stood riveted. I had seen this trick, but they had not; they were glued to the sword and the fight as it continued. I trained my eyes and used the heightened senses his blood gave me to follow their strikes and parries.

I could smell her blood in the air as he sliced away at her using his magic and his blade. The speed was beyond anything I could have imagined. His silver power mixed with her red as they fought. Aiyana looked as fast and as strong as Aedan in those first moments, but once the opening moments of the fight passed, it was apparent that she was no match for him. He didn't even break a sweat as he tore her apart.

Power flowed from him, raising goosebumps on my arms and bringing terror to the hearts of almost everyone in the room. It was beautiful and horrible at the same time. He flowed like water around rocks in a river; it was a dance. A deadly dance. The smell of her blood drifted in the air.

She fought well. A lesser vampire would have been dead already; I had no doubt of that. As his sword moved, she countered, but she was always on the defense, never did she have him on his heels, not once, and she drew not one drop of blood from his perfect body. He did not allow that.

In the end, she crumbled at his feet, dropping her sword in a clatter of steel after he struck her through the heart in a final deadly blow. He removed his blade casually, sheathing it behind him.

"Aiyana has betrayed me with the help of my former second, Mikolosi. I take responsibility for this. I have been too lenient a Master. I tried to be fair with you. I tried to raise you up from the shadows. I gave her a place in my city and made her successful. I brought peace. I brought change. I brought you all freedom.

"She could have had the world, but instead, she went after something that is uniquely mine, but I know something you do not. The real face of my monster is much, much more than she has ever seen- more than any of you have ever seen.

"Tonight, I usher in a new era. Any who stand against our forward progression shall die. No rules. Just death. You may challenge me in the ways of old for the House I hold, and I will honor that but make no mistake, I will fight with any and all strengths that I have; there will be no holding back for the sake of fairness." He let the shields of his power drop, and it staggered me back a half step.

Every other creature in the room dropped to their knees, but I pulled my shields tighter and straightened. This was Faerie magic, and I had my own. I didn't know if I could meet him head to head magically and never wanted to find out, but I could stand up straight and watch him make his point. A slow smile spread across my lips as the feel of his true power kissed my skin, and even as it terrified me, I basked in it like I would the sun. This was something entirely other. And it felt right.

Aedan raised his eyes to me and bowed his head in acknowledgment. It was not lost on a single creature in that room that I still stood.

"This is my city. Mine," he continued. "The only House here is mine. Let there be no misunderstanding." He picked up Aiyana by the back of the neck and sank his fangs into her neck, drinking long and hard. "Let there be no more mistakes. Grania is named my second," he said, pausing at Aiyana's neck. A line of blood dripped down his chin. "I will no longer suffer a weak second for the strongest House in the world." Mikolosi paled, and Grania's eyes leaped to Aedan as he made his announcement official.

Aedan pulled Aiyana back to him and drained her dry. The feel of his power grew as he took the last of her blood in. I was not jealous. Not at all. I did not want this kind of feeding by him. I watched in fascination as he finished, dropping her dried husk to the ground.

"As you took every drop of my blood, I take every drop of yours," he said to her still form, as her eyes still watched his face in wide-eyed horror, then he snatched her up and took her head with his sword. It was so fast that I couldn't see it, and I am guessing that no one else could either as there was a gasp when her head hit the floor in a dull thud.

"Anamcara, would you be so kind as to join me?" Aedan asked, meeting my eyes. His were perfectly whiskey-colored; they glimmered and sparked in the light like a thousand facets on a crystal chandelier.

My heart sped up, and my breath caught. This wasn't my fight; I didn't want to be involved. I moved anyway, walking down the stairs on shaking legs, I went to him.

"Gregory," Aedan started. Gregory stood up under the force of Aedan's power. "Aaron." Another man stood. "Carissa." A woman stood.

He called name after name, and each vampire stood, suddenly able to move under the suffocating weight of his magic. The vampires he called stood and awaited further instructions. More and more vampires had come into the club as he called their names, and now dozens of them stood while a hundred more knelt, crushed under the weight that is Aedan.

"These are but a fraction of my children. They, in turn, have hundreds more children, and they, in turn, have hundreds more. I have lived for two thousand years. Two Millennia. I am not sure if I made that clear before, but I make it clear now. While there is room for civil dissension and discourse about where we as a people go as we move forward, there is no room for any attempt to usurp my leadership and our legal position in this new world. I am concerned that there has been a misunderstanding and that you think my leadership is optional. It is not. My Children are loyal to me, as are their children, and so on. If you cannot join me in the future, you will be deemed superfluous. I do not need you. Are we clear?"

There was a mumble among those vampires that knelt on the floor. The feel of Aedan's power flowing from him stopped before disappearing again behind his iron shields. The absence of it was painful to me; I felt its loss on a visceral level. The vampires on the ground stood.

"I ask you again if I am clear?" The Ireland in his voice was deeper than I had ever heard as his gaze swept over the crowd above and across the dance floor.

"Yes, my Lord," they said in unison.

"Mikolosi," Aedan dragged the word out, and once again, the hair rose on my arms. Grania pulled him to where we stood.

"Someone in my House has been aligned with Aiyana beyond Daniel. I had many long hours during my absence to ponder who that person is. Daniel knew too perfectly when I would be unavailable on the night of your attack, Lara," he said, turning to me. "Items in my House have been missing, and information is known in the community that should not be. Information that was stolen by someone who had intimate knowledge of my affairs.

"Word about events that should only be known to a small, private circle in my House have become common knowledge. These events have directly affected the safety of all my People and ultimately cost the lives of five of those under my protection.

"A war was almost begun to fight for my position that would have, most certainly, involved humans and other supernaturals. This war would have been long and bloody had I not returned to stop it. Many lives would have been lost, and any and all advancements we have made as a People would have been overturned. Not only that, since we are now known to exist, but we would also have been hunted mercilessly for allowing this war to happen. Mikolosi, have you anything to say about this?" He turned to the young vampire I had once found attractive but now only saw as pathetic. Inside I froze at the truth of Aedan's words.

Something had been off about the night Daniel attacked me. I felt it then, and I saw it now. The timing was too perfect. It always struck me how Mikolosi behaved that night and how long it took him to get to me.

I also went back over the night Aedan went missing. Only someone Aedan trusted would have been able to walk up to him and begin the process of poisoning him. Aedan told me he was poisoned similarly as I, only worse. He doesn't remember exactly what happened, but Noah smelled Mikolosi in the field. I chalked it up to him being there the night before when we all searched for Aedan, but what if that isn't true?

From the beginning, something about him had always been off to me. The night Aedan disappeared, he acted appropriately, shocked for about a minute. Then he took over and started bossing everyone around. Again, as Aedan's second, that might not be unusual, but looking back, he wasn't all that helpful. He never offered to do anything at all to find his Master, not like the others did. In fact, he refused to help at all. Everyone stepped up but him.

He was also quick to refuse to attempt to foster Grania, the only other very strong vampire left in the House of Aedan, that could have been a roadblock for him. Instead, he planned to stake her at the earliest opportunity, and it was only after I bound her to me that he left.

It came together in my mind, and anger forced the walls holding my power in check to crack. Aggression and anger poured out of me. It felt different than Aedan's power, cooler but no less intense. I was furious. Mikolosi had almost fooled me. Almost. He had almost cost me my life. Every head in the room turned to me.

"I have served you well, my Lord," Mikolosi lied, his face cocky under Aedan's scrutiny. He did, however, watch me out of the corner of his eyes. I felt Aedan reach for him with his compulsion, and I saw his face crack.

"I ask again, did you betray your House, even after renewing your blood oath to me?"

"Yes. Your power is too great, and it is time for there to be more equality among us. No one person should get to decide all for us as a people. Not everyone wanted to go public." Mikolosi tried to shut his mouth but couldn't. "Your influence is too great," Mikolosi said, his body stiff as a rod as he fought the compulsion to speak.

"My influence is too great?" Aedan laughed at that. His laughter rolled out across the crowd, causing their collective breaths to catch. "Do you prefer to hunt in darkness and feed in shadows? Do you prefer to have to move every natural lifetime, ripping out long-established roots, to keep from being detected? Do you prefer to be hunted by those who know of our existence and have no legal check on them?

"The world knows you can live forever. No more hiding that you own property or have amassed a fortune. Your families are free to walk in the open and be what they are. The majority of you wanted that and enjoy the rights and freedoms we all now share. Only a few wanted to remain in the shadows. So, tell me now why this decision was not a good thing, and why the desires of a few outweigh those of the many?

"I have been more than fair to all of you. You have brought your individual Houses out as a whole. You have a chance to build strength, wealth, and power through a long, well-lived life.

"You, Mikolosi, joined with a member of another House and helped her attempt to destroy me, not through legal or proper channels, but by cheating. If you wanted my power, you should have challenged me for it. You helped Daniel poison and attack my mate and me instead of issuing a direct challenge that you knew you could not win. You refused to act as a true second to me, as you were sworn to and undermined me at every turn. You nearly caused the death of the only True Healer our community has seen in eons, all because you could not stand against me in an honorable challenge.

"Fourteen humans died in Atlanta as part of Daniels ruse to draw me there. Fourteen. New laws threaten to take away our rights because of this, because of what you conspired to do. Tell me again how I have too much influence." His voice boomed out across those who had gathered. The crowd had settled into an almost perfect silence as his last words rang out.

His compulsion reached out again, filling the air around us in heaviness. "Are there others here who agree with what Aiyana, Daniel, and Mikolosi believed or who attempted to subvert my House and the legitimacy we all share?"

No one stepped forward, and there is no way they could have avoided doing so if they had been involved. Aedan's compulsion was too strong.

More and more anger built in my chest. Three vampires caused this. Three. There may be more out there somewhere, but here tonight, in this club, that is the grand total of betrayers. Three vampires and their human agents. Anger I never allowed myself to feel during Aedan's captivity, and even before then, rose inside of me. Anger over everything that had happened.

I had taken this all in stride and barely blinked at the changes in my life, but once it started to build, the door holding it in broke, and anger crashed out of me, filling the room with the chill of it. Fearful eyes turned to me, and I didn't care. I was pissed.

Why is it that a rash few can threaten the peace of many? Aiyana was a power grubbing bottom feeder, picking up the likes of Mikolosi and Daniel to do her bidding. She knew she couldn't beat Aedan, so she tried to take what was his the easy way, by going through his People. That's bullshit.

"Lara, it is you he has hurt the most; what do you wish his punishment to be?" Aedan turned to me, reaching for my hand. He looked tired, tired of fighting these stupid battles.

"I think it is your People as a whole who he has harmed the most. He helped Daniel attack me, but I lived. What he did to them has more far-reaching consequences. Their very existence is threatened, their livelihoods, their families, everything, by the actions of one House, or at least a few members of that House.

"Daniel is dead. Aiyana is dead. What would you like to happen to the last one? It's your decision," I said as Aedan's eyes fell to mine. I looked out among the crowd, clamping down on my errant power and cutting it off. No one spoke.

"I'm asking you, as a People, what do you think the appropriate punishment is for this crime?" I said, turning to them and making eye contact where I was allowed.

Aedan was wrong. I had been hurt but not damaged. They had been damaged, if not hurt. Their consequences had the potential to be far worse than mine. I couldn't let my anger cloud that.

"Kill him," one person yelled. That voice was joined by a chorus calling for Mikolosi's death. When the voices stopped, and the silence turned expectant, one more voice spoke in his clear Middle of America accent.

"Heal him, Healer. Make him mortal again," Gregory Cavanaugh said from the balcony. No one spoke for a moment, then a cheer of agreement went up from the crowd.

"You do not need to do this, Lara. I will take his head for what he has done to you." Aedan bent to my ear and spoke so that only I could hear him.

"I think your people have spoken on this, Aedan. He hurt them a lot more than he hurt me. Let them decide. It will strengthen you in their eyes," I said, looking up at him.

He looked at me a long moment without saying anything, then dipped his head to me. I could Heal Mikolosi; I knew that. The Goddess had taught me how to unmake any magic, and all a vampire truly is, is magic. A curse. Misbehaving blood cells.

I would rather heal him than see him dead. It was a far greater punishment for a man like him. I was a Healer, after all. I didn't enjoy the loss of life. Even I could smell his fear at this point. This was a sentence far more punishing than death.

I had promised to stay myself. This was the only outcome I could knowingly be okay with. I walked to him; he fought, kicked, cursed, and tried desperately to get away from me.

Grania pulled his arms from behind and restrained him with ease; she really was the strongest of them all. Aedan said they underestimated her; I could see now just how right he was. He used all his strength to get away from her, but she didn't budge. Her face was glued to mine, watching. No judgment. No concern. Just acceptance. She agreed that this was the best way. I could feel it through our bond.

He fought and spit like a trapped animal, calling me every name there is. I ignored him. Giving him one mercy, I built a calming ball of blue upon my palm, the way Grania had taught me, and I pushed it into him. He sagged in her grip, his eyes almost closing, and his loud shouts quieted to whimpers. She caught my eyes and gave a half-smile in approval.

I laid my hand on his chest and felt the pounding of his heart. His lungs didn't rise and fall. I turned my other sight to his blood, isolating the cells that made him a vampire, those cute little hemophagic cells that ate up red blood cells, digesting them, before spitting out the shell. They were similar to Aedan's but not the same. I could see, finally, the wrongness in them. I had never been able to see it before, but I had never been looking with this much intent at them.

"Through Aedan's blood in both our veins, I call you," I whispered to Mikolosi. No one but Aedan, Grania, Mikolosi, and I could have heard my words. He straightened, arched his back, and let out a howl that rocked the club as hard as any song ever played.

"By the power of the Goddess, I release you." I found those cells and pulled their threads. All of them. They fell apart with my unmaking. Not the healthy, once human cells upon which they fed, just the other cells that made him a vampire.

He collapsed to the ground, and Grania let him fall. He had been a puppet anyway; I just cut his strings. His chest heaved as he breathed in his first human breath. I knelt before him and did one final thing. I wove a spell around him that would never again allow him to be turned. I don't know what I did or how I did it, but I knew that it would work. In the end, Mikolosi would live his life as a human and nothing more. That was his punishment. He coughed and heaved as oxygen once again flowed through his body. He spit up dead tissue on the floor, and his heart pounded before settling into a slow and steady rhythm.

The room watched in silent horror. The terror was palpable. I had just done what they all feared I would. The whole reason Daniel attacked me the very first time all those months ago was because he feared this. Holding my head high, I met the eyes of the vampires that allowed it before placing a chaste kiss on Aedan's cheek, reminding them that I was an ally. At least I could be if they let me.

"I'm going to get a drink, babe. Can I get you anything?" I asked. One side of his mouth quirked up in a grin, and he rolled his eyes just a little.

"I will take mine to go. We are done here. There will be a meeting for those formerly of Aiyana's House, and I will expect you to take a blood oath of loyalty. Your other option is to move far away from this place. My second will arrange the meeting and make you aware of the details. If you intend to leave this city, advise her of this as well and plan to never return. You are all excused," he said, watching my face. Vampires shuffled out any and all available exits, talking among themselves. Taking my hand, Aedan walked us to the stairs, leaving a crumpled Mikolosi on the floor. Grania stepped in beside me.

At the top of the stairs, Gregory waited. Charles stood at the bar frozen; I had never seen him any other place and wasn't sure he knew how to do anything else.

"Clean this mess up, Charles, and plan on opening the tomorrow night. I will get with the staff later."

"Yes, my Lord," the bartender said, dropping his eyes. He slipped away from the bar and scurried out of sight.

"Miss Hennessey, it has been a pleasure. It truly has." Gregory took my hand in his and placed a kiss on it. "Sire, should you need anything, just call. I should go see to my House." He faced Aedan, and they clasped forearms, a look I could not interpret passed between them.

"Thank you, Gregory." Aedan smiled at him, holding the other man's arm for a heartbeat or five.

Emily walked from the corner of the balcony, where she stood with Paul. I didn't know whether he came back in after the fighting was over or avoided the compulsion and stayed.

"Are your nights out always so interesting, Lara?" she laughed, meeting my eyes with a smile. Lights sparked off her dark irises in merriment.

"Lately? Yes." I laughed loud and long, tossing my head back and sending my hair flying.

"Thanks for the invite; I'm glad I didn't miss it. Come by, and I'll have some new designs ready for you. Maybe something in solid Emerald?" She winked at the look of horror that crossed my face. At least she wasn't afraid of me.

Aedan watched the exchange with narrowed eyes but said nothing until she was gone.

"Aedan, Emily made me my own House color," I said with a chuckle.

He let loose a long-suffering sigh, scrubbing his hand down his face.

"Apparently, Hennessey House is emerald." I nodded firmly, and any tension that was left seeped out of us.

"Oh no," he said. "I am not changing my wardrobe, and green is not as flattering on me as it is you." He smiled down at me, pulling me to him. I rested in his arms and let the emotion from the evening drain out of me. It left me tired and ready for the night to wrap up. Alisondro and the others looked ready to go, too.

We got back in the limo and headed to the Four Seasons. Grania was restless, and I could tell she wanted to say something but was holding back. It was making me antsy through our bond.

"Spit it out, Grania; you are getting me wound up." I lifted my head from Aedan's shoulder just long enough to glare at her.

"Father," she stopped. A long silence filled the space between her and Aedan. The other vampires around us stilled. Having been around Grania and me the last few weeks, they knew what was coming. Alisondro sent me a worried look.

"Yes, Child?" he prompted when she didn't go on.

Gathering herself visibly, she continued, "I can't be your second." She dropped her eyes, waiting.

"Why ever not?" His eyes narrowed on her, his face holding a challenge.

"I'm not of your House. We have no blood bond," she whispered so low that I strained to hear.

I understood her fear immediately. She was afraid he would take her back, and she didn't want to be bound to him again. Not like that. She had gained a lot of power in her binding with me, and she didn't want to give it up.

I understood her fear. She was happy now, and we were almost back to where we had been. I didn't want to see her lose that either. In a flash, he was on his knees in front of her.

"Daughter mine. You are bound to me always; I will not change you again. I swore to you then, and I swear to you now, I will keep my word. You are strong, brave, and I believe you are loyal to me, even if we do not always see eye to eye. You are my first child and the only one I kept by my side. I am not asking you to be anything other than what you are when you stand for me as my second. Understand this. You can drink from me, or not, but I will ask nothing more of you, only that you stand with our House and me as you always have."

She wilted, and he pulled her to him. She cried. The quiet sobs shook her shoulders. I had suggested Aedan make her his second before we left the hotel, but he had already been thinking along the same lines anyway. Who better to be his second than the very strong vampire that had been by his side for nine hundred years?

Operation Best Friend was rolling right along, the momentum at which it grew unstoppable.

Chapter 16

The limo pulled up to the hotel, and the concierge rushed to open the door for us. Sarah and Jeremy were at the desk checking in; Alisondro crossed the lobby in three strides, scooping one up in each of his arms. He held them for a long time. I was glad to see them back. The little boy waved at me over his shoulder, but his father wasn't letting him go just yet. We parted ways, planning to meet tomorrow and figure the rest of it out.

I kicked my shoes off at the door and walked to the kitchen. The plate of steaming food laid out on the counter stopped me short, making me look around for the short brown-haired perpetrator. I would recognize those green beans anywhere. The little almond slivers gave it away. Aedan came to stand beside me and laughed a deep belly laugh.

"That little bastard," he sighed. I shrugged my shoulders and began shoveling food into my face with abandon. I never asked questions about the cook's abilities because I was just happy to eat. Aedan poured a glass of wine and leaned against the counter, watching. It was almost perverted the way he stared. I grabbed the French press that sat beside my platter of food and poured a steaming cup of the best black coffee there is, gulping it down. Aedan pinched the bridge of his nose.

"You were amazing tonight," he said as he watched forkfuls of rotisserie chicken get rammed into my face.

"You weren't so bad yourself," I mumbled around bites.

"Did I frighten you?" he asked, his brows knit together.

"I'm not afraid of you, old man." I scowled at him. And I wasn't. He let his power out tonight, and if anything, I felt better about it. I always wondered about just how much he had. Now I knew. It was a lot, but I could stand in the face of it. Yay me. I wasn't going to ask if he was afraid of me, though. I didn't want to know. He watched me unmake one of his former vampires. What he thought about that was his to think.

"I am no babe," He griped.

"Baby?"

"No."

"Sugar pie?"

"I do not think so."

"Love muffin?"

"Absolutely not."

I downed the coffee and grabbed his hand. "Let's go to bed, babe," I said, arching my eyebrow at him. He scooped me in his arms like I weighed nothing and had me up the stairs faster than I could watch the scenery go by. My laughter filled the room, and I punched his arm lightly. I could feel the goosebumps on his neck where I had my face buried. I gave him goosebumps. That thought pulled at things low in my body, and the mood shifted from light to something else.

In the bedroom, he stood me on my feet, reaching around to unzip my jumpsuit. I stepped out of it and let it fall to the floor. I stood naked in front of him.

"I need a shower, Aedan."

"No."

With that simple word, I was wetter than I could have imagined. I groaned, pulling myself to him. Pushing me away, he began to unbutton his shirt. I slapped at his hands, fighting to take over. I undid each button, placing a kiss on his chest. I took my time. When the shirt was free, I pushed it down his shoulders, running my hands down the hard planes of his chest.

His eyes never left mine, his lips parted, and a soft sound came from them. I reached down, unbuckling his belt. I let my fingertips dip below the waistband of his underwear and graze the hard head of him. Never letting him drop my gaze, I watched as his eyes paled, just a shade.

Dropping to my knees, I pulled his pants to the floor and slid my mouth down his hard length. His hands buried in my hair, holding me in place. I ran my hands up his thighs then clenched the cheeks of his ass, pulling him to me, taking all of him to the base. His salty, sweet taste slid across my tongue, and I wanted more.

"Not tonight, wicked Faerie," he said, his voice husky with desire.

He pushed away from me, his eyes once again their multifaceted, beautiful whiskey color. He pulled me to him, surrounding me with himself. Lifting me up, he spread my thighs. I wrapped my legs around his waist, and he pushed into me with a groan. I clung to him while my body adjusted to his. Kissing along the soft hollows of his neck. I wanted him so much at that moment that I thought I was going to come just from this.

He tilted his hips into me. Like it was nothing, he lifted me against him over and over. Our position had the heart of me pressed against his body, and I knew I wasn't going to be able to hold out. He stripped layer after layer away until I was raw with need. I bucked against him wildly, out of control. I crashed hard. The moan started deep in my core and vibrated out. Power leaked out of me in thin, rose gold waves, and I thought I was going to break into pieces. Keeping my face buried in his neck, I came. My body tightened against his, and I felt him shudder, but he held back.

When I was limp in his arms, he carried me to the bed, laying me down. Meeting no resistance, he stabbed into me in one stroke. I was so slick he went straight to my cervix, and his pressing into it brought pleasure so sharp it took my breath. I watched between us as he pulled out of me and entered again with agonizing control. He watched me, watch him, fuck me. It was the hottest thing I ever saw. I didn't want it to end. I wrapped my feet around his calves and tilted my hips to him, taking him all in, bringing him to that spot. He hit against it, and I arched into him, panting for more, but he held back. His control too great.

He reached down with his mouth and took first one nipple between his teeth and then the other, rolling them with his tongue, hard enough to hurt in a good way. It took my breath. There was no trace of his fangs as he nipped at me, bringing out little whimpers.

"You don't have to be gentle, babe. I won't break." I licked along the curve of his ear, grazing it with my teeth. His movement stuttered, then he grabbed my hips and pounded into me without restraint. Hitting that spot over and over. I felt myself stretch around him, deeper than I had ever been pulled before, and I cried out.

He had been careful with me. At that moment, I found out just how careful. Our first time together, he had been gentle, even when I thought he hadn't been. He unleashed himself, and I thrilled in it. Pain had never felt so good. I rose to meet him, bracing myself against the headboard with my arms so that my body couldn't evade his.

Hot power flowed over me, bowing my spine. My orgasm ripped out of me, and the headboard cracked under the force of a Master Vampire fucking against it. I felt him swell inside of me, and a snarl sounded in his throat. He pulled me to him and sank his fangs into the hollow of my neck. I came off the bed, clawing at his back. I couldn't breathe, my heart pounded against him, and the most agonizing ecstasy I have ever felt threatened to drown me.

I felt Aedan pump into me one more time before he held still, warm fluid pulsing like a heartbeat. He dropped on top of me, and we both fought to catch our breath. His heart raced against mine. I loved that I did this to him. That I could cause this ancient, powerful creature to lose himself.

"You undo me, Liomsa," he whispered into my hair. "I love you so very much."

"I love you, too, Aedan." I pulled the covers over us and snuggled into him. The soft sound of his breathing tickled my ear, and I slept. I dreamed nothing.

I slept for about an hour until the stickiness between my legs woke me up. I slipped out from under Aedan's arms and into the bathroom, closing the door behind me. It was only five in the morning; I didn't want to wake Aedan. I turned the shower on oh-my-what-have-you-done-hot and slipped in. I let the water sluice over me. I leaned against the shower wall and relaxed into it.

I never heard him enter, didn't hear the door open; his lips were simply on mine. He kissed me like it was the last thing he would ever do. I sank into the kiss and explored his mouth, taking my time. He tasted amazing. He didn't move to touch me with anything other than his lips. I opened my eyes and saw him watching me.

"Hi." I smiled into his mouth.

"Hello." He grinned back. "Are you okay?" he asked, worry creasing the lines of his eyes.

"Of course, I'm fine, Aedan. You aren't going to break me. If we are going to do this, then you can't hold back any part of yourself. Otherwise, it will all be a lie." His eyes darkened a shade, which was a new thing.

He dropped his barriers, and I felt the weight of his feelings crash into me. The Goddess was right; he did love me. Fiercely. Absolutely. Dangerously. Any worry I had in the back of my mind that this was all related to the feelings brought on by sex or the sharing of blood evaporated. I could feel him. He finally had something that was his.

He had said it last night, and I misunderstood, thinking he was talking about his House. I got it now. I was uniquely his, and the world had better look out. The funny thing is, I felt the same way. My feelings for him could make me very dangerous, indeed.

He washed me from head to toe, taking his time. He explored my body with soapy hands, bringing tingles of pleasure everywhere he touched. He washed and conditioned my hair. I let him explore me in a way he never had before. He looked at me like he was memorizing every hair, every spot, every scar.

We didn't talk; we just absorbed each other through little touches and gazes. I washed him too, tracing the hard lines of his muscles, watching them flex and relax with my touch; I drank him in. Turning him away from me, I traced the lines of scars along his back, pressing my breasts against him, placing kisses down his spine. I washed him until he was clean, and when I was done, he pulled me to him.

I could see the need in his face; it hardened the lines of it with longing and some distant pain. Maybe it would ease with time, and maybe it wouldn't. His needs had gone unfulfilled for longer than I knew, so they may never be satisfied. I told him I was in, and maybe he hadn't understood what that meant, but I had given myself to him.

I think at that time, he didn't understand just how much of myself I would give. I had never, ever, given myself freely before and didn't know how. Maybe you weren't supposed to do it this way, but I gave him everything I had. I was his. He was mine. I had never experienced anything like this before. It was reckless, terrifying, and by far the most pleasurable, frightening, and exhilarating feeling I had experienced in my life.

He turned me away from him, pulling my hips to his. I took him into me, shifting until it was comfortable. He splayed one hand across my back and held it there as he slid inside of me. The other he ran down my sides, touching me everywhere, all at once. He said a lot of things in a language I didn't understand.

Where before had been about power and letting go, this time was about need and desire. Everywhere he touched, he lit me on fire. It didn't take long, emotion flowed between us, and we let it, neither of us hiding anything. I let him know my thoughts, my feelings, my everything.

He came into me with a soft moan of release, taking me with him. It was gentle this time. He held his weight against the shower wall as my body finished milking him for the last drops he had, then he rewashed me. We toweled off and curled around one another under the covers as the dawn took us both down.

Chapter 17

I woke up a few hours later. Aedan was still out and curled around me, his nose buried in my hair. I untangled myself from him and headed into the bathroom to get dressed. I needed to go home and see to the horses and open the clinic. I slipped on jeans and a soft sweatshirt, threw on a dab of makeup, and headed out. Downstairs in the kitchen, I found coffee and breakfast waiting on me; it was hot as usual. I didn't understand Aedan's Brownie. One of these days, we were going to have a chat, though. I fixed an egg and sausage sandwich with what he left me, then poured the entire contents of the French press into a to-go cup. I texted Grania and Aedan, letting them know I had snuck off, then headed downstairs.

The lobby was bright; sunlight rippled off the Inner Harbor, making the day look warmer than it was. The concierge waved at me as I walked out.

The minute my feet stepped on the pavement, I was approached by the press. Ten or more reporters from various news organizations, some national, some of them local. They all shouted questions at me. I stopped, stunned, not knowing how to handle it.

"Miss Hennessey, what is your relationship with the Governor?"

"Miss Hennessey. What happened at the Spring Conclave, and can you explain the video footage of you taken that night?"

"Miss Hennessey, what are you?" I stilled at the last question.

The shouts came from everywhere, leaving me no safe place to go. I put my head down and walked to the garage, pushing through the crowd of people shouting questions.

Someone had finally asked. I knew it was coming. We all knew it was coming; I was not ready to answer the questions. I pushed my way to my truck, never saying a word.

Pulling away from the garage, I desperately hoped no one would follow. I didn't think these guys were like paparazzi or that they would chase me to my house, but I couldn't be sure. On my way down Pratt street, heading out of town, I called WBAL and asked to speak to Cindy.

She had done interviews with Aedan before and was very glad to hear from me. I knew I needed to get ahead of this, somehow. I could plan with the others, but I needed to make some kind of statement. Immediately. I agreed to be there the next day at nine for a taping; I did not agree to do anything live. That could go badly for me.

Traffic going in my direction was light, even as the traffic heading into the city was log jammed. I jumped on I-83 and then onto the Outer Loop heading to the Northwest Expressway and home. It was about a forty-minute drive on a good day, and I should be home by noon.

I came off the expressway and merged onto Route 140. A red light loomed ahead of me, and instead of slowing, I checked the light in the other direction. Seeing it yellow, I kept going, knowing by the time I got there, my side would be green.

Reaching down, I turned up the radio. I started flipping stations, wondering what had set the reporters off and if there was a story I should know about. Glancing up, I saw that my light was indeed green. I grinned as I sped up, loving it when they worked out like that.

I heard the scream of brakes and the crash of metal before the impact ripped through me. I hadn't seen it coming, but I saw it now. A semi had run the light and come across Route 91. All I could see was the huge grill smashing into me on the passenger side, pushing me into oncoming traffic.

Everything slowed.

They say these moments are measured by heartbeats, and everything moved so slowly I thought my heart would stop.

The scream of brakes coming from eastbound traffic was deafening, and I was hit again. And again. My truck rolled over once, twice, and the semi went with it, rolling over top and trapping my Chevy underneath. Airbags exploded from everywhere. I felt the crush of metal on me and heard the hiss of the engine. Everything stopped.

I felt Grania scream in my head, "LARA!"

I could feel her panic; I tried to let her know I was okay, but my peripheral vision closed in on me, and all I could see was black.

I heard voices before I could force my eyes open. My head was screaming, and I could feel blood running down my face. I couldn't move. My legs were pinned under something heavy. I tried moving but found all I could do was lift my head.

"We got a live one!" I felt fingers on my neck and knew someone was checking my pulse. "Get Trooper One out here now! Ma'am, we are going to get you out. Hang in there." All I could do was moan.

I was hurt. I knew it. I could feel the damage, and it was extensive. I kept my eyes open and got a good look at my surroundings. All I could see was twisted metal.

The smell of diesel fuel clouded the air, and smoke blew in wisps through shattered windows. I was covered in glass and smelled my own blood. I tried to look around, but the white of the airbags blocked my view. I was encased in metal, surrounded by unrecognizable shapes.

My legs were twisted underneath me at an unnatural angle. I knew they were broken. Metal protruded from my side; I could feel where it entered my body. I was impaled on something. I could breathe, but just barely. No part of me did not feel pain.

I heard yelling and screaming; I could feel Aedan in my head. I don't know how long it had been since the accident, but it had been long enough for him to fight through traffic and get here.

"Let me go to her!" he shouted at the medics or police, trying to hold him back.

I tried to let him know I was okay, but his mind was such a jumble I couldn't make sense of it. "She is Mine. Let me go to her," he shouted. He wouldn't hurt the humans or physically fight them, but he was trying his best to intimidate them into letting him through.

"Sir, as long as she is in that vehicle, she belongs to me. I need you to step back and let me do my job." The paramedic must have done something because Aedan stopped yelling.

I could feel the panic in his mind. I tried again to reach him, but I could only moan out loud. I tried reaching Grania, but that did not work either. I wondered, finally, if I had a head injury, possibly a severe one. That would explain my inability to reach them. Blood trickled into my eyes, and I let them drift closed.

I heard the HURST jaws of life start as workers struggled to unravel the mess I was in to get to me. It seemed like hours, and maybe it was. I felt the helicopter drop in and land; the blades shut off, waiting. I heard ambulances come and go, taking others away.

I tried to listen to the chatter of the firefighters and the medics working to free me. I knew the driver of the semi was dead. They thought I was, too, until they heard me moan. They said it was a miracle. They said my truck didn't even look like a truck anymore. I listened to what they said while I tried to reach Aedan. I knew he and Grania were out there, waiting. I could feel them, but I could not communicate with them. The sound of metal screeching and the hum of motors around me lulled me into a restless sleep.

I was tired, I could feel my heart slowing and my blood pressure dropping, but I held on anyway. I could heal the damage if they just got me out so that I could do it right. Using what energy I had, I constricted the blood vessels in my arms and legs, bringing my blood pressure up to a more normal level. It was all I could do until I was out.

Arms reached in and held my neck in a midline position, waking me up. A cervical collar was placed so I couldn't move. I screamed as they straightened my limbs and pulled me from the cradle of metal. I couldn't help it. I screamed again when they laid me on the backboard and strapped me down, securing me.

Aedan growled and rushed to my side. I felt his warm, strong hand grab my cold one. I tried to open my eyes but couldn't. I squeezed his fingers as they lifted me into the helicopter. The doors slammed shut, and we lifted off.

"Trooper One to Shock Trauma, on the roof in ten multiple injuries. BP 50's palp. Transfusing one unit. Heart rate 140s. Maintaining airway. Going to offload hot."

I felt the pinch of the needle as they started my IV, and the sting of thick blood run into my veins.

They were so worried about me that they weren't even stopping the helicopter blades before they got me off. I looked inside my body and categorized my injuries for them. Both my femurs were broken in more than one place. Blood pooled in my thighs from the trauma of the breaks. My left lower leg was shattered, and bones stuck out through the skin. My left upper and lower arm was also fractured, probably from the impact.

The semi had hit me on the right side, pushing me to the left. My pelvis was fractured, and I was bleeding from one of the arteries there. It had been sheared from the force of impact. I had fractures to my spine, but they did not intrude into my spinal column. I had neck fractures at the cervical levels three and four, which sucked. Like, extra bad. I also had injuries to my spleen, liver, and left kidney. I used what energy I had to work on those before I got into the trauma bays. I did not want to lose an organ over something I could fix.

I couldn't fix it all before I got there, but I could fix it in time. My body had started to heal before I turned my attention to it anyway. I would have survived regardless of my abilities to Heal myself.

Lights flashed over my eyes as the flight crew whisked mc into the trauma bay. The press of cold steel ran up my legs as I felt them cut off my clothes. Had I been watching, it would have been kind of cool. I had seen traumas run like a well-oiled machine before. Shock Trauma is the best of the best. I'd like to see them in action, on someone else. They log rolled me and took my clothes, covering me with a warm blanket. I let the shouts soothe me.

"Unit three up on the Level One."

"Hemoglobin is five. Initiate Mass Transfusion."

"We are at ten minutes; let's get packed up and get to CT scan."

"FAST exam is positive; there's blood in the belly."

"Get the OR ready."

"We need to intubate."

"No," I croaked.

"Let's get to CT and see what we've got."

I felt my stretcher move, and off we went to CT scan. In smooth, effortless movement, I was placed on the table, and pictures were taken. My head was clearing up, and I reached out to Aedan and found him close. Relief poured through him at the feel of me in his mind, and I let him brush through me. I kept the connection open, even as I rested again. He didn't fuss or rage; he just sent me his strength.

I was wheeled back into the trauma bay, and for the first time, most of the team filtered off. A nurse stayed behind and spiked another bag of blood product into the machine that would pump it into me within minutes. Soft beeps from the monitors were the only sound in the room. The warm blankets they placed over me cooled, and my naked skin beneath them began to chill.

"Sam," Will you pop out and let me talk to the patient alone for a second?" I heard a voice say. I couldn't see who was talking. I was flat on my back with my neck in the collar to keep me from hurting myself worse with movement.

"Uh. Sure, Dr. Abrams. She'll need a unit of platelets in just a few minutes."

"I'll get it," he said.

I heard the door slide shut as she left.

A man's face came into view. He was probably in his sixties with gray hair at his temples; his skin was dark brown with a cinnamon tint to it.

"Miss Hennessey, my name is Dr. Abrams. I'm the trauma surgeon today. That was quite an accident," he said.

"Yes, sir," I whispered.

"Ortho will be in shortly to straighten out your extremities and get you casted. Are you sure you don't want to be intubated for pain control?" he asked.

"No, thanks. I don't want that," I said.

"You're a nurse, right? One of the medics recognized you from the Emergency Department at Carroll Hospital."

"Yes, Sir."

"I need to ask you a question, and I want you to be honest."

"Okay," I croaked, knowing what was coming.

"You aren't human, are you?"

I sighed, "Not entirely, no, but doctor-patient confidentiality is going to not let you say anything to anyone about that," I said simply. I could feel my strength coming back. The blood had helped, but my body was healing itself, I worked on the big stuff little by little, but my magic was doing the rest.

"I'm a friend of Dr. Breger's," he said, meeting my eyes.

"Oh."

"Your injuries were severe, they still are, but I watched your brain bleeding improve from one CT frame to the next. You are still very injured. I think I know who you are, just based on your name and the fact that you are healing yourself. I need to keep you overnight so that there will be no suspicion unless you want to come out now. Let ortho straighten your limbs and cast you. You can take the casts off at home. Your brain is already healing. Your spleen laceration has healed, and your liver laceration is almost healed. The ball is in your court on how you want to proceed," he stopped, waiting for my response.

"My boyfriend is here; can I talk to him?" I asked.

"Is he the vampire tearing apart my waiting room?"

"Most likely."

"I'll be right back."

The second Doctor Abrams was gone, a nurse hustled in and changed bags around, hummed over my blood pressure and, adjusted a few other things, and walked back out.

Dr. Abrams came in, trailing an irate Aedan and Grania behind him. He slid the door shut and leaned against the counter.

Aedan rushed to my side, grabbing my hand.

"Anamcara," was all he said. He held my hand, and tears rolled down his face. Grania slipped to my other side and picked up my broken arm, cradling it to her. I didn't have the heart to tell her how bad it hurt, but she noticed the crunching noises and laid it back down on the bed, stepping back. She buried her head in her hands and sobbed.

"Ortho is here, Miss Hennessey; what do you want to do?" Dr. Abrams asked.

I explained everything to Aedan, who said nothing until I was done.

"You are not coming out, Lara. I forbid it," he said when I was done.

"Forbid it? Are you fucking kidding? You don't get to decide this for me, Aedan," I yelled. It lost some of its intensity coming from a naked woman flat on her back, but I put some extra oomph into it anyway." I saw Dr. Abrams turn away to hide a chuckle. "I already called WBAL. I am going on tomorrow. I want the orthopedic doctors to straighten my arm and legs before they heal crooked, and they have to rebreak them, Aedan."

"No. You will stay in the hospital and keep your secret."

"Do you hear yourself? Do you want me to let them do surgery on me too?" I yelled.

"Whatever they need to do, let them do it," he growled at me, leaning over so I could see that his eyes had paled a shade.

"I am not. Absolutely not doing that. Dr. Abrams, let ortho in, please."

"Do not let the others in yet, doctor. Lara, listen to me. You cannot come out. You will have a target on your back," he said, scrubbing his hand over his face.

"I already have a target on my back. They already know. Reporters were waiting for me at the hotel today, asking questions. They know. We knew this was coming. We need to get out ahead of it. We'll come up with a plan together, but this is what I'm doing, Aedan. I love you, but don't try to control me. Understand?" I said, sinking back into the stretcher, suddenly tired. "Groups like the Watchers or whatever are getting dangerous. More the more supernaturals that come out, the less influence these groups have," I finished, rubbing my good arm down my face.

My other arm began to throb painfully, and I knew it was starting to heal. I didn't want them to have to crack it up again to make it straight.

"I just worry for you, Liomsa." Aedan squatted down, getting on my level. I turned to face him as much as the collar would allow. "I thought you had died. Our link was severed," he whispered.

"I had a head injury, babe. It mostly healed before I could get into the CT scanner. Everyone is going to know. We need to control the spin. That's the best we can hope for, okay?" A tear slipped from my eyes. "I know it's going to cause trouble, but it needs to be done anyway. They were asking about the video, Aedan. They already know." I grasped his hand, pulling it to me, and kissed it.

"Okay," he said, taking a deep breath and letting it out. "Okay. We will come up with a plan. You are right. He stepped back, and Dr. Abrams slid the glass door open to let the Orthopedic surgeons in.

Orthopods are the most focused group of individuals in medicine. They see a broken bone and dive on it like it's gold. I've seen them jump in on a broken bone before the patient was even stable enough to tolerate their not-so-tender attentions. The muscled, young residents clucked and conversed over my legs under the watchful eye of their attending, taking portable X-rays to see which way would be best to straighten them.

"Call the nurse and get some Versed and Fentanyl for sedation."

"No," I said. "Let the Governor do it." I used Aedan's official title to get their attention. "I don't want narcotics. Aedan, please," I asked. He came to my side and leaned over me, pulling my hair through his fingers.

I surrendered myself to his compulsion. I had to let down every shield I had and pull him in so it would work, but as he spoke in his sing-song voice of Ireland, in a language I did not understand, I gave myself over to him.

I felt the pull on my legs and heard the bones crack into place. Each leg took a long time, but I felt them straighten. There was almost no pain, but I saw Aedan flinch and wondered about that meant. I heard Dr. Abrams tell ortho not to cast them. The argument was quick and loud over his instructions, but it was settled when Aedan said in a low and dangerous voice that I was not human.

A hush settled over the room while everyone looked at each other, unsure how to proceed. Eventually, medical training took over, and they moved to my arm. When their focus was off my legs, I began to heal them, weaving the rose gold threads of my aura over the bones until they were whole again. I knew the doctors would not see the magic. At least most of them. Dr. Abrams watched with rapt attention.

When they were finished with my arm, I moved to it, weaving until it was also whole and unbroken. I fixed my back fractures and sat up, taking off the collar.

"Take me home, Aedan. This may be the last night I have peace."

The doctors in the room froze. I wasn't sure I could stand; I was sore all over. So, I sat while my blood pressure normalized from too quick a motion. The nurse walked in, saw me sitting up on the side of the stretcher holding my blanket to me, and simply walked to the level one infuser, turning it off.

Just another day at Shock Trauma.

She took my IVs out and held gauze over both spots, like this kind of thing happened all the time. I knew where she was coming from, and I gave her a small smile. She was a good nurse.

"Thank you all for saving my life; I couldn't have done it myself without the support. I appreciate everything you did except maybe the rectal exam. I could've done without that," I chuckled.

"Send the bill to the American Vampire Association along with a list of any new medical equipment your trauma center needs, and I will see that you have it. Thank you for caring for her when she could not care for herself. Also, any money you need to explore what it will take to work on Supernatural creatures, please feel free to ask for. There is always room in the budget," Aedan said, scooping me up. He walked with me to the doors, Grania dropping in beside him.

"Wait. Sir." One of the orthopedic surgeons touched Aedan's arm, effectively stopping him. "Is there any chance there is one of, uh, you, that would be willing to work with us on traumas? Usually, we have to give a ton of sedatives to do what we just did with nothing. Those were the easiest reductions of the most complicated fractures I've ever done. Someone with the ability to ease the pain would be a huge help around here.

Aedan stood, considering. "I will go through my files and find someone appropriate. Thank you again for your services, call my office, and I will arrange whatever you need," he said, pulling me to him and walking out.

Chapter 18

The ride home was quiet. Grania drove, and Aedan sat with me in the back. I looked out the window at the passing lights and held my blanket close around me. Aedan held my hand and watched me watch the lights. Grania said nothing, but I saw her check the rearview mirror often. My thoughts were heavy. This day had been an eye-opener for me.

"My mother isn't dead, is she Aedan?" I asked, not looking over at him.

"I do not see how she can be, Lara," he said, using my given name instead of one of his pet names. I nodded my head in acceptance as a tear slipped down my face.

"After today, I don't either," I said. "That's all I could think about while I was in the truck, waiting to be cut out. There's no way I should have survived. I'm not even a little bit human anymore, am I?" I tried to make it a question, but it came out as a sob. Grania and Aedan looked at each other through the rearview mirror but said nothing.

"Tell me, Aedan, tell me what happened. You know. Don't keep this from me." I looked at him then, turning my angry eyes to his sad ones. He took a slow deep breath in and let it out.

"We do not know exactly what happened, Lara. I swear to you, we do not. But on the night you were poisoned, something changed. I do not know what, but it was significant," he said, looking sad.

I still thought he was holding out and maybe even outright lying, but I let it go. That night had been horrible for everyone. If Aedan didn't want to talk about it, then it was probably worse than I knew. I would have to live with that. The body I had a year ago would not have survived the car wreck. I didn't know what that meant, but it meant something.

Maybe it was just the natural progression of my power and the fact that I was getting older by Faerie standards, or maybe whatever part of me that was human had died during one of my more extreme moments of late. I wasn't going to poke it. I just couldn't.

We pulled into the drive, and I was surprised to see the spot where Aedan's house once stood lit up as bright as daylight. A crew of fifty or more men worked on framing up his new house. Trucks stood at the ready, filled with supplies. Concrete trucks poured basement walls into forms, and men hauled supplies into the empty space.

"It will go up very quickly. I have teams working around the clock," he said at a loss to say anything else.

"It's going to be great, Aedan. We are all going to love it." I reached for his hand, and he gave it.

Grania parked in the garage and pulled out a key card, letting us in. I was able to walk on legs that had been shattered into pieces a few short hours ago. I was weak and tired, but I could stand. I hugged her to me.

"Thanks for being there," I said.

"Thanks for not dying," she answered. "I don't want to go through *that* again. She rolled her eyes so hard no iris showed.

"I'm glad it's all about you," I said, punching her in the arm.

"Me too," she said, walking away.

In the kitchen, a meal was laid out. That tricky bastard must have a bell on me to know when I'll be home. I appreciated it. Grania grabbed a plate and piled food high. I joined her, tying my blanket in a knot so it would stay up.

Aedan had apparently not been made aware of this change in her because he stood slack-jawed and staring at us as we shoveled chicken teriyaki, rice, and broccoli down our respective throats. I don't think she needed to eat, but she enjoyed it for sure and was maybe stress eating a little. We finished our meal in silence that was only broken by grunts and groans as we ate. Aedan sipped wine and watched it all with a lopsided grin. When we were finished, Grania slipped out, and I heard her shower turn on. I stood and piled dishes in the sink.

"I will get those," he said. Go shower. We need to plan your press conference before you rest. I didn't say anything, just walked away.

I turned the shower on not-as-hot-as-normal hot. While most of me had healed, there were still glass shards and the tiny cuts from them on my skin. They burned when the water touched them. I rinsed the worst of it off first, then scrubbed my skin around the abrasions. I heard Aedan come in and shut the door to our bedroom behind him. I got out, dressed in soft pajamas, and opened the door between us. He lay on my bed, his head thrown back, arms crossed over his chest. He looked tired and did not sit up when I edged in beside him.

"I want you to drink from me," he said, not looking at me, you need strength.

"Tomorrow, after the interview, I will. If any of these marks are left in the morning, it will help my story," I said.

"And just what is your story?" he asked, covering his face with both hands and scrubbing it hard.

"I'd like to out us all as a race. I mean, I don't know anyone else, but that actually helps me. I'm going to say I am part human, part Fae, which is the truth as I know it," I said, not meeting his eyes. "I'm going to explain that there are a lot of us out there and that most people just don't even realize they have the mix in them."

"I see," he said, still not looking at me.

"I'm going to be as vague as possible and not admit to any of the magic I have. As far as the Spring Conclave? I'm just going to outright deny everything. There is nothing on the video with Noah that they can prove."

"I see," he said again.

"Aedan, talk to me. Please. What is going on? Why are you so unhappy about this?" I asked, not reaching for him.

"I am unhappy about this entire day. I thought you died. You were just…gone from my mind. It felt like a part of me had been ripped away. Now I fear that you are putting yourself out there where there is no buffer. You being the only one to out means that you are the only one under the spotlight. You will not be safe. I have waited too long to have you by my side, only to lose you to what could be if this goes badly," he said, looking at me then.

"Aedan, how is this any different from when you came out? How? You are the face of vampires all across the world. You. The world knows others exist, but you are the one on the cover of Time magazine. You're still here. It will be easier for me.

"It will be a free for all. Every human with a green thumb or a sixth sense is going to guess they are part Fae. There is no test, or we would've been found out a long time ago. All those folks that never get sick or can wiggle a pencil with their mind are going to go to the media and say 'Me too!' There will be such a rush that I will end up insignificant in the whole thing," I argued.

"Besides, the real Fae, the ones still in Talamh na Sithe, need help. One of them came to see me already. They should have a choice to stay in this world and be free.

They could get away from the twisted politics of the place if they want to," I sighed.

I had made a promise to the Goddess that I would bring her People out into the world. She never said I couldn't tell Aedan. I didn't want there to be secrets between us. I took a big breath and continued.

"When I went there, I met the Goddess, like the actual one. She taught me how to do her magic," I started.

"I know she did, Anamcara. I saw you unmake my chains. No one else could have taught you that," he said, his face clenched in worry.

"Okay, well, she also gave me the means to find you, but I had to make her a deal." He stiffened at the word, his eyes snapping to mine. "It wasn't a bad deal at all; she actually helped us both out a lot. I had to promise to bring her people out into the world. To give them a choice. I'm saving myself the aggravation at the same time, but I am just keeping that promise, Aedan." I finished.

"What else did you promise? What are the other parts of her deal? I must know." He asked, looking away. I could tell he was thinking the worst.

"It was simple, I swear, and she got me out of a deal with Aramea that probably wouldn't have ended well for me, knowing what I know now. I had to bring you home for starters." He looked at me again; his brows flew to the top of his head in surprise. "I had to heal the land, which I already did, and I have to stay myself, which I am going to try hard to do. She gave me keys to a shit ton of power, and I'm not going to lie and say it doesn't scare me, but I have you, her, and Galahad to keep me straight.

"Yes, you do." He came to me then and wrapped me in his arms, placing a kiss on the top of my head. "I still do not like it. It is not my wish to see you hounded."

"It's already started; I honestly believe this will make it better. People are getting curious, laws are being passed that hope to limit your rights, and more and more groups want to come out. Maybe outing the Fae will make such a stir that no one group will be the focus anymore. It might help us all, actually. We still have to figure out the Watchers and Sheriff Collins. We need to stop reacting and get ahead of some of this," I said, curling into his arms.

He sighed, inhaling the scent of my hair. "You are right. I have been so focused on national and worldwide issues that I let my personal ones fall apart. We do need to start getting ahead of this, as you say. Regardless of what happens, you will have the support you need."

"I know, thank you."

I laid down to sleep and, even though it was early for Aedan, he lay down with me until I drifted off. I felt him get up when he thought I was out. I knew he was worried. He didn't leave to go back to the city. Instead, he spent the night on the phone talking in hushed tones. I couldn't hear what he said, but his accent was deep, as it often is when he is more emotional. I drifted in and out of sleep. My body was stiff and sore, making it hard to be comfortable.

He came in not long before dawn and slipped in beside me, I curled into him, and he pulled me to his side. I could feel the tension in his body ease, but not completely.

Chapter 19

My alarm went off a little after eight. I didn't need long to get ready, so I had decided to sleep in. I eased from Aedan's side, feeling the pull of my muscles. I was still sore, but I was better. In the bathroom, I turned my flat iron on and brushed my teeth while it heated. My face was pale, and there were dark circles under my eyes. There was harsh bruising on my jaw, and the side of my head was still sore where it had bounced off something.

My arms were covered with bruises, and my left arm was almost a solid purple, but I could move everything, and there wasn't much pain when I did. I dusted my face with powder, put on mascara, but did not downplay the fact that I had been injured. It would make my story go further.

I straightened my ratty hair since I had slept on it wet and moved through the bedroom to grab the coffee and muffins waiting for me in the kitchen. I laid money on the counter for the cook since he was working for me now.

Aedan walked past me, grabbed the cash, and put it back in my hand before heading for the garage. I stopped, staring after him. He was dressed in clean clothes and smelled like he had showered. I looked around, wondering what the hell.

"Old Vampire. Do not need to sleep. We should go." He grinned over his shoulder at me, smiling at my gaping mouth and shocked expression. I followed him out.

"You don't need to go, Aedan," I said, buckling my seat belt.

"Actually, I do. You did not give me much time, but I managed to get my PR people working on this so that the spin, as you say, goes your way and not another. If I had more time, I could have had legal protections in place, but as you are going to claim to be human, I am hopeful they will not try to whisk you away to study," he stated, not meeting my eyes; his jaw was tight. There was a trace of anger in his posture.

"Babe, I'm sorry. I am. I just thought this would be the easiest way. I don't think we will need all that other stuff," I said, reaching for his leg across the seat.

"Let us hope not." I knew he was still unhappy, but then he is also used to always getting his way. Too bad that part of his life was going to change. Rapidly.

At the studio, we were ushered into a taping room, and makeup people descended on me in a flash as introductions were volleyed around, and people moved fast to make things happen.

"No. No makeup," I said, moving away from them. "What I have on is enough."

"You look half dead," one of the young makeup artists said, offended that I pushed her away.

"She looks fine," Aedan said, ending the debate. How come everyone argues with me, and no one argues with him? I hate that. Cindy came in, and the interview started. Aedan stayed off-screen but alert. This was a taping, and so anything I didn't want to answer or that needed to be edited out could be, he assured me of that.

"Miss Hennessey," She started.

"Call me Lara, please." I smiled at her, not looking at the camera.

"I hear you were in a serious motor vehicle accident yesterday after agreeing to this interview," she stated, leaning forward.

"Yes. I was. One person was killed, and many others were treated as well," I answered. "I was t-boned by a semi that ran a red light." I kept my face impassive.

"Yet here you are today, even though the hospital said your condition was critical at the time of the accident. How is that?"

I took a deep breath and straightened my spine, wincing at the soreness. I hoped the camera caught it. "I am part of an extensive and very diverse group of people whose ancestors mixed with an old supernatural group of beings called the Tuatha de Danann. So, basically, I am part human and part Fae, or Faerie if you will," I said, meeting her eyes but keeping my face pleasantly bland.

"A Faerie?" she asked, too calmly. Aedan must have warned her. "And that makes you what? Hard to injure? Judging by the pictures on the scene of your accident, I'd say impossible to kill," she asked, getting a gleam in her eyes that I didn't like.

Aedan growled from behind me in warning. The editor was going to be busy. Aedan said the final taping had to be approved by him before it could run. He made them sign a contract.

"I am more resilient than I would be without that mixed heritage, but that's all. I heal faster than average and don't usually get the flu or whatever bug is going around, but I'm a nurse and have good immunity, so there's that," I answered.

"How many others are there?" she asked, slowing her roll and taking the focus off me.

"Many thousands, most likely. I didn't know about my mixed blood until I met the Governor of the Eastern Region of Vampires, and he explained it to me. In his many years as a vampire, he has come across thousands like me. It is common knowledge among them that humans with mixed Fae blood exist. Maybe you have a talent for growing things or a sixth sense. Maybe you see things others don't or have a strong talent with animals. If so, then you probably have mixed heritage," I said, banging home my point.

"What does this mean for the rest of us, the regular humans that don't have this mixed blood as you call it?" She leaned back, looking at me intently.

"Nothing. It means absolutely nothing. I'm just a regular person. The same person I was last week or last year. It means I'll get better from the bruises a few days earlier than someone else might. I have an inborn knack for being a nurse, but that's about all," I answered.

"Rumors are going around that there is much more to you than that, Lara," she said, trying to slip one in.

"I date the Governor of The Eastern Region of Vampires, I go with him to a lot of places, and he is an incredibly powerful individual. Being around him, I have no doubt, fuels those rumors, but he is the power player in our relationship, I assure you," I laughed a little, evading the actual question by throwing her an even juicier bone.

"So, you are a couple?" she asked.

"Yes. We've been together a few months now, and he is helping the Fae transition as a group the way the vampires did. We don't pack the same punch as they do since we are simply humans with a few faeries on the family tree from a long, long time ago. I'm not going to name the names of the others I know, but I am sure they will be trending on social media since, to us, it's a big deal. Hashtag Faelife," I said on a whim. I was going to break Instagram.

"What are your plans for the future?" she asked, "and how does the Governor fit into this? Word is he is tightening the reins on his People since the Spring Conclave and that there was some controversy over you being his representative," she asked, digging again.

"My plans are simple. I work in a private health care clinic in Westminster that sees the human families and employees of local vampires. They have dealt with prejudice and lived in secret for a long time, and current health care settings aren't equipped to deal with them yet. The doctor I work for prescribes medicine for them, and we treat things like the flu, colds, lacerations, or whatever needs to be managed. It's a home setting that makes them feel at ease.

"As far as Aedan, he is working with Shock Trauma to develop a program to treat humans, vampires, or whatever else may come in. I'm sure there have been plenty of vampire car accidents, and there may be times when a supernatural ends up in the hospital. He is hoping to bridge any gap in knowledge there might be. As for any other plans? You will have to ask him; I try very hard to stay out of it," I said, wanting that sip of Aedan's blood. I was tiring too fast.

"What happened to the old Tuatha de Danann? My research cited the fact that they were immortal." Her face was careful, and I was guessing she was toeing some line Aedan had laid down. I answered anyway, even though I felt him stiffen behind me.

"They were forced underground," I answered quickly before Aedan could pipe in. "There was some kind of war between them and the Milesians in Ireland a long ass time ago, and their homeland got pushed out of this one. If I am honest, I don't understand all that, but that is the history anyway."

"Are they still around? Can they come here?"

"I would say yes. Speaking from the standpoint of legends and histories, there are ways to travel back and forth. Hypothetically anyway. I can't speak to that, though."

"Are there wedding bells in your future? That would be the event of the century. A beautiful Faerie Princess marrying the Governor of the Eastern Region of Vampires," she asked, a wicked grin flashing across her face.

Behind me, Aedan choked on the water he must have been sipping, and my eyebrows flew to my hairline. I threw my head back, laughing for the first time in a while. I mean belly laughing.

"Look, Cindy," I said when I could talk again. "I'm just trying to get through this week. I'll worry about the next one when it comes." The interview cut to an end. That last exchange did not get edited out. You could even hear the sound of surprise from Aedan in the final cut.

The interview played nationwide within the hour. It was edited to perfection and had turned out better than I hoped. My too pale skin and bruises left from the wreck made my point for me. I was just a human. By the end of the day, there were millions of hashtag Faelife posts on every social media outlet there is. It trended for days. Not only did Instagram break, but all of the internet suffered.

I was right when I said I would be forgotten in the grand scheme of things because I was. My phone didn't ring. Not once. Actresses, novelists, television personalities, and single blue-collar moms and dads posted about their Faerie heritage and made up the best stories. Most of them far grander than my actual truth. There was no backlash and no legal rumblings. No one came to take me to study.

So many humans came out that it was a cliché in hours. It was perfect. No one can fake being a vampire, not beyond fake fangs and trying to drink blood, but anyone can fake being a Faerie, and everyone did.

"You did not say no," Aedan said as we drove back to Westminster.

"Say no to what?"

"Marriage." He looked over at me, his face deadly serious.

I punched his arm and sighed with a soft grin. "Slow your roll, old man." He grinned back, a wicked light in his eyes. He looked like he had won something.

"You still did not say no. I will take that as a yes." He raised one eyebrow and gave me a rakish grin.

"Uuuuuuuugh," I said. "Why are we going this way?" I asked, changing the subject. He had taken Route 26 from Baltimore, which was a roundabout way to get to Westminster.

"I need you to pick something out," he answered.

"Oh, God. What did you do now?" I asked, sinking back into my seat. I had the seat warmers on to ease the soreness in my muscles.

"You will see."

I glared at him, but he ignored me, as usual. We pulled into the Chevy dealership in Eldersburg, and I got a hint of his plan.

"You are not buying me a truck, Aedan." I glared harder at him.

"I already bought you a truck; you are just here to pick out which color you want," he answered, a shit-eating grin on his face. He moved out of the door so fast I couldn't hit him again.

Asshole.

He strolled to the line of one-ton diesels parked at the side of the building. I sat in the Escalade, refusing to get out. I watched him open doors and sniff interiors. When the salesman came to talk to him, I decided I had better get out.

"I can buy my own damn truck, Acdan," I snarled, stomping up next to him.

"I know you can, but it made me happy to buy one for you," he said, looking bland. The salesman just stood there, grinning. I wanted to punch him too.

"You aren't buying me a truck," I said, folding my arms across my chest. I had to clamp down on my hands because I was all too tempted to blast him.

"As I said, I already paid for the truck; you must simply pick the color."

"I'm going to strangle you."

"Pick the color first, Liomsa," he said, picking fake lint off his jacket.

I glared between them and knew this was another fight I was going to lose. Maybe he was still getting his way.

All the damn time.

I looked at the trucks lined up; they were so pretty. I hadn't had a new truck in forever. These were four-door High Country editions, so they were top of the line.

"Aedan, these are seventy thousand dollar trucks. I can't accept this," I said.

"I already paid for the truck," he answered.

"Tad more than that, ma'am," The salesman said at the same time. We both glared at him.

"Aedan."

"Lara," he said, using my name to let me know I wasn't going to win this.

"Fine," I growled.

I stomped the line of trucks and checked them out. There was a black one, a gray one, a red one and a white one. They were all beautiful. Some had tan leather interiors, and some had gray. The leather was butter soft, and there wasn't an option they didn't have. I narrowed it down to red and white, but the red one was the only one with gray interior and a sunroof, and although that seems like a non-issue in a truck, to me, it is an issue. I had always wanted one. The salesman gave me the keys to the thing, shook hands with Aedan, and walked away. I kissed Aedan's cheek.

"Thank you, Aedan," I said, using his name to let him know I was serious since that is apparently a thing now.

"You are welcome. Thank you for taking my gift. It makes me happy."

"As expensive as it is, it should make you very happy then. I never give you anything, and you always get me the best stuff," I whined.

He grabbed my face in one hand. "You give me the world. That is your gift to me, and you give it every day. I love you," he said.

"I love you, too," I said, overcome with emotion.

Chapter 20

I followed him home, breathing in the smell of leather and a new vehicle. The Chevy drove like a race car compared to my old one, and it took a little getting used to. I wanted to touch everything and play with the buttons, but I didn't. I kept my hands on the wheel and my eyes on the road.

We were parked in my driveway in twenty minutes. There were cars already here and people waiting to be seen. I opened the doors to the clinic and let them in, asking them to wait while I changed clothes. I don't usually open until noon anyway, so they were a little early.

My house smelled of spring rain and damp earth.

"Son of a Bitch," I mumbled, grabbing Aedan's hand as we walked through the living room.

"Grandmother, you need to start calling." I sighed. Aedan tried to drop my hand, but I wouldn't let him.

"Ah, Granddaughter. I wondered when you were going to get home after your busy day." Her eyes glittered with finely controlled rage that slipped just a little further to the edge when she saw my hand in Aedan's.

The TV was on Fox News, and the interview was playing. She slowly changed the channel to CNN, then the local news, and I saw that it was on all the channels. That was quick. Maybe that had been arranged as well.

"What did you think you were doing," she said, stalking to me. "Remove your filthy hands, Oathbreaker, or I will make you," she snarled, her expression dark and furious in a way that I had never seen before.

"He's mine, Grandmother." I leaned up on my tip-toes and kissed his cheek. Staring at her, matching my face to hers, and daring her to say something. Anything.

Her spine stiffened as he brought his arm around my waist and let it drift lower. He said nothing.

"So that is the way of it. You have no right. None. No right to go public with our secret. My People do not need to be of this world, they have their own, and I will see you trapped in it as well, you haughty little bitch. You will not waste yourself on Fae trash that I failed to take out. You will recognize your place, and I will see to it that you fall in line," she said, taking the gloves off and proving that she never, ever, had good intentions toward me.

Any act of kindness, any act of caring, had been fake. My heart sank a little. She was the only blood I had left. Not the only family but the only blood. I stopped letting it matter.

"It was OUR secret, not yours, and my story to tell. You ruined your People. Let them come here and be free of you if they want. You have no say in my life. Zero. You are a cancer to your kind, and I will never bow to you," I said, my voice shaking from anger. I didn't let the doors to my power open, which showed a lack of control, and I was getting better. I didn't need much time to waste her ass anyway.

"And who will protect them here in this strange land? You?" She laughed at that, tendrils of her power leaking out around her.

"Better than you. Better than what you did to them. You ruined their homeland. You. Your actions ruined any future they had. Well, I gave it back to them when I healed it, and now all they have to do is survive you. I will lay my hands on them and heal them all. Not you. Them. They will do what you never could, and I will laugh when your head rolls," I said, dropping Aedan's hand and advancing to her.

"I will see you in chains, little girl. I will see you punished for this. Ask your lover what that means," she said, advancing to meet me. We stood eye to eye.

"Try me," I threatened, raising my eyebrow. Aedan tried to pull me back, but I refused. I could take that bitch. I know it.

"Ask your lover what it felt like to be under me. Ask him what it felt like when I fucked him to the point where he emptied himself into me. You aren't the first in our line to sample Coimeadai Lasair's pleasure, Lara Hennessey. Ask him what it felt like when I rode his very fine cock to completion," she said, sneering into my face. I felt Aedan crumple behind me.

"Answer me this, Aramea, was he in chains when you felt his so-called pleasure?" I asked, knowing the answer in my soul. I wove a sword with my aura and my intent, and it glowed a soft rose gold in my hand. I don't know how I did it, but I did. I held it to her throat, and I could feel it pulsing with my magic. Her eyes went wide. She would know who's magic I used to make it; she would have to. For the first time, I saw real fear in her.

"You don't think I know the story? You don't think I guessed what part you played in it? There is nothing you could ever say. Nothing you could ever do to make Aedan the guilty party in your awful but pretend vengeance. Torturing him only made you a sick, weak, and pathetic imitation of what he was, is, and always will be compared to you. It's you that I hate. Now get the fuck out of my house before I kill you and find a way to make it permanent." I snarled in her face, my power finally leaking out and causing the hair on my arms to stand.

She snapped out of my sight and was gone.

I pulled the sword back into me and turned to Aedan to find his face twisted in agony. I didn't need to ask him if what she said was true. I knew it was. I could see it and my heart broke for him. I would end her for that look she had put on his face.

"Aedan, listen to me," I said, grabbing his face in my hands, trying to force his eyes down to me. They stared at a spot above my head, frozen, relieving some awful memory.

"Aedan... Coi," I demanded, using his other name when he refused to acknowledge me, the one his mother, the Goddess, calls him. His eyes came to mine.

"I don't care. None of it matters. Not to me. Not to you. Not anymore. None of it. Come back to this time. Come back to this place. What she did to you is not your fault. It never was. Ever. You aren't the same person, even if she is." I leaned up as tall as I could and placed a kiss on his lips. At first, he just stood there, still living a memory I never wanted to share. Then he bent to me, wrapping his arms around my waist, pulling me to him.

"I will never let her touch you," he said, burying his head in my neck.

"I know." I could feel him shaking against me. I let him scoop me up and sit me on the counter. I had worn a skirt to the taping, and he pushed it roughly around my hips, burying his face in my hair as he pushed inside of me. I wasn't ready, and with his size, it hurt a little, but my body made the adjustment, accepting him into it anyway.

I licked a line on his neck, infusing enough power into it to open his vein and drink from him until the pain and soreness from the accident were gone. He dipped his head lower and groaned into my hair. I let him take what he needed at that moment, and I gave back all I could.

He needed to have a different memory in his head, and I gave it to him. He moved inside me, kissing and touching my face, watching with open eyes as I came against him. I dropped the walls I shielded my emotions behind and let them lick over him. He would not have to guess what I thought because I showed him.

I would not let him think, not for one minute, that Aramea could change what is between us. If anything, she made it stronger.

This was a secret he didn't have to keep anymore. It could be just him. Just me. Nothing dark waiting to jump out from the past. With delicate slowness, he eased his long fangs into the spot he so loved, and it was like being entered again. I felt each glorious inch they sank into me. I shuddered against him until the only thing on my mind was how ecstatic it felt as he drank his fill. Groaning low as he came, he sagged against my chest, pulling me in tight.

"Anamcara."

"Babe." I stifled a grin.

"You need another nickname for me," he smiled into my hair, and I knew I had accomplished my goal.

"Pookie?"

"No."

"Studmuffin?"

"Absolutely not."

"Snookums?"

"I will strangle you."

"Ok, babe, I need a quick shower so I can get to work. There are folks down there waiting." I kissed the tip of his nose and pushed him away from me, walking to the bathroom. He followed, staying close, and I let him because I knew he needed it.

Aramea had ripped open an old wound he probably thought long healed. He might need a minute. I wanted to kill her for that. She had no right. I tried to push it out of my head. It was hard, but I managed to tamp it down into the pile of things I would deal with later.

It was a huge pile.

He hung out as I showered and dressed. We talked about everything but nothing of significance. He kissed me before he left. I promised to see him at the hotel later. We were fine. We would move on from this.

Chapter 21

I felt like a million dollars when I went downstairs. I was loose and relaxed from good sex and pain-free from sucking on Aedan's neck. I could get used to this. Boyfriend perk number three. Or was it four? It was hard to count. The clinic had a ton of people waiting. Mostly little things, a few lacerations, a fever, some end of the season flu, and a bellyache. Everyone was talking and laughing about the interview. They knew it was ninety-nine percent bullshit and congratulated me on selling it. Pictures of the accident had played before the interview, and I got some worried glances, but the fact that I had healed myself shocked no one here.

I didn't know any of these people, but they knew people in my life, and they knew me. I had them sign the confidentiality papers that Domingo dropped off anyway. Not that it would matter, but at this point, I had outed myself, and if they went around spreading rumors, it wouldn't change anything.

I was busy; I saw double the people I had on my busiest day and everything from kids to grandmas. The hardest thing I did was unmake some kidney stones, so it was all simple stuff. If my announcement caused me to be busy like this every day, I was going to have to hire a helper.

Alex came in with a few of his friends in the mid-afternoon. They all had varying stages of Vampire Infectious Disease, judging by the graying edges of their auras. I had them wait while I came up with a plan and finished my other patients. Since the clinic was busy, it was easy to slip away and draw my own blood. I placed it in tubes with a blood thinner component, shook it up to keep it from clotting, then drew it into syringes.

I worried, just a little about blood type compatibility, but knew I was O negative, the universal donor, so I figured they should be fine. Also, I didn't think that my blood would do injury to them anyway, what with the Healer thing and all. I was betting that I only needed to give them just a little in the form of a 'vaccine' to cure their disease. Noah had not gotten back to me about his research, but I was going to do a little of my own.

"Alex, are you ready? I've got to warn you that this vaccine is still being tested, but so far, it has worked. I just don't want you to get your hopes up," I said, calling him to me.

"I'll try it. I saw your interview, but I know you're more than you let on, just judging from what happened at Fangs Amillion," he said. "I have a daughter at a college in West Virginia. She is studying to be a nurse. I need to be able to help her through school. I'll try the vaccine."

"What is your daughter's name?" I asked.

"Michelle. Michelle Milan. She will be one heck of a nurse someday," he answered proudly.

I filed that information away for later. I did not want this man to sell his blood to vampires anymore. If Aedan could buy me a truck. I could give this girl a full scholarship. We needed nurses; I would pay it forward.

After they signed my confidentiality agreement, the men lined up and bared their deltoid muscle. I gave them each a shot of my blood, telling them that I needed to watch for a reaction. While they waited, I took the opportunity to clean up the mess the day caused.

After half an hour, I went back to them and placed my hands on their arms. All of them were healing. With my other sight, I could see my blood cells multiplying and tearing through the VID virus. It worked. The gray around their auras faded, and I sent them home, asking them to follow up with me in a week to make sure there were no issues. They left feeling better than they had in days, and I felt good too.

I called Noah and left a message for him, unsure if he was avoiding me or just busy. I hadn't talked to him since the night of the Spring Conclave when I called him and his Shapeshifter friends to me in their cat form. I shouldn't have been able to do it, and he had been furious at the new development. I put that with the other things to worry about later.

An hour before dusk, the door opened, and a tall woman came in with Keelin, the Fae I had seen a few days ago. The new one had dark, almost black hair and wide gray eyes. Four men stood behind them and waited, saying nothing. They were all exceptionally beautiful and as different from each other as they could be in coloration. Still, there was no mistaking any of them for humans.

"Lara," Keelin said, drawing my attention from them. "This is my friend Finley, and these are my mates Bain, Faolan, Adair, and Max." She didn't walk forward, seeming to sense that they made me nervous.

"You have nothing to fear from us, Healer. You gave us a child, and we thank you for that," one of the men said, drawing my attention back to him. He was so blonde he was almost white-haired, but his eyes were dark and kind.

"Um. What? It's been like two days," I answered. "And you paid me way too much. You've got to take those diamonds back." I rose from my desk, moving to get them.

"Time passes differently in Talamh na Sithe, but Fae know immediately when they conceive. Our child grows in her womb; we will not take your diamonds," one of the other men said. Moving beside Keelin, he placed a tender arm around her. She just smiled. "You are right; she has her mother's fire," he said, smiling down at her.

Ignoring him, "What can I do for you today?"

"Aramea has made it nearly impossible to travel the ways. She is outraged, ripping, and tearing apart any she thinks might be a threat. The others are afraid to come to you, but Finley wants to know if you will help her the way you helped me," Keelin said.

Finley just stood there, staring. Her gaze was riveted to the TV I had on in the corner. The room silenced as they listened to my interview, and their eyes widened at my explanation. One of the men laughed at my oversimplified explanation of things.

"Yeah, I'm sorry about Aramea," I said, drawing their attention back to me. "We got in a fight today, and I kinda threatened to kill her. I imagine she is pissed about that, but the old bitch deserves it," I said, half under my breath. One of the other men choked on his spit, his face paled.

"She is definitely Ari's child," he laughed when he could breathe again. "Your mother was always fighting with the Queen. It became quite comical, really. Your fathers will be proud of you, little one."

"Well, this wasn't comical. I mean it. She fucks with me again, and I'll find a way to take her out." I felt the hair on my head rise with my anger, and I tamped it down as best I could. The eyes of the six Fae around me sharpened to attention.

"Sorry, it's been a long day. Week. Month. Honestly, I've lost count. So, Finley, let's take a look at you. Hop up here, sister," I said, patting my little exam table. She paused, looking at the others for guidance and back to me like she thought I had lost my mind. Again, probably not an unfair assessment.

"I don't bite. I swear. Aramea just set me off today. You know you guys can come here and stay. I mean, not like Here as in my house although that's cool too if you need a place to stay. After I came out to the public, everyone is Tuatha de Danann, or so they think anyway. You would fit right in. You could buy an entire town for what those diamonds are worth. You should take them and run." They stared at me like I had lost my mind. Which maybe I had.

"She's cute, isn't she." Keelin beamed with pride.

Sighing, I rolled my eyes and waited until Finley slid herself onto my table and laid down. I placed my hands on her abdomen and felt them warm. "How many pregnancies have you had, Finley?" I asked.

"None," she said, her voice so soft that I had to strain to hear her.

"None. Okay," I said, shifting to my inner sight. I ran through her systems and could find nothing wrong at first glance. Her uterus was in good shape, Fallopian tubes were open, and there were no fibroid tumors that could cause infertility. "Is the land over there getting better?" I asked, not looking away from Finley.

"Yes, things are beginning to grow and flourish. The taint is gone," Keelin answered me.

I found an area of gray hovering just around her cervix and thought that maybe it was keeping sperm from reaching her uterus, but I couldn't be sure. As it was the only thing I could find, I cleared it away and got her the same vitamins I had given Keelin.

"Take these until further notice and come back when they are gone. I fixed a little something in there, but it could be that the land kept you so undernourished that your body wouldn't…accept a child." I tried using words I thought they might understand better. They nodded in agreement. "Come back if it doesn't work or if you run out of pills, and I'll try something else. Maybe wait more than two days since Keelin over there is probably an anomaly." I smiled at the woman, and for the first time since she came through the door, she smiled back.

"Can you look at Keelin and check that all is well?" one of the men asked.

"I can look; it's so early I might not be able to tell," I said, waiting for her to lie down.

They said nothing as I placed my hands on her, opening my sight into her uterus. I grinned when I was rewarded by finding not one but two little blobs in there. I looked even more closely at them. I don't know if it was Aedan's blood or just dumb luck, but I could feel their gender thrumming through them.

They were right; time must pass very differently there than even I understood because these little blobs were a lot further along than two days. At least going by human intrauterine development.

"Do you want to know what they are?" I grinned, unable to help it, when tears popped into my eyes.

"They?" Keelin asked. The men by the door gripped each other tightly.

"Yes. They. You are having twins," I answered.

"What are they?" She asked in a careful whisper.

"One of each. A boy and a girl." Her face fell and tears formed in her eyes.

"What? No," one of the men said, and another sucked in a deep breath.

"Why is that bad?" I said, my brows knitting together and my temper rising.

"The Queen will kill the boy. New males are not permitted as it takes from the existing ones," she said, her tone sad. "There were twenty children that survived birth in Ari's and our time. Only eight were girls, and only seven remain," she finished.

I felt the wall to my power drop. I was unable to hold it back anymore. That bitch. Those poor women. Their girls farmed out like prized heifers, and their boys killed.

I have never felt so much anger toward any one person. These people did not deserve to be at Aramea's mercy, and she did not deserve to lead them. My hair rose and swirled around me, unbidden, and power crackled along my fingers. I itched to get my hands on my grandmother. Taking a deep breath, I closed my eyes and forced it all back down. She would present the opportunity, and I would take it.

"I'm sorry," I said, opening my eyes. Their faces were slack and staring. They weren't afraid, but they were stunned at a minimum. "Look, I don't know everything that's going on. I don't. But I can tell you this. She won't touch a hair on either of those little heads floating around in there." I waved to Keelin's belly. "My word. You can stay here, you can stay in the city, you can do whatever you need to get away from her, and I will help you. It's that simple."

"It's not that simple," Keelin interrupted.

"Yes. It is," I said with finality. I have a house on the beach where I grew up. It was safe for my parents and me; it will be safe for you. Whatever it takes until I can figure out a way to get her out of your lives. I mean, you guys are like my aunts, right? You are sisters to my mom, in a way; are you not? That makes you my family. I don't have much of that left, and I seem to be getting very protective of what I do have. Other than your

Queen, that is," I said, stumbling over my words. "She does not deserve protection."

"Rumor is the Goddess wove you together from the seed of all your mother's mates," Keelin started. "There is a lot of power in the number five. It is a symbol of great magic, and you were born from that. It was spoken about in worried tones and hushed whispers, for the Goddess gives only the most powerful of gifts to her people. Gifts she seldom gives, but make no mistake. That is what you are, Lara, a gift from the Goddess herself. There is not a Fae in the land that did not see the magic skies in the days before Ari and Seal fled Talamh na Sithe. You are the reason. I will bow to you as Queen someday."

The only man who had yet to speak stepped forward. "We are honored."

"Hush with all that. I am no one's Queen. That's a job I would never want. Surely someone else can step up." I smiled at them.

I felt Aedan coming, my Vampire Detection Syndrome singing in my veins. The six Fae in front of me looked around, confused.

"That's my, uh, boyfriend. You get used to the noise in your head after a bit. I went to the door and let him in.

"Liomsa, I was meeting with Guy about our house and thought I would stop by." He came through, turning to see the basement full of Fae.

"Aedan, these are friends of my mom's." I hurried to introduce him. He froze, his eyes paling just a fraction. I doubted anyone else would notice. "Keelin, Finley, Adair, Faolan, Max, and Bain. I don't know who is who beyond the ladies, though. Sorry. This is…"

"Coimeadai Lasair," he said, with a half growl, half-whisper, trying to maintain his calm.

"Yeah, um, so, they are here to get checked out," I finished. The Fae eyed him curiously, scenting the air and staring openly, not realizing that there might be an issue. "They aren't, uh, you don't know them, right babe?" I asked, sliding next to him.

"No. I do not."

"I know you." Keelin stepped forward. I had her pegged as the brave one of the two women. "Ari talked about you. We all did. You're the one whose blood still scents the Great Fae Hall, the one Ari's mother cocked up that made the rest of us suffer all these years. The Goddess plagued our land after your, uh, expulsion," she said, stepping to him until she was right in front of him; she looked him over.

"Keelin. Hush." One of her men, God, did I need to learn which one was which, stepped up and put his hand on her arm.

Aedan's face broke out into one of the biggest smiles I have ever seen, surprising me.

"Yes, that would likely be my blood, but I don't feel all that cocked up. At least not anymore," he said with a chuckle.

"The stories that they tell about you are incredible," she said, standing on her tiptoes and looking him in the eyes before dropping them quickly.

"Yes, I imagine, and they are true, I have no doubt," he said, sliding his arm around me, just a trickle of his power leaking all over me. "Anamcara, You make the most interesting friends," he said.

"We are like her aunts. It has been decided. We all despise her grandmother and love her mother; Ari and I grew up as sisters. All of The Eight did, and Lara has given us twins. I am at your service, should you need anything." She bowed her head slightly.

"Oh Geez, none of that. I'm glad I could help," I said, thinking it was time for them to go before something happened or Aedan happened. Whichever came first.

"Is he one of your mates?" the quiet Fae, Finley, asked.

"He is the only mate." I grinned up at Aedan, catching his surprise at my words. I patted his arm. "We do things a little differently here, not better, not worse, just different. I'm sure your way works great for y'all," I answered. "Please let me know if there is anything I can do for you, and feel free to bring others if you can. I meant what I said. You would be safe here. My offer is open if you need it."

"And we thank you," Keelin said, bowing again. "We will keep you posted as we can. I imagine your fathers will be around as soon as they can get away," she said, shutting the door behind them as they all left.

"I don't think I can do this," I said, leaning against the door. "They are so hopeful that I can change things. I just don't think I can do anything but help them get knocked up and encourage them to make a home here," I sighed.

"Do not underestimate yourself, Lara. To the rest of the world claiming Fae blood, you mean nothing, but to the Fae, the real ones, you represent a great deal. You are still young and are not yet at the apex of your power, Mo Chroi." He hugged me to him, smoothing my hair. It had been an emotional few days, and it was dragging on me.

"Let's go to the city and have dinner. I have some late work to do, and you can sleep while I finish up."

We took care of the horses together before heading back into Baltimore. Tomorrow was supposed to be nice, and I planned on taking a ride in the morning. I could use some dinner and a good night's sleep. Maybe a swim, yes, a swim would be nice. I had seen the hotel's pool, and it looked amazing.

"I'd rather order in. You can work all you want to, and I can take a swim in the pool. Since I'm treating this like a vacation, I might as well vacation a little," I said, reaching for his hand.

Chapter 22

We drove into the city in comfortable silence. Aedan pulled up under the canopy and let the valet take his Escalade. Grania was already there, and I called to let her know we made it.

"Ask her to meet me in our rooms around midnight," Aedan said when he figured out who I was on the phone with. Ask. Don't tell. It was a big step in their relationship. I passed along the word.

Upstairs the air in our room was crisp and fresh. It smelled like lightning and ozone. As we walked through the door, the air shimmered, and the Great Goddess walked through the shimmer into our living room.

We stood rooted and staring at one another. Dani's breath caught in her throat at the sight of Aedan. She came to him, bowing on the floor in front of him, holding herself there with the tips of her fingers; she kept her back straight and bowed her head until it touched the marble floor.

"I have done you a disservice, my Son," she said, her voice breaking.

Aedan stood frozen and unmoving.

I had forgotten how small the Goddess is. Standing straight, she would come to just below his ribs. She looked like a child.

"I do not understand," Aedan whispered. "Why are you kneeling before me, my Goddess.

"Because I failed you, and I must ask your forgiveness." She stayed where she was but raised her eyes to his.

"If anyone has failed, it is I, my Lady. Please do not stay at my feet; I am not worthy." He shifted, looking between his mother and me. My face must have shown all the shock I felt. He looked between us, sensing there was something he missed.

"It is I who am not worthy. We must talk, my Son," she said, rising to her feet

"I can go," I said, moving to the stairs.

"No." Dani placed her hand on me. "This involves you as well. Please stay." She looked between us, gauging her words.

"How are you here, if I may ask? You said you couldn't travel to this plane."

"If you remember, I stole a drop of your blood after your mad dash through Talamh na Sithe; you provided me with an anchor that allows me to go where you are. Since you are often with my son, I hoped I would find him here.

"I do not understand, Goddess. Why would you seek me out?"

"I must tell you a story," she started.

"Why don't we sit down. Can I offer you a drink?" I asked them both, moving to the kitchen.

"I'll take a whiskey," he said softly, following behind.

"I will have what you are having, Lara," Dani said.

"Coffee it is, Dani."

Aedan startled at my use of her pet name, then chuckled, knowing none of the Fae seem to like coffee. "Perhaps a nice wine instead," he said on her behalf.

I put on a fresh pot of coffee, waiting in silence for it to finish before pouring two cups, a whiskey, and a glass of wine. I handed out drinks then sat on a barstool next to Aedan. Dani moved to sit across from us, taking a sip of the fine black coffee Aedan stocked for me. She didn't wrinkle her face; in fact, she closed her eyes in pleasure.

"This is amazing," she said, making me like her more. She closed her eyes and waited a minute. I reached for

Aedan, placing my hand in his. He watched us through narrowed eyes.

"Once upon a time," she started over, taking a deep breath. "A mother failed her son so badly that she lost an entire People and set about ruining a kingdom mourning his loss. Never had the mother loved one of her children the way she loved this one, and all knew him to be her favorite. In her arrogance and overconfidence, she left the child to fend for himself, trusting in her allies to keep him safe, and their jealousy brought him low. She did not hear his cries for help in time to save him, and he was taken from her for what seemed like an eternity," she paused, not meeting his eyes.

"Then he fell in love for the first time, and she heard his prayers again. A young Healer, barely old enough to have stopped growing, told the mother that life encompasses many things and many beings. Told her that her son was not truly lost." She looked at me, and I felt tears form in my eyes and stay on my lashes.

"Coi, you are my son, truly born. I failed you so horribly that I can never expect you to forgive me, but I must ask all the same. Through conceit and faith in my own power as the Goddess to all, I missed the one person's prayers who needed me in his most desperate time. The only being's prayers I actually cared to listen to. I can never, ever make it right, but I beg your forgiveness." she finished, looking at him even though he refused to meet her eyes.

He sat still, looking out across the living room and through the windows to the water beyond, saying nothing. Moments passed into minutes, and still, he stayed silent.

"I'll go," she said, rising with a sigh. She came to me first, placing her hand on my cheek. "Thank you for bringing my son home." I nodded my eyes only for Aedan. I could feel his pain. She kissed him on the top of his head, inhaling his scent deeply, closing her eyes.

"You are still you, Coi. Lara is right. You are now and will always be my son. I failed you once, but I haven't failed you again since I knew you lived. And I never will." She disappeared in a glimmer of red, leaving behind one thin red feather.

Aedan moved slowly; taking it in his hands, he turned it over and over, not looking at me. The silence stretched for a long time.

"When I was a boy, no bigger than my bow," he started. "I got lost hunting a large stag that I hoped would feed my foster family for the coming winter. Night was coming, and fearsome things hunt Talamh na Sithe after the sun goes down. I came to a lake, and sitting in the reeds was the most beautiful red bird I have ever seen. I followed it back to my village and away from danger. That scarlet heron saved my life not just once but twice. I know this," he stopped, walking to the window to look out.

"I will not deny my mother the forgiveness she seeks, for I have fought to find it, myself. I will not. I assume that this is some part of the story from your trip to Talamh na Sithe that you could not tell me."

"It wasn't my story to tell, Aedan."

"I understand. I do. I need to get ready for this meeting. The others will be here shortly. If you would still like to swim, perhaps you should go before they get here and delay you." He didn't face me. It was like he couldn't look at me. I closed my emotions down and shut them away. I was getting better at this. If I didn't want them to leak, they wouldn't.

"Okay." I walked upstairs, got my bathing suit, my cell phone, and left the suite, shutting the door softly behind me. He could be mad or not. Not my problem. Then again, he just found out his mother was the Great Goddess of All Things.

He might need a minute.

Chapter 23

I texted Grania in the elevator and told her I'd be in the pool awhile with Chinese delivery if she wanted to skip the meeting. She texted me back with an eyeroll I could feel through the phone and our bond, telling me she wished because Aedan was cranky. I snickered at that, ordered Chinese, and walked to the pool, my flip flops slapping the marble floor.

I changed into the little white bikini I bought with Aedan in mind and mentally congratulated myself on the fact that he'd be irritated that he missed it. I had gained a little weight since Cook had started feeding me, but not much. My hips were more rounded, but my waist was still a lot smaller than I was used to, as were my breasts. Where once I had been a solid size eight, I was more like a six on top. I didn't like it. I liked my curves and wondered if they would ever come back.

The smell of chlorine hit me when I opened the doors to the Olympic-sized, heated indoor pool. I loved the smell for some reason and inhaled deeply. Dropping my towel on a lounge chair, I dove into the deep end and swam almost the whole length in one push.

My mom had taught me to swim at a very young age, and I could swim with the best of them. I was at home in the rough surf of the ocean or the still water of the pool. It didn't matter; I loved the water.

Taking a breath, I dove back under the thin glass divider that separated the indoor and outdoor sections of the pool. The cold air hit me, but the water was so warm that I didn't mind. I swam to the edge of the pool that was designed to look like the water never ended. It blended seamlessly with the water of the Inner Harbor. I floated at the edge, looking out into the night to watch lights dance across the small waves. Diving under, I did one more lap through the end before coming back to my spot at the edge of the world.

Technically, I was a fire sign, a Leo, born at the height of the summer's heat. In reality, I was a water sign at heart, always more comfortable when I could feel its cool soothing brush on my skin. Unless maybe, it was the fire the water soothed so completely.

I floated, staring up at the enormous hotel laid out in front of me, counting the floors up and wondering about the meeting going on at the highest one. Lights shone from the windows, and the curtains were open to the night.

I dove under again and swam to the section of the pool that was partitioned off and jetted, letting the pounding water soothe the tense muscles in my back.

I heard my name called from the pool area and ducked under the partition, popping up on the other side.

"Miss Hennessey, your delivery," The bellhop sat my Chinese on a table.

"Hang on, I've got cash," I climbed out of the water and went to my towel.

"It's been taken care of, ma'am."

"Please don't call me ma'am, geesh. I'm not that old," I muttered under my breath as I grabbed my dinner. I was starving.

He chuckled, looking over my shoulder before turning to leave. I paused, turning. I had been alone when I came in but apparently wasn't alone any longer.

Across the pool on the other side sat a tiny, red-haired woman with a huge man that towered above her by close to two feet.

Apparently, it was mother's day.

"Mom?" I almost dropped my Chinese; I did sit heavily on the lounge chair. Keelin had been right. I looked nothing like her, and she looked nothing like I remembered. My mind had filled in the blanks as her memory faded, making her look more like me and less like herself. She wore a bathing suit and was wrapped in a towel, but she was dry. Her long, fire-red hair hung in waves that were not quite curled, just like mine. My hair was much darker, almost brown with streaks of red. Her skin was pale, and freckles dotted her face and arms. She looked like a teenager.

Next to her sat my father, his smooth olive skin contrasting his light brown hair with platinum blonde highlights. His brown eyes glittered with every shade of brown in the box of Crayolas. He was partially wrapped around her, and she was melded into his side. He was beautiful. They both were. I froze. They froze. None of us moved.

"Lara?" She finally stood, clutching the towel to her. She looked down at my dad, but he just sat, staring, his mouth open in shock. "Oh, my Gods, it is you." She walked around the pool to stand in front of me. "We were coming to see you tomorrow; we just flew in."

I couldn't breathe, I tried to catch my breath, but it caught in my throat, and I gulped like a guppy. Words wouldn't come, my heart raced, and my vision narrowed. I had to force myself to calm down. Doors crashed open, and swords were drawn.

I was pulled to my feet and shoved behind six angry feet of blonde vampire and six and a half feet of angry Aedan.

"I'm fine, I'm fine. Stop. Relax." I forced myself to breathe.

"We felt your panic," Grania said, turning to me and keeping herself between my mother and me.

"I can take care of myself, Grania." I didn't take my eyes off of the couple in front of me.

Aedan said nothing, just looked between my mother and me. He did not drop his sword. It glowed a soft silvery blue, and my father's eyes were glued to the sight of it. "I don't want to interrupt your meeting; I'm fine."

"The meeting is over," Aedan said, looking at my face for the first time. "What is going on that caused your excellent shields to crash, Anamcara?"

I stepped out from behind them, looking at my parents.

"Aedan, Grania, meet my mother and father." They stood just a few feet away, not close enough to touch, but close enough to see the details in my mother's multi-faceted eyes that were a much brighter shade of green than mine.

"I am Airmed; my friends call me Ari," she said, formally addressing them.

"Are we to be friends?" Aedan asked, still not dropping his sword.

"You have a sword made by one of my mates, and you hold it between my daughter and myself. It glows with the veracity of your feelings. I do hope that we can be friends and not enemies," she said, eyeing him sharply.

"This sword is much, much older than I imagine your mate is. I am Coimeadai Lasair; you may call me Aedan." He sheathed the sword behind his back and reached for her hand. She took it, glaring up at him.

"You are the Fae, my mother killed, fucking up everything." My dad put his hand on her arm, urging her back.

"Ari, hush," he said as she pulled back against him.

"I am that Fae. Although I do not feel exactly killed." Aedan grinned, releasing her hand. "And you?" He looked pointedly at my father, who was a match in both height and weight to Aedan. The look on neither of their faces was pleasant.

"You may call me Seal," he said, reaching for Aedan's forearm in the handshake of old. Aedan took it.

"This is Grania, my best friend," I said. Grania inclined her head but didn't move forward.

"You surround yourself with interesting people, Lara," my mom said, moving to sit on a lounge chair near me.

"I surround myself with powerful, interesting people, mom. Why are you here, and why did you leave me?" I asked, getting down to the heart of it all.

"Sit down, and we'll talk. Your mate looming over me ties my tongue." She looked between Aedan and me expectantly.

"I will go," Aedan said, moving to the door.

"You can stay if you want, babe." I didn't look away from my mom but did move to sit on the lounge next to hers. Aedan shuffled in behind me, and Grania sat one behind. My dad came to sit next to my mom.

"I saw your interview, Lara. Your dad and I planned on seeing you tomorrow. We got here as fast as we could."

"Mom, why did you leave? Why did you let me think you were dead all this time? Was it so you could go back to Talamh na Sithe?"

"No small talk then? Let's get down to it, I suppose. As long as your grandmother is Queen, we can never go back. Not until we are ready to challenge her for the throne."

"Then, why?" I asked again. I wanted to hug her and cry, but so much had happened to me after she left, and I needed to know why.

"I got pregnant," she said, staring at her hands. "The Goddess had given us the means to keep your power in check, but even that wasn't absolute, and occasionally it would leak out. Without my other mates, Seal and I struggled to keep the three of us hidden. As your brother grew inside me, it became impossible. We decided that the only way to keep you both safe was to go."

"So, you chose him over me?" I asked, feeling like a spoiled brat for saying it. Aedan placed his hand on my back.

"No. We chose to keep you safe by leaving. The spell would protect you from your grandmother's prying eyes, but it wouldn't protect all four of us. She had spies and contacts everywhere; we were constantly hunted and exhausted from it. We had found peace in South Carolina and hated to leave, but we couldn't let her find you."

"The spell didn't protect me, mom, not really," I said, a tear sliding down my cheek. "Where is this brother? I should get to at least meet the kid that ruined my life."

Everyone around me stiffened, and I didn't care. At that moment, I was a selfish thirteen-year-old child abused by those who should have protected me and the foster care system that turned a blind eye.

"He lived forty-three minutes after taking his first breath. His chromosomes were misaligned, or so the doctor said. There was no saving him. By then, we were gone and had no way to come back into your life. We had everything set up for you though, Caro should have taken you. You should have been happy with her and the horses," she said, searching my face. "We looked for you afterward, hoping that if you were older, we could find a way to explain, but you were gone. We looked for signs that your power had broken through but still couldn't find you."

"Caro was an alcoholic back then; the state wouldn't let her take me. Instead, they sent me somewhere else," I looked away.

"We didn't know," she said, reaching for my hands. I let her take them. "We called Caro pretending to be one of your old teachers, but she wouldn't say where you went.

"She is very protective of me. It doesn't matter anymore, mom. I don't guess any of it does." I stared at her tiny hands on mine.

"Did your power break through the spell then? At such a young age?" my dad asked, his light accent taking me off guard.

"No. I was raped a few months ago. It broke through then."

"Oh, my Goddess," she said, gripping my hands harder.

"It wasn't the first time, mom. I was a kid the first time." Aedan stiffened and growled behind me; I imagined his eyes paled. My dad watched his face transfixed, the look on his own face equally dangerous.

"He intended to kill you," dad said, scooting over to placing his hands on mine."

"Which one?" I asked, twisting the knife a little deeper.

"The spell concealing your heritage was designed by the Goddess to protect you until you could either grow into your power or your life was threatened.

"It was definitely threatened."

We sat in silence for a few minutes.

"So much has happened. I just don't know what to say right now," I said.

Despite her tiny size, She pulled me off my lounge and crushed me into her, surprising me with her strength. "We love you, Lara, your dads, and I love you more than anything. You are all we ever thought about, all we ever cared for. We don't even remember a time when you didn't exist.

"The Goddess came to me before you were made. She told me that she was going to give me a gift. A gift I didn't want. At the time, I never wanted a child. Never. Your Grandmother would have taken and twisted any child born to us, or worse. She said with this gift came a great sacrifice. I didn't understand anything she said. Not then," she stopped, holding my dad's hand and looking down as tears dripping from the tip of her nose.

"The capital was attacked by Trolls, and many of our people died. Two of my friends were taken, and one was never found. I fought them as best I could but ended up falling over a cliff and into another realm. This realm, actually. I was here for over a month and unable to get home. Seal came to get me," she stopped, looking over at him fondly.

"When we got home, you were conceived, and I knew the gift of which the Goddess was speaking. She bound the five of us together with lavender threads and took the best of each of them, and made you. That is how you became what you are, but your power was so strong. From moment one, it was so strong. We couldn't stay and risk the Queen finding out. We had to run.

"Seal can travel the old ways, and he went with me. The others stayed behind to gather armies and begin the slow work of rising up against her. We intended to take you back with us, to wage war against her, together. We never planned on another pregnancy. I know I can't take back what happened, but I want you to know we had nothing but love in our hearts for you."

"You gave up a lot too. You gave up your life, your, uh, husbands. Your friends. Everything to come to a strange place," I said.

"We would have sacrificed anything for you. You are alive, and you are safe. We obviously made mistakes, and for that, I'm sorry, but we love you. Look at how strong you are. Brave, strong, kind, powerful, and amazing. Your interview blew my mind, so calm and poised. I didn't play a part in that, and I wish I had. But looking at you now, I'm not sure I would change you either."

I nodded into her, not trusting my voice.

"When did you get so big?" she asked.

"When did you get so small?" It was an old thing we used to say to each other.

I remembered the little things I had forgotten. A silver-haired man playing with me along the shoreline because he was afraid of water. A dark-skinned man making me fight with a wooden sword and a quiet man who looked more like me than any of them. I remembered mom making cakes and baking for days. I remembered calling them dad. All of them. Some part of me had buried those memories, but here in her arms, they came rushing back.

"We'll catch up tomorrow, Lara; you look exhausted and haven't even had your dinner yet," she said, letting me go and rising to leave.

"We are in the presidential suite should you need anything," Aedan said, rising too.

"Thank you, Aedan," dad said, watching him with predatory eyes. No one would have ever thought he was human, not in my opinion, anyway.

"Where are the others?" I asked.

"The Queen watches them so closely now; we haven't been able to travel the ways in ages," my mom said, her face crumbling. I could see in that look just a little of what her leaving Talamh na Sithe had cost her. I couldn't imagine spending thirty-five years away from Aedan. Not for any reason.

"For them to come here will mean they can never go back, not until the war we intend to wage begins in truth. The work they are doing there uniting the Queen's enemies is too important for them to abandon." Her green eyes shone with such fierceness at her words.

"Aramea is a horrible person," I said, barely above a whisper.

"You've met?" She pulled back like she'd been slapped, her eyebrows pinned to her hairline.

"Yeah, sadly. It's a long story. Come to the clinic tomorrow. We have all day to catch up." She had done what she thought was right. Maybe it had been right at the moment. She was younger than me when all this had gone down if what Keelin had said was true.

I've made a ton of mistakes myself and still make them every day. I wouldn't hold it against her. She was my mother, and she was a good person. Unlike her mother, who did everything for her own selfish gain, she had given up her life for mine, and her motivations were pure.

She was right, too; I had grown into a strong woman with a fighter's soul. I can't say I would change the past that had built me into what I became. To say that cheapens everything somehow. I loved my life and everything about it.

Had I stayed in South Carolina with a doting mother and father, I likely wouldn't have ended up in Maryland, and even more likely, I wouldn't have found Aedan. Even if I had found him, it would have been after my heritage was already out in the open, and we probably would have been on opposing sides of things. No, I wouldn't change anything. I had mostly good years and only a few bad. That's all anyone can ask for.

I hugged her again, then my father, for the first time. He held me to him, smelling my hair for what seemed like an eternity, rocking me side to side. It felt very nice. They left with promises to see me tomorrow.

When they were gone, I sank down onto the lounge chair, feeling suddenly cold. No one said anything for a few minutes.

"I'm eating your Chinese food if you don't," Grania said, opening the bags and spreading things out.

"You wouldn't dare," I answered from behind the arm I had thrown over my face.

"I would," I heard her crunching noodles instead of putting them in the soup. "Dad didn't feed me a damn thing during that meeting." She gave him a wicked side eye and chuckled.

I grinned to myself. She loved calling him dad and thought no one noticed, but I did. Before, he had been Aedan or master, now he was just dad. I rose and went to the table, sorting through containers until I found what I wanted. When I ordered, I was starved and could have eaten a horse. Now, not so much, so there was plenty to share.

Aedan lounged back on his chair, closing his eyes, not saying anything. His shields were so tight there was no getting through. I clamped mine down a bit harder, too. It had been a long day; it was a lot to process for both of us.

"I was angry at your parents, Lara. I did not think that they cared enough for you, and I did not understand why they left you alone when I knew they had to be alive." Aedan didn't move his arms as he spoke, and I still could not feel him. "I thought my own mother had done a much better job finding a family for me when she felt she could care for me no longer. My mother is the Great Goddess of all Things and could not hear my prayers in my darkest hour? I do not understand. I may never understand." He finished, moving to stand.

I put my hand on his arm and drilled onto him with my eyes. "Would you change it, Aedan? Would you change your life if you could? Would you change your past if it meant you changed everything that came after?"

He didn't say anything; he just walked away without looking back.

"Your mom looks like a firefly." Grania laughed, trying to break up the heaviness in the room.

"Yeah, she does. Damn, I didn't remember her being so short." I smiled too. I had my parents back. I wasn't going to ruin this day with what-ifs. "Hey, I was going to ride in the morning, but I think I'd rather fight. I need to blow off some steam and maybe practice some stuff. I think I am ready to disappear. I actually think I can do it." Her eyes narrowed on me with glee.

"I would love to spar with you," she said, rubbing her hands together.

"Perfect. We can ride together if you can get your vampire ass out of bed before noon."

"I'll meet you in the lobby, weakling. Muahahahaha." She threw her head back, her fangs flashing in the reflection of the lights on the pool.

"That's the worst evil laugh ever," I said, shaking my head.

I cleaned up our mess and delayed a while longer before going upstairs. I had asked Aedan a question; I wasn't sure if I wanted to hear the answer.

Chapter 24

The lights were off downstairs. The door to our bedroom was shut, and soft light filtered through beneath it. Walking to the kitchen, I poured myself a shot of Grey Goose. Then I poured another. I took the stairs to our room, opening the door and closing it behind me.

"I would not," Aedan said as soon as I walked in.

"You want me to leave?" I whispered, watching him through half-closed eyes.

"I mean that I would not change my life." He sat on the bed, his back to me. His head was in his hands, but when he brought his eyes around to find mine, they were serious. He stood, turning around, but kept the distance between us.

"If the Goddess had heard my prayers and come for me, Elizabeth and my child would still have been dead. I would have still wreaked havoc on Talamh na Sithe but would not have been forced out by its magic. Maybe I would have been king, but I doubt I would have been a good king after all that happened to me. I likely would have been no better than Aramea.

"The damage was done before I uttered my first prayer to the Goddess. Had Aramea died that day, Airmed would not have been born. Had Airmed not been born, I would have deprived the world of a True Healer and myself of the one being with whom I found peace. With whom I found life. I would never have met my true mate because she would never have come to be.

"As much as I say you are mine, you are not. You belong to something much larger than myself," He sighed, closing the distance. "As much as I would like to stand on the moral high ground, I cannot. Your mother is right. I would change nothing about myself, and as much as your past hurts me, I would change nothing about you either." He pulled me into his arms, holding me lightly. "There are no mistakes. Not really. There are bad choices, but the big things? Are not mistakes. I believe this.

"Whether it is fate, a God, a Goddess, or something else entirely. There are no mistakes. Had events played out differently, all the realms would be changed today. I do not believe it would be for the better because a world without you in it is no place I want to live." He took my towel, dropping it, and slowly untied the strings on my bikini.

"I do believe that white is my new favorite color," he said, kissing my hair. I watched him watch me as he took my little bathing suit off to leave me standing in front of him naked.

Taking a step back, he pulled his tie off, his eyes raking over me. I stepped toward him, unmaking his clothes with a thought.

"Are you kidding?" He quirked his eyebrow up at me. "That suit cost me a thousand dollars." I shrugged, moving into him now that the playing field was level. I pushed him back until the backs of his knees hit the bed. I pushed a little harder until he sat on it.

Holding his eyes, I sank down, nestling between his thighs. I took him in my mouth all the way to the base in one quick motion. He wasn't quite hard, so it was easy. That softness didn't last long.

He wrapped his hands in my hair and pressed me down. I moaned around him, causing goosebumps to run up his thighs. With one hand, I gripped his base, and the other, I pressed against the smooth flesh behind his balls, using my knuckle to massage the gland there. He bucked against me, making me dig in harder.

As slowly as he has ever teased me, I teased him. Using my hands and my mouth to make him squirm but not enough pressure to make him finish, I just worshiped him with licks, kisses, and strokes.

I rose up and sucked his head hard, increasing the speed of my hand. His arms had gone limp at his sides, my hair still tangled in them. His eyes were closed as he focused on the feel of my hands and mouth. I drew my lips and tongue along the long underside of him then took him to the base harder. His hands tightened in my hair again, and I felt his hips quiver. I took him to the base and moved my hand to get him all the way into my throat. My hand was slick from spit, and as he came, I slid my finger into his ass and hit that gland hard. He cried out. Never before had I heard such a noise from him. I drank him down as he came, prolonging his orgasm with my finger until he lay limp and empty.

I took my towel and dried him off. Good blow jobs are messy and wet. If you don't need to dry off, you didn't do it right. He seemed very pleased with this one. A soft snore came from him. Feet planted on the floor and back resting on the bed, he slept.

I smiled all the way to the bathroom. Maybe you can still surprise an old vampire.

I jumped in the shower with my toothbrush to rinse off the chlorine, and when I went back to bed, Aedan was curled on his side, under the covers, asleep. A soft sigh of happiness left his lips when I snuggled into him.

He slept through the night, which floored me. I half expected him to wake me up a few hours later by banging my head into the headboard. Again.

Possibly breaking the headboard.

Again.

But no. He slept the sleep of the righteous all night. I set my alarm and was gone before he woke up. He had a long few weeks, and I knew he had a busy day planned, so I let him sleep, dressing quietly, unlike the days before we shared blood freely when he would sleep through anything. I did not want to wake him.

Grania met me in the lobby, and together, we drove to Westminster. She had on black yoga pants and a white tee shirt that was tied at her waist. Her hair was in a ponytail on the very top of her head. It wiggled when she talked and was absolutely adorable. She chatted animatedly about everything and nothing, enjoying herself.

Work on Aedan's house was being done at a wicked pace, and the entire thing was almost under roof. I couldn't believe it. It was going to be huge, larger than anything I had ever seen.

"You're going to live there?" Grania asked, giving me a look.

"Not all the time, but yeah. I'm going to live there."

She nodded her head. "I'm going to manage Fangs. I'm changing the name to just Fangs and am going to try to get the shifters involved. I want to close the place down and redecorate a little."

"No way! That's awesome. You're going to be busy." I let out an evil little Muahahahaha on the inside.

Never on the outside.

Just on the inside.

Operation Best Friend was just about complete. Grania was nearly independent now. I wonder if she even noticed. Yeah, we spent time together, and she could feel me, but we didn't spend every minute, and when I shielded hard from her, she didn't freak out. That was wonderful. With the club and being Aedan's second, she would have her hands full. I was a proud mama. I would never tell her that.

Nope.

"I know what you're doing," she said, popping her gum.

"No, you don't," I said, palming my face as soon as the words left my mouth.

"Yeah, I do. I'm not mad, but I'm going to kick your ass anyway," she laughed.

A few weeks ago, when I bound her to me, she couldn't even raise her voice in anger against me. The fact that she could physically fight me now meant I was winning. Oorah.

Inside, I flipped lights on and put on a pot of coffee since the French press was nowhere in sight. Grania and I went out to feed horses and look things over. Jeremy and Sarah had been coming to help feed and brush them so that he could spend time with Foxie.

Sarah could ride and was getting him through the basic stuff until I could be here full time and get him up and running. Literally. Stalls were clean, and horses were brushed, so I let them out to enjoy the spring sun.

Back inside, food was placed on platters, and I didn't even question how Cook knew what he knew. I no longer cared. We sucked down coffee and piled food high on our plates, eating until we popped. I knew when the action started that I would regret the last piece of sausage I shoved down my face, but I did it anyway.

Patients were coming earlier and earlier, so I wanted to get in some exercise before I had to work.

"Let's go get this over with, vampire," I sighed, regretting my chosen exercise already.

Chapter 25

Outside, birds chirped, the sun shined warmly, and spring flowers bloomed. I hid behind a tree, keeping my head from being too visible.

Grania skulked fifty yards away, searching for me. I had my strongest shields to date jammed into place, and it was working. Also, Grania wasn't freaking out a bit. Not one little bit. I sent a stream of power straight to her, flattening her to the ground, feeling very proud of myself for flattening my bestie.

My snicker did me in.

I had a face full of blonde vampire punching me in the kidney. It seems that since I didn't die in that pesky crash, now she thought I could take a little more of a pounding. I bucked her off me, sending enough power into my hips to send her flying. I pounced. Sending a flurry of punches into her side before jumping up and getting into a fighting stance.

She faced me, wasting no time with a kick to my ribs. I blocked her kick, ducked under her leg as she aimed higher to my head, and punched her in the hamstring.

"Ouch. Bitch. Where did you learn that?"

"I watched an MMA fight on TV when you guys were holed up a few days ago. Bring it," I panted at her.

"An MMA fight? Are you serious? You're an idiot." She landed a flurry of punches on my abdomen, but I used just enough power to shield myself from damage. On her last punch, I landed an uppercut to her chin, a knee to her gut, and in a sweep of her legs. She went down.

She lobbed a fireball at me.

I ducked and sent one into her, knocking her back.

"MMA style right there, biotch."

"MMA fighters don't use magic, asshole."

"This one does." I did a little side to side happy dance, feeling cocky. She punched me so hard in the face that I saw stars.

"Damn. Ouch. Not the face. Man, that's the moneymaker," I yowled.

"I don't think your face is your moneymaker, sister. I feel like you should know that by now. Well, maybe one part of your face." She gave me a wicked grin.

I leaned backward in slow-mo, pretending I was in the Matrix movie, and swept her off her feet again. She dragged me down with her, flipping me to my back. I flipped her back and did an elbow jab to her gut. She rolled on her side, grabbing her middle when I moved in to check on her; she got me in a chokehold. I smashed back into her nose with my head, and we both said ouch.

"Ouch."

We lay in the grass, breathing hard; blood trickled from both our noses and various other places. My heart pounded.

"Good talk," I said with a groan.

"You need to start training with Aedan," she said. "I can't take you anymore."

"I will train you."

I jumped to my feet, readying my power. I threw up a protective shield around Grania, looking for who had spoken.

Three very large men relaxed against trees, watching us with smirks on their faces.

"I told you my child would be a force to reckon with, said the darkest one. His skin was a deep mahogany brown with just a hint of cream blended in.

"Your child? She's not just yours." The lightest one pushed off from his tree and started coming my way. "She gets her fierceness and beauty from me."

The third just stared. His green eyes met mine, and I saw myself in them, despite what the silver-haired one said.

Grania eased to her feet, stepping in beside me. I could tell by the way she looked back and forth between us that she could see it too.

"She needs a sword in her hand," my dad said, proudly joining my other dad in his slow stroll to me.

"I brought her a blade, but it may be too small for her hand. She is much larger than I remember."

This four dads thing was going to be complicated.

"I'm not a sword fighter," I said, a slow smile spreading across my face. "I prefer a Glock to a sword."

"Bah, if you can fight like that without a sword in your hand, then you will be magnificent with one in it." He reached out, shaking Grania's hand. "I am Lara's father, Lann." He wrapped me in a big hug and swung me around like a kid before popping me back on my feet.

"I am Saige, her favorite father, and that sulking one over there is Laith, ignore him." He shook Grania's hand too, then wrapped me in a hug, placing a kiss on my forehead.

"If I recall, you hate water, so I'm not sure you can be my favorite," I said, pulling back with a wink. He stilled in front of me.

"You remember?"

"Some things, yeah. Not everything. I didn't until I saw mom yesterday.

"She's here?" The quiet dad finally joined us. I did have his coloring, but my features were the others blended together. Keelin was right.

"She will be; she's in Baltimore." They looked at each other and smiled.

"Gods, it's been so long since we've seen her," Saige said with a soft sigh.

"Well, it's time then. Come inside? Have breakfast? There will be food, no doubt," I said, waiting for an answer.

"Just like that?" my quiet dad, Laith, said.

"Well yeah. I mean. Right? I'm starved. Again."

I walked away from them, Grania followed quietly behind. Inside I picked leaves out of my hair while my dads squeezed through my doorways. I never dreamed anyone could be larger than Aedan, yet here were three men as large as or larger than he.

On the table, fresh food was laid out family-style on large platters, and dishes were stacked and ready. Maybe Cook reads my mind. I understand he is lesser Fae and that this is his magic, but his awareness is uncanny.

I grabbed a plate and piled it high. Again. MMA fighting is hungry work.

Grania followed, and we said very little as we shoved our faces full of food and filled in the cracks with black coffee.

After a few minutes, the dads joined us.

"She does not eat like her mother, that is for certain. I like it." Lann dropped down beside me with a wide grin.

We ate until everything was gone. I had to make more coffee. It was a good morning.

They asked a lot of questions about my life. I was hesitant to answer, but I tried the best I could. As weird as this moment could have been, it wasn't. It felt natural.

I knew what they said was true, that despite what genetics teaches us, they are all my fathers. I can feel that link to them and see parts of them in me.

They asked Grania questions too, and if they noticed she was anything other than Fae, they didn't say. I wondered what they would think of Aedan and groaned inwardly. One father's approval is hard enough.

Grania went to clean up, and they went down to the clinic with me when the first patient rolled up the drive. I explained to them what I did and how I did it. They had some knowledge of this realm since they used to visit, but they needed some updating. Cell phones were new since their last trip, as were tablets and real internet. I gave them a laptop, a desktop, my phone and showed them how to Google. It was all over from that point on. I left the remote for the TV with Laith and worked on easy ailments for the first part of the day. Give a man a TV, and he will watch it, teach a man to surf channels, and he will be entertained for a lifetime.

Noah came in the early afternoon, a naked, bleeding man slung over his shoulder, and that's when my job got a little more complicated.

He stopped when he saw the three huge Fae sitting glued to my electronic devices. I saw the question in his eyes, but he had bigger worries and continued into the room. I cleared off one of my lounges and watched as he draped the man onto it.

"He was hit by a car," he said.

"Hit by a car? Naked?"

"He was a wolf when he got hit."

"Oh my god. Okay." Noah was the leader of
the shapeshifters, not only locally but around the
country. Noah shifted into a giant black panther. He was
pretty cute that way too. He hadn't returned my calls
since the night of the Spring Conclave when I used
magic to call him and a bunch of other cats to me.

They were waiting anyway as a show of power to help
me calm the supernatural community in Aedan's
absence. Shapeshifters were being killed, and everything
was going to hell fast. They were going to fake like I
could call them, only I actually did. He had been less
than thrilled at this new aspect of my magic.

The dads had stopped watching SportsCenter and
turned a wary eye to Noah. Lann's hand was behind his
back like he was reaching for something.

"It's okay, dads, stand down."

"Dads?" Noah croaked, just realizing what he might
have walked into. What do I call them? Dads? The
Quads? Their names? This was way too complicated.

Ignoring them all, I placed my hands on the naked man
in front of me.

He needed a helicopter to Shock Trauma almost as
much as I had after my accident; he was a mess. I could

see that his body was fighting to repair the damage, but it was too extensive. He had massive internal injuries, and pretty much everything was broken. His spinal column had been severed at one of his lumbar vertebrae. Scratch that; he needed the helicopter more than I had.

His blood pressure was undetectable, and his heart rate so slow I wasn't sure he was savable.

"He's going to die," Noah said, his voice cracking.

"Not today he's not," I said.

I focused on his vital signs first, constricting the vessel in his extremities and forcing the blood to centralize.

"Noah, start an IV on him and give him some volume while I work on this other stuff; it will buy me some time." He moved to do what I asked so I could focus.

I felt his blood pressure come up and his heart rate increase enough for me to move on to his other problems. His liver, one kidney, and his spleen were torn badly. Blood pooled in his abdomen instead of running through his veins and arteries. I worked on his spleen first, bringing the jagged edges of the thing back together. You can live with one kidney, so I moved to his liver next. The organ was dead from lack of blood flow due to a severed vein, so I fixed that next, allowing blood to refill the organ. I healed it by pushing power until it was a normal reddish-brown in color. I felt him strengthen under my hands and his own natural healing ability move in once the major damage was fixed.

I moved to his spine next. He could probably heal the bones himself, but that spinal cord was going to be an issue. Gods, but I hated neurological stuff. It was not my strong suit. The spinal cord is made up of twisting nerves that each performs specific functions. In nursing school, I had to learn what each of them did and where they went, but I promise, as soon as I took my nursing boards, that knowledge went right back out the window.

His cord was not cleanly broken. In my sight, it looked frayed and torn. I took the pieces and treated them as a puzzle, this frayed end matched that one, and so on. After what seemed like forever, I had the pieces together.

I felt Noah's healing power blend with mine as he worked on some of the man's bones. I pulled a little power from him and joined with it to soothe the spinal cord and bring the swelling down. A paralyzed shapeshifter could not be a good thing. I sent power down each nerve, weaving magic around it for added stability. When I finished the last one, I felt muscles and bones shift like liquid under my hands. I opened my eyes and found a beautiful silver wolf lying on my lounge, watching me with ice blue eyes.

Noah hugged me to him, breaking into short sobs. "I can never repay you."

"There's nothing to repay, Noah. Thanks for trusting me with him."

"You don't understand, Lara. He's my mate. My everything. We got into a fight. He ran off to cool down, and I let him go. I found him discarded on the side of the road like roadkill. I waited to look for him for hours. I have no idea how long he laid there and suffered. He was so broken. I tried to heal him myself, but he was too far gone. All I managed to do was help him shift to his human form so he could die easier." He took a shaking breath. His mate crawled forward, licking his hands and whining softly.

"No, Liam," he said, growling at the wolf. "Do you see now? Do you see what I mean?" Noah buried his face in his hands, scrubbing them hard against his skin.

"You were arguing about me, weren't you?" I asked, knowing the answer.

"Yes. The shifters don't trust you. Many of them want to find a way to remove you as a threat." He stared down the wolf until the wolf averted his eyes.

"It's okay, Noah. I get it. I'm not a threat. You know that."

"I do," he said, glaring at his mate. I wondered what fights were like between them. Cats and dogs. And I thought my life was complicated.

"I'm no threat to you. Not to any of you," I said to the wolf, looking him in the eye. I wasn't his alpha, but I wasn't prey either. He looked away first.

"Noah, I've said it before; I'll say it again. You are all welcome here." I looked Noah over. He looked thinner than when last I saw him, exhaustion rode the lines of his face, and I could sense that he was weary to his bones.

"You're getting stronger. A few months ago, healing like that would have made you black out."

"I've been practicing." I gave him a wink. Rising from the side of the wolf, I moved to introduce Noah to the three hulking figures staring at us with rapt attention.

"Noah, these are my dads Lann, Saige, and Laith. Dads, this is Noah, local werepanther extraordinaire and multiple time savior of your daughter. Without him, I would've been toast. A few times.

"That's hardly true." Noah clasped arms with each of them. They were wary but accepting of the gesture.

"Any creature that tries to eliminate our daughter, threat or no, will have to go through us," Laith said, his eyes hard and feral. I watched his face thin. Magic rippled over him, causing him to step back, and a slow grin spread across his face.

"There is no threat to Lara, I assure you. I will deal with my people," Noah turned his back on them, giving me a curious look.

"Have they met Aedan?" he asked with a low chuckle.

"Uh. No."

"You have your hands full with that. Good luck."

"Thanks?" I said with a laugh. I caught my dads casting worried looks at one another.

"We're allies, Noah. You know that," I said as he moved to the door. "I've got a lot on my plate; I don't need to be worried about shifters."

"I said, I'll take care of them, and I will. My word. I'll send you a check for Liam. We need to get together and talk about VID. I heard there was a vaccine of sorts, but it didn't come from my people."

"You don't owe me anything. You saved my skin more than once. That's what friends do for each other. No payment is needed. As far as the vaccine, it's simple."

"Don't say it. Not out loud." He glanced around, and I realized just how concerned he was and how little he trusted his mate.

"Knowledge is power, Lara. Don't forget that. I'll come back, and we'll talk about it."

"Over coffee?"

"Over coffee."

He hugged me once more then moved to leave. His wolf jumped soundlessly off the lounge and walked to me with his head down. He nosed his way between my arm and my body, forcing my hand to go to his head. I rubbed behind his ears. Noah waited for the wolf before shutting the door behind them.

"You live in a strange community, Faeling. That was incredible. You are incredible. Your mother thought you might be a True Healer; I never imagined she was right." Saige came to me, wrapping me in his long arms.

"Thanks, dad." I heard the driveway sensor beep, letting me know someone was coming. I opened the door to watch a silver sedan wind up the drive. "I think mom's here."

They fought, shoved, and pushed their way out the door, three large bodies trying to squeeze through one little space. There were swearwords and grunts before the doorway cleared again, and I could go through. They rushed to the drive, and before the car could stop, my mother threw the door open and fell from it, running to them. They scooped her up and hugged her between them before ripping her from each other violently, squeezing her to themselves. I've seen toddlers fight more gently over a toy than how they scrabbled for her. She looked like a tiny doll held in the arms of overgrown children. There were words in another language and tears. Lots of tears.

Seal came to stand by me. "When did they come?" he asked, taking my hand.

"This morning," I said, unable to take my eyes off the scene in front of me.

"It begins," he said.

"What begins?"

"War." He walked to my parents and pulled the other men into long hugs.

Giving them privacy, I walked around them to the barn to check on the horses, Seal's words heavy in my mind. I knew there was trouble in Faerie, but a Fae war was another thing entirely. I pulled Galahad into the aisle and ran a brush over him. He rubbed his head against my belly, letting it rest there a moment.

I just wanted to ride. So many things were happening, and it was almost too fast to follow.

"You have a Guardian."

"I've had two. This is Galahad." I turned and faced my mom. She stood a few feet away, looking at my horse with awe-filled eyes, her mouth open in a soft 'o'.

"He's magnificent. May I?" she raised her hand, wanting to touch him.

"Sure," I said.

She walked forward, bowing deep to him.

"See, that is how I should be treated. I think I like this one," Galahad said, giving me a horse smirk.

"Maybe if you didn't buck me off in snowdrifts, I would be nicer," I grumbled at him.

"Maybe if you didn't make me wear that ridiculous saddle, I wouldn't buck you off into snowdrifts."

"Maybe if you didn't buck me off, I would skip the saddle.

"I bet she doesn't use a saddle," he said, lowering his head to her so she could pet him. I rolled my eyes. Behind me, Lann laughed out loud.

"You can hear him?" I asked, surprised.

"I can. It is part of my magic." His smile was wide, showing his beautiful white teeth.

"So, I have you to blame for this." I threw my head back, laughing. Galahad glared at me.

"Galahad, these are my parents," I started.

"I know who they are. Knowing things is my job," he stood just a little straighter. "If you are here, that means the war has begun."

Lann filled in those who couldn't hear the Guardian, and they stilled at his words.

I forgot what he was. I treated him like a horse in my barn, rode him, brushed him, fed him, loved him, but at the end of the day, he was magic. He was Goddess blessed magic and not a horse at all. He knew things. Things I didn't and things he didn't share. He was Dani's creature, not mine.

The five Fae in front of me watched Galahad. I watched them. The truth of his words on their faces.

"It has not begun but will soon," Laith said. "Aramea is tearing apart the land, trying to root out rebels. The tide is turning against her."

"I see," my mom said, stepping back into them.

"It's time, Ari," Saige said, placing his hands on her shoulders.

"Yes, I suppose it is." She smiled at me, reaching out with her arms. I walked forward and was pulled into the biggest hug I've ever had in my life.

"Let's have coffee and talk about it," I said, pulling away. I was overwhelmed by the feelings of love and strength that surrounded me. I could feel their foundation, and it was secure. The love and faith they had in each other bled into me and filled the cracks life had created in my own base, making me whole again. I knew then that none of the other things mattered. This mattered. This love. This strength. This family.

Chapter 26

I felt Aedan coming, felt the brush of him in my mind, and the buzz of my vampire detection syndrome. This would be interesting. He was family too. Sometimes family was complicated.

Lann pulled his sword.

Aedan's Escalade slowed to a stop, and he stepped out of the driver's side.

He grinned. It was wild, fierce, and meant everything.

"Anamcara, more fathers, I presume?" Aedan said, pulling me to him and kissing me roughly despite the glares from my dads.

"Umph."

"I take that as a yes." He released me, stepping to the side.

"Is this the lad then?" Lann said to me, his eyes narrowed. "The Aedan fellow that the shifter wished you luck with?"

"Yes. Saige, Lann, and Laith, this is Aedan."

Aedan drew his sword.

I wondered if all daughters from ancient times went through this. Date comes for prom, dad draws sword. Date draws sword; swords clash. I sighed, rolling my eyes. My mother grinned. She looked like she wished she had a sword; her eyes glinted with glee.

I was glad her sword hand was empty.

"Dad. Aedan. What are you guys doing?" I said, "We were just going in for coffee."

"Liomsa, it can wait. I insist," Aedan said, circling Lann; they both grinned like fools.

"Oh, my goodness, come on, y'all," I sighed.

"My daughter is not yours, so keep your pet names to yourself, Flame Keeper," Lann said, his sword glowing faintly orange.

I sighed again. Deeply.

"Liomsa, are you not mine?" Aedan said, his grin widening, his sword glowed a soft silvery blue. Beside me, Laith gasped.

"I'm yours, babe. Let's all have coffee and talk about it," I sighed again, sounding like a petulant teenager.

Swords clashed.

The men fought and whirled like dancers. It wasn't serious; they weren't trying to draw real blood. It was a dance that fathers and suitors have engaged in some manner since forever, I imagine. They were testing. My dads were old, and Aedan was older. Back in the day before the caveman dragged the cavewoman by the hair, I'm sure he had to get into rock fights with her dad.

Ridiculous.

Grania moved in beside me.

"Are we doing anything about this?" she waved towards the sword fighters.

"Nah. It's testosterone-induced," I said.

"I see. Your parents are interesting." She cocked her head sideways. "You should let him train you; he moves well."

"Yeah, I'm pretty sure I don't have a choice with that anyway. They seem to take this stuff seriously." The sound of swords clashing emphasized my words.

We watched as they sparred. Their movements so fast I could not make out the details. They were both masters for sure. I hadn't seen Aedan use a sword, not like this, and he was magnificent.

The rest of my family thought so too. We stood together, watching them fight. The men made sounds of appreciation, and my mom just smiled proudly.

It ended as it began. Quickly. They stood apart; their sword hilts raised to their foreheads in salute.

"You are worthy of our daughter, Son, welcome to the family," Lann said, reaching to shake Aedan's hand.

Aedan smiled from ear to ear. "I would speak to you all about that later. How long will you stay?"

"Are you kidding me?" I glared at all of them. Beside me, Grania chuckled delightedly. Traitor. "I'm standing right here."

"We cannot go back. Not now. Not until the war is won and Talamh na Sithe is safe again," Saige answered.

No one said anything to that. The moment passed, and hands were shaken and introductions made. Aedan introduced Grania as his daughter, and she smiled the entire time, showing lots of pointy fang. It was a day for smiles. We went inside to another full meal laid out family-style on the table.

"You have a brownie," Saige said, taking in the spread.

"I wouldn't say I have a brownie so much as the brownie has me." I poured coffee into cups and passed them around. It was mid-afternoon, there was also wine and a pitcher of sweet tea set out. I let the others pour what they wanted.

Grania sat down and piled her plate high with beef tenderloin and gourmet macaroni and cheese. My parents watched her, then looked at each other, something passing between them that I didn't catch.

"May I hold your sword?" Laith asked Aedan.

Aedan handed his sword to my dad, then folded his arms.

"Iomproir Eadrom. This sword is a myth. I thought it lost all these centuries; legend says it was destroyed by the Queen after your supposed death. My grandfather made it and passed its story down." Closing his eyes, Laith caressed the sword. As he did, Aedan's sword glowed a soft yellow under his touch. "He said he made it for the boy who would be king. It has soaked in the blood of your enemies, and its magic has only gotten stronger. I feel it in every part of the blade. You are a true warrior, Sir. It is an honor to meet you and for you to hold the blade. Thank you." He passed the sword back to Aedan, who sheathed it behind his back.

Aedan inclined his head, watching them closely but said nothing.

As they ate, it became more than obvious that my parents wanted nothing more than to be alone. Together. Minus the rest of us.

We talked and caught up; they asked questions about my life and the things that had happened. We talked about Aramea and my trip to Talamh na Sithe. I filled them in on everything. We talked and laughed and talked some more. They told stories about each other, and it was plain how much they loved each other.

My dads each told the story of how my mom came into their lives and what a pain in the ass she was to them. As the minutes turned to hours, the glances between my parents turned heavy, and the silences stretched out. They had been without each other for a long time, and as different as it was from what I had with one man, I could see that those five needed to be together. Now, preferably. As much as I wanted to shudder at the thought of my parents having sex, I recognized it for what it was. Love. There is nothing gross about that.

"Mom, I have a big house on the beach in Pawley's. Why don't y'all go down there, spend a few days, a week, months, whatever," my voice cracked with emotion. "You need to be together again, I'm sure."

Her entire face smiled. Goddess, it was the most beautiful thing I have ever seen. She transformed into something entirely other, and the years fell from her, not that she looked aged. Not at all. She just looked burdened. That bright smile lifted the heaviness from her, and she looked angelic and light.

"That is very kind," she said, her hand gripping mine.

"Take my plane. I will have it fueled and ready before you can get to the airport. I insist." Aedan wrapped me in his arms, holding me to him.

"Thank you. I. Yes, we would love that," she said, meeting his eyes and holding them.

Aedan pulled out his cellphone. "I'll make the call," he moved to the living room and spoke in hushed tones. Making two phone calls, no doubt. One to ready the plane and one to warn his Southern Representative of a friendly Fae invasion.

"Lara, I hate to leave you. We just found you again," she said, taking my face in her hands. She had to reach up to do it.

"I'm not going anywhere, and you have a lot of time to make up for with them. Do you need anything? Money?" I asked.

"We need nothing. I can't thank you enough. I love you. We all love you."

"I know, mom. This is a good thing. They need time to get acclimated too. When you guys are all ready, I'll be here. When you come back, I'll have someplace ready where you can all be together." I smiled at them. Aedan walked to the door alone, and the dads followed. I watched them go, wondering what they were up to.

"Gods, you are so beautiful. I'm glad I did one thing right."

"You've done more than one thing right. Go. Make yourself at home and stay as long as you like. Call me, text, whatever. I'll be here. There's time."

I went outside and caught the guys in what appeared to be a serious conversation. They stopped talking when they saw us, moving away from one another sheepishly. We all hugged and said our farewells before they crammed into the silver sedan and drove to the airport.

Paul came to get Grania as they had plans to spend the night hours working at Fangs, and over the rest of the night, I closed the link between us in little increments so it wouldn't be sudden and she wouldn't feel its loss. She would be busy and hopefully not notice. Paul would text me if she got antsy.

The text never came.

Things were changing. The air was heavy with it, almost expectant.

Aedan went to talk to Guy about construction, and for the first time in what seemed like a decade, I was alone in my house. It was nice. If there was a war brewing in Talamh na Sithe, this moment of peace would not last. I had offered the Fae sanctuary, and if the fighting began, they would come. They would keep coming until Ari, Seal, Saige, Laith, and Lann took the fight back to Faerie, and when they did that, I had some choices to make myself. I would keep quiet about that for now.

I mixed a drink and soaked in the tub, thinking deep thoughts about the long game.

I fell asleep after my bath. Sometime during the night, Aedan came in and curled up with me, but in the morning, he was gone.

Chapter 27

I dressed in the soft emerald green shirt I got from Emily, throwing on a pair of comfortable jeans, ate the breakfast Cook had laid out and took care of animals before nine.

Jeremy and Sarah came to ride Foxie, and I gave Jeremy a lesson on the sweet little pony. Jeremy was a natural rider, and Sarah and Caro had gotten him up to speed quickly. He took what she had taught him and was able to manage the pony reasonably well on his own. I had him walking, trotting, and cantering with his heels down and his head up.

When he was done riding, they walked over to the new house to check it out, and I was alone again in the barn.

"She thinks I'm cute," Galahad said to me as I brushed out his tail.

"Who?" I asked.

"Foxie. She says I'm cute, and then she swishes her pretty little tail and trots along the fence with me.

"No. Nuh-uh. Not happening."

"What's not happening?" he said, flicking an eye at me.

"You and Foxie. Ain't happening."

"Awe, come on. I like her; she likes me."

"No."

"We just want to hang out, scratch each other's necks and stuff." He stood in the aisle the picture of innocence.

"Galahad. You would crush her. Like an ant."

"I will not. I am quite the gentleman," he said, shifting from foot to foot, eyeing Foxie in her little pen.

I stood back, glaring at the beast of a horse. He may have been a magical creature, but he was packed inside the body of a giant warhorse.

"Galahad, you are five times her size. No neck scratching, no tail swishing, none of that. You keep to your side of the fence.

"Goddess, you are mean. I'm telling Dani to rethink her deal with you. Total pony blocker. Not cool," he said with a stomp of his front foot.

"Go ahead, I betcha she'll be on my side here. Maybe I can take you to Faerie, and you can find a nice mare your own size." I finished brushing the horse off and put him back in his stall.

"You would do that?" he asked, his eyes brightening.

"I'll think we'll be there soon enough, Gally, maybe for a different reason, but you never know. I saw lots of other horses there, so anything can happen."

"The war? You will fight?" he asked.

"I think so. I'm not much of a fighter, but I am a Healer, and I'll be needed, I'm sure. Keep your trap shut, and don't say anything to anybody else. Aedan will flip out, and Grania will build me into the walls of the new house." I scratched his ears fondly, and he closed his eyes in pleasure.

"You could be Queen; Dani has said as much." he turned his head so I could get to the other ear better.

"Not a job for me. Let my mother have it or someone else."

"Maybe not now, but someday," he said with finality.

"No day, Galahad. My dream for the future involves more beach house and less trouble. I'd love to be able to travel freely and learn of my heritage, but I don't want to be trapped there. I like my life here." I stepped back from the Guardian, turning to leave.

"Immortality is a long time, Lara. Never say never."

I walked out of the barn, leaving the thoughts of being Queen with him.

I was in the kitchen, texting Aedan, when the doorbell rang. I was thinking about him and completely distracted, so I opened the door before checking to see who was there.

The blast of the twelve gauge slammed into my chest, pushing me into the wall behind me. Sheriff Collins racked the slide, stalking up to me.

"Son of a Bitch, I just bought this shirt. What the fuck Collins?" I groaned, pulling a shield in front of me and sliding up the wall to stand. I used power to push the projectiles out of my body and heal the damage before they could do any real harm.

"Why won't you die? Why. Won't. You. Die!" he shouted at me.

"I don't know. I'm a pain in the ass like that," I shouted back, moving the business end of the Mossberg 500 Tactical shotgun he had pressed into my chest away from me. "Why the fuck did you shoot me?"

He sagged against the wall, running his hand through his hair. I pulled power to me and waited. He had a decision to make, and so did I. I would kill him if I had to. I didn't want to, but I would.

"It's over. It's all over," he said. The shotgun fell to the ground, clattering on the tile.

"Good. I hope so. Whatever you are up to and whatever bullshit you are into needs to be over, Devers. The Fae and the vampires are out in the open now, and the Shapeshifters will soon follow. There is no longer a point in protecting humanity from what they know exists and can deal with themselves. The Watchers are no longer relevant." I kept my power pulled in tight, but I could see the defeat on his face.

"That's not what I meant. I'm leaving. I'll not be a problem for you anymore. I came to let you know that. I don't know why, but I felt compelled," he stopped, walking into the living room and sinking down onto the couch.

Unsure, I followed. I could see his age in the lines of his posture and the look on his face. I dropped my power. He was no match for me.

"Aiyana came to me. She said that she had found a way to end you. To end the Governor and to take the vampires back into the shadows. I believed her, and I shouldn't have. I should have seen her lies for what they were. I sided with the enemy to take down what I perceived as the greater threat. You. Only you turned out to be more than I expected and maybe not the enemy at all, but now the Watchers are going to kill me for my betrayal. I'm running, leaving, and never coming back. There's just one thing I wanted you to know first." Taking a big breath in, he waited. I stayed silent, still unsure why the man was here in the first place, other than to ruin my new shirt.

"You didn't destroy all of the blood," he said, meeting my eyes for the first time.

"What?" I whispered.

"At the farm."

I stilled at his words, my focus on him laser sharp.

"At least one box was taken immediately to a lab in Morgantown, West Virginia. Aiyana said something about making a race of super-beings from that blood. They were doing experiments. Whatever she said about wanting Aedan out of the picture, while true, was not her ultimate objective. I know from the records that the Governor has had thousands of years to learn to control the power he has. Whatever Aiyana was building with his blood will not have that kind of time. That kind of power in something newly made will only mean disaster for humanity. She may be gone, but that work is still being done. That is why I'm here now. That reason alone. Whatever you are and whatever your power, you have proved to me that you are the lesser evil here."

I nodded my head, a chill settling deep into my bones. This was not good. Not good at all. I imagined all kinds of things that could be done with those vials. Each box had contained hundreds and hundreds of them. One box, possibly more, had gotten out of that dungeon. Aedan's blood made me a superstar. It sharpened my senses and made me stronger. Just a few sips with no magical intent and my own power intensified and sang in my veins. His blood in the wrong hands could mean disaster. The possibilities were frightening and endless.

Ben Devers let himself out of my house.

I sat in my formal living room in stunned silence.

When I could stand, I called agent Johnson and filled her in, then I called Aedan. That conversation ended in a long silence. He told me he loved me and hung up the phone without another word.

The clinic was busy that day. Shifters, humans, mixed Fae from around the state, and a few of Aedan's new People came to me. He had taken over every House in and around Baltimore, just as he said he would. Those vamps had been bound tightly to him, probably during the nights I slept and days I worked. Now their humans were coming in to be seen, and I knew not one of them.

It no longer mattered since I had already outed myself as Fae. Hollywood might think I was a watered-down version of the Fae ideal that they had, but the people who sought me out knew the truth, and I took care of them all.

My parents called and told me they made it safe and sound to the beach house, and they were working on shoring up the protective spell around the place. I doubted very seriously that was true since I had seen the way they looked at each other before they left, but I let it go.

I closed the clinic for the night and drove into the city, even though I hadn't heard from Aedan since this afternoon. I found him moving through forms with his sword again, classical music playing through the Bose speakers in the room. Light glimmered off the sweat on his body, and the planes of his muscles shifted as he moved. I have never seen anything more lovely than him. The sword my dad gave me lay on the floor next to the entrance to the room.

"Pick it up, Anamcara," he said when he saw me.

"I'm not a sword fighter, Aedan," I said, picking the short sword up and turning it over in my hands. It was lovely, the steel had a hint of blue to it, and it was patterned and layered beautifully.

"Anyone can be a sword fighter, Mo Chroi." He turned to me, taking my breath with his beauty. His molasses-colored hair had grown a bit; the top was tousled and swept down into his eyes. His whiskey eyes glittered in the light.

"Maybe anyone can be a sword fighter, but I have you and four large fathers who already know how to sword fight," I said, walking to him, our swords between us.

"Lann says your mother can beat him in a fair fight, and he is the best in the land." He raised his sword and narrowed his eyes.

"Then, I have six strong Fae that stand between my enemies and me. I have magic. I don't need a sword." I took another step closer, still not dropping the blade.

"Keep your tip up, Lara," he said.

"I'm not going to fight you, Aedan."

"Then dance with me." He brought his sword down and clashed it against mine. The sound rang out and echoed through the large space he had dedicated to this particular dance.

Slowly I countered him, bringing my sword against his. With his form and his hands, he took me through the basic dance, eye to eye, and sword to sword.

There is something incredibly sensual about two blades clashing together. A parry here, a strike there, a slip now and then. He moved carefully, his eyes never leaving mine. When fighting with a sword, you must never lose eye contact. You can't possibly watch the blade or your opponent's arms, you must watch their face, and so I did.

He twisted around me, spinning on his toes and taking me off guard. I caught his sword with mine and ducked under his reach. My arms were tired, but during our slow dance with Fae steel, I learned something important.

I can be a sword fighter.

The sword is an extension of my arm, and I am quite good with hand to hand combat. My arm is an extension of my magic, and I only had to let the sword become one with me to feel the rightness of it. Lann's blood sang in my veins, the spirit of a Master swordsman flowed within me, I felt it settle in and take hold, the sword knew the dance well, and together we moved.

At that moment, Aedan crushed me to him, his speed and strength far greater than mine. He captured my mouth with his, crushing me. His tongue slipped across mine, caressing it. I sought out his fangs, nicking my tongue on them to let my coppery blood flow. He groaned in my mouth, pulling me closer to him. With one arm, he disarmed me, taking my sword and his, laying them on the floor. Then he scooped me up, Scarlett O'Hara style, and took the steps two at a time to our bedroom.

He took my shirt in both hands, ripping it down the middle, then pushed me backward onto the bed, following me down with his body. I would need to go shopping again. I lost two shirts today.

He moved his mouth over the healing marks the shotgun had left on my chest. By morning they would be gone, but now they were still light pink, and my chest was riddled with them.

"Why did you not kill him when he did this?" he asked, tracing the marks with his tongue and igniting a fire down low in my groin.

"It wasn't necessary. He's the hunted one now, not me." I arched against him as his mouth went lower. His fingers hovered in the air, and a light blue flame that was almost white formed in his hand. I breathed in sharply. He rarely showed his fae magic. He did so now, using it to light my jeans in cool flames, burning them painlessly from my body.

"Those were my favorites," I whispered into his mouth as he leaned down to kiss me again.

"As was my suit that you unmade," he said, nibbling up my neck and to my ear.

"Touché." I pushed him away, taking his buttons and undoing them carefully, one at a time. "This new addition to our magics could cause difficulties for our closets."

"Mmmmmmm, I do not care. There are other suits and other jeans. I will have twenty pairs just like them in your closet by morning," He growled low at the hollow of my neck as I pushed the shirt behind him, trapping his arms.

I reached up and tangled my hands in his hair, kissing him deeply, taking my tongue, and shoving it into his mouth as deep as it would go. He ripped the shirt neatly by merely flexing his muscles, freeing his arms, and gripping my hands in his. He hauled me up to the center of the bed, pinning me with one hand as he worked his pants off with the other. His eyes had bled a pale yellow, and I knew he had no desire to be gentle with me tonight.

I was okay with that.

My bra disappeared, and he entered me in one stroke. I reached up and licked along his neck, drawing blood with magic and my tongue. He sucked in his breath, and his eyes bled paler still as I sipped from the wound, taking him into me. He tilted my hips and buried himself deeper, making me cry out and release his neck. His eyes never leaving my mine, he pounded into me at a punishing pace before flipping me over onto my knees and taking me to my cervix. I moaned low, feeling it starting in my core and working its way out. He pulled me up to his chest, reached down, and flicked his finger across my core, calling on his blue flames and using them to tease that sensitive flesh until my thighs shook from need. I felt the release coming, like a flash flood destroying everything in its path. It washed through me, taking my voice. Magic pulsed out of me, hitting him hard. I tried to pull it back, but instead, he released his own, allowing his power to dance and mingle with mine, caressing the air around us with silver-blue and rose gold threads. The feel of it across my skin had my nipples tightening. It felt so good that I wondered why we ever used shields when we were together.

When my orgasm was down to the last spasm, he pulled out, soaking his hand in the wetness between my legs. He coated me with it, slipping a finger into my ass and pushing me back to the mattress. Where he had pounded into me moments before, he gently probed the entrance there, making me suck in a sharp breath.

"Aedan. I haven't done that."

The rest of that thought vanished as he pushed inside me millimeters at a time, allowing my body to adjust to him before pushing forward. I wouldn't have thought he would fit, but he did. He never let me feel pain from it. His painstaking patience paid off, and he was finally buried inside me, making me pant with need. When my body melted around his, he began to move.

I never would have thought you could come from this kind of sex, but I was wrong. Really, really, wrong. My body tightened around his, and instead of spasms, it was one long torturous clench, pulling an uncontrolled grunt from me. I made noises no animal has ever made until my throat was raw from them.

When he came not long after, his cries met mine. He poured himself into me, soothing any sore spots there might have been before taking my hair in his hands and my neck in his fangs. He drank deeply, and I came again, not from vampire compulsion but from the sensation of him sucking at my neck. I collapsed under him, and he rode me down, taking more than he ever had but leaving me full despite his bite.

He licked the pinpricks on my neck and nuzzled my ear. My heart hammered in my chest, and my chest heaved until my breath caught.

"I love you, Lara. More than anything. You make me everything I am not." His tone was serious, and I turned into him, catching his eyes.

"Aedan. What's wrong?"

"Nothing is wrong. I'm just concerned for what is to come," he said, his whiskey eyes meeting mine. I started to say something back to him to reassure him everything would be okay, but we didn't know that. Instead, I wrapped my arms around his neck and kissed him.

"I love you too, Aedan. With all that I have and everything that I am.

"Marry me, Liomsa."

"Oh. Hey. Ho. Whoa, there, fella. I. Oh. So. Yeah. I don't know about that," I stammered, trying to pull away from him, but he held me tight, his eyes twinkling with delight. My own rounded with terror at the intensity of his gaze.

"Do you fear forever?" he asked, smiling at me.

"I mean, fuck yeah, I'm afraid of forever. Forever is a long ass time. It's like. Forever." I sank into his embrace, rubbing my face on his chest. A low rumble of amusement ruffled my hair.

"What's so funny?" I said, rubbing the other side of my face on him.

"You mark me like a cat as your possession, and you have yet to actually say no when I ask for your hand in marriage. You will say yes. One day, when I ask you properly, you will say yes." I felt the corners of his mouth move into a smile. I snuggled in tighter. Who knows, maybe he was right. Maybe eventually, I would say yes.

I was afraid of forever, if I am honest. Forever for Aedan and me would be a long time. As much as I loved him, as much as I never wanted to be without him, I was still uncomfortable with the idea of forever. Would the magic we shared together dim over time or grow stronger? I didn't know, and I was almost afraid to find out. Right now, at this moment, with this man, everything was perfect, and I didn't want there to be a day when I learned it wasn't. I wasn't sure I could handle it.

It was early yet, Aedan had work to do, and I needed a shower. We took one together, washing our mixed sweat and other things off one another. Aedan washed my hair, massaging shampoo and conditioner into my scalp, trailing his hands down my back, and I washed him, top to bottom. When we were clean, he went to the office downstairs to make calls, and I went to the kitchen to find food.

Tonight's meal was a twelve-ounce filet mignon, grilled rare, and some kind of potato casserole with a hint of onion and a ton of cheese dripping off of it. It was terrific, as usual. After I ate, I touched base with Grania and asked her to go with me to Westminster again in the morning to work on my magic. She agreed, and we planned on a fairly early morning for us.

I slipped into bed around midnight. Aedan came much later. He slid in beside me, pulling me to him, kissing the line of my ear to the shoulder. His soft sigh of pleasure at holding me tickled across my neck, and I snuggled into him, falling back to sleep with my own sigh.

I used to dream crazy things. Sword fights and sex, running from danger or flying on a horse. Lately, I dreamed nothing. Whether it was peace, satisfaction, or exhaustion, when I slept with Aedan, I rarely dreamed at all, and I never had nightmares. So, as he was pulled into sleep when the dawn came, all I did was burrow deeper into him and doze until my alarm went off.

Chapter 28

The next morning, Grania and I sat in my kitchen watching the morning news and cramming French toast, eggs, sausage, and grits down our throats. Steaming cups of coffee sat next to us, and I resolved to give Cook every penny I had to my name and possibly the diamonds Keelin had given me, too. He was worth every bit of it. We were talking about life, nothing, boys, and everything in the way girls do. When Noah's face came into focus on the news, all talking stopped.

The shifters were coming out.

Dr. Noah Breger, respected physician and panther shifter, talked to Cindy on WBAL about his kind. Her questions for him were sharper and less friendly than mine had been. She asked him to shift for her, and he declined. She pounded him with question after question about the night of the Spring Conclave and the video of him and me together. She asked about love triangles.

Aedan would be furious, and I knew that Noah hadn't come to him for advice because his interview was not scripted or contracted the way mine or even Aedan's had been. It was almost adversarial, and I wondered how smooth their transition would be.

The shifters numbered far fewer than the vampires, especially after so many had died in Aedan's absence. I worried about my friend, but he was tough and smart. I had no doubt they would be okay in the end. I would help where I could, just as he had helped me. Aedan would get over any irritation he had, and if not, then oh well. This wasn't his battle.

Grania and I worked on my magic the rest of the morning and into the early afternoon. Gone was the slow and easy way we used to practice. We both knew that something big was on the horizon. It approached through that weird yellowed atmosphere like the first bands of the hurricane before the full storm truly hits. It was coming, and we needed to be ready.

I learned to disappear that day. I could see the tree and be the tree. One minute she was hammering me with fireballs that felt all too real, and the next, I was gone from her sight. It was like I was unmade. My particles floated in the air around where I once stood, and I felt myself just be one with the nothingness of it.

Then I remade myself behind her, taking her to the ground. I pinned her arms and held her, using Aedan's blood and the strength I gained from it to keep her there. We fought for real then, so evenly paired that we protected ourselves from each other. Had I used magic, I could have destroyed her, but she is my best friend, so I just used my hands and roughed her up a bit.

If Aramea came to my home to fight me again, I would take her down. No question. Whether I used magic, my hands, or a sword, I would never let her win. Not here. Not in my land. If it came to war in Talamh na Sithe, well, time would tell.

In the afternoon, it started.

Refugees from the Fae lands poured across the old ways as the veil between this place and that one all but disintegrated. They didn't ask for healing; they didn't ask for food; they asked for safety. They asked for the protection I had offered when those first Fae came to me.

Aramea had gone mad.

I don't think she had ever been sane.

Her soldiers were tearing through the land, imprisoning any and all who had ties with my mother and her mates.

Any they had ever talked to or associated with were either captured, dead, or on the run. She and her loyal core had turned on their own people, and blood ran through the streets of the capital. Keelin came with her mates, and I met the rest of The Eight and their men, minus one girl that was missing after having been taken by Trolls. Trolls. Yeah, that made me glad I grew up here and not there.

I still couldn't wrap my head around their arrangement, but it worked for them. Oddly, even though they had been forced into it, they were all still together and seemed happy. They didn't see themselves as forced, but then marriages have been arranged in many cultures throughout history, and they still are arranged in some today. Those marriages work for many. I guess it worked for these women.

Grania put them up in the sunrise rooms at Fangs, as the club was closed for renovations anyway. Aedan arranged for them to have drivers available and helped them convert the gold and jewels they brought with them into cold hard cash. In a week, when my parents came back, they would get together and plan. For now, they were safe.

I called Noah to let him know I was available, should he need me. Cook kept food on the table and coffee in the French press. I taught the Fae refugees everything I could, as fast as I could. They didn't want to be here long, but they were here now and needed a concept of this world that was so different from theirs. We piled them in vans and took them shopping for necessities before taking them into the city and showing them the ropes.

They attracted quite a crowd. There was no denying that these beautiful people were something other; the news was on them in a minute. Ravena, with her nearly blue skin and Keena with her striking hair and eyes, were obviously not human. Not to mention Baltimore had never seen the kind of beauty the Fae men as a whole represented. Since they were seen with me, the resident Faerie Princess, their identities as Fae, came out almost immediately.

They didn't care and were enamored by the technology and lifestyles that humans take for granted daily. They hid their swords and other weapons with glamour.

One of The Eight named Arlie explained to me that the moment I healed Talamh na Sithe from the poison allowed to fester there that their magic had begun to come back, setting the Queen even more off-kilter. She wanted her populace weak and at her mercy. The Fae surrounding me exuded magic and strength, making me wonder what strength my grandmother had gained as well.

Aedan hired security guards for them who dressed up as tour guides so as not to draw even more attention. It didn't work. The attention was intense, and our group was often followed by reporters and gawkers alike.

That night we closed down the local Cheesecake factory and took the Fae and many of Aedan's new vampires there. They mixed and mingled; each creature fascinated with the other.

"This is a beautiful thing," he said, sipping his glass of wine. I sat at the head of one of the long tables; he sat to my right.

"It is. I never thought I would see so many beautiful people in one place," I laughed.

"That is not what I mean," he said.

"No, I know. It's incredible. The Fae blend so seamlessly. Gods, they've survived so much, and here they are in a room full of vampires like it's nothing." I smiled, watching mixed groups talk and laugh.

"It can be like this. It can. Let Aramea have Talamh na Sithe. The rest can be happy here," he said, watching the room.

"You don't mean that, Aedan." I took his hand in mine, pulling his eyes to me.

"No. I do not." He kissed my fingers one at a time. I felt the eyes in the room turn to us. I caught Keelin's knowing smile. "War is coming, Mo Chroi," he said, taking the smile off my face.

"I know. For tonight though, let's not think about war. Let's think about these friends and this place. Let's go back to the hotel and swim in the pool and make love after we dance together with swords. Let's do that now and think about war later." I took his hand, placing it on my lap.

"Done."

After we saw the Fae safely home, we went to the hotel and did just that.

Chapter 29

The next morning Aedan and I toured the new house. Not only was it entirely under roof now, but much of the interior was also done too. Drywall finishers smoothed mud, and stonemasons worked on the many fireplaces throughout the house. There had to be sixty people working on finishing it. The kitchen and bathrooms had tilers elbow to elbow, and only Aedan's rooms were devoid of workers. Our rooms. Not his. Ours. He had asked me to live in this beautiful monstrosity of a house, and I said yes. Kind of.

"I can't believe how big you made just these rooms alone, Aedan. It's nuts. You don't need all this, surely. It's like a house in a house," I said, taking in the layout.

"We need this space, Liomsa. I plan on working here as much as I can. My House is much larger now, with all of the Baltimore vampires in it. I assure you; this space will not be wasted."

"If you say so." I turned, walking down the hall to what would be the bedroom. His. Mine. Ours. Whatever. The sound of my shoes echoed through the empty space. French doors opened out to the highest wrap-around porch, and I could see my house and barn from them. Jeremy rode Foxie in the field, and Sarah stood watching. I smiled at the sight and turned to find Aedan on his knee with a box in his outstretched hand.

Sunlight streamed through the window, catching the highlights of his molasses-colored hair, making them gleam. He took a big breath he didn't need and turned his gorgeous, whiskey-colored eyes to mine.

"Marry me, Liomsa. Do me the honor and grant me the privilege of being your husband and having you for a wife. Forever is not long enough for us to share all we have to offer. I know this."

I took a step forward, my hand flying to my mouth before I could stop it. My gut tightened in visceral fear of what he was asking of me.

"Aedan, I. I just. I love you. God, do I love you. I have never loved anything more than I love you."

"Then say yes," he said, not moving from his knee. He held the ring up like an offering.

It was stunning. A huge ruby surrounded by perfect, glittering diamonds. It was a match to the necklace and earrings he bought me, and I knew. I knew he had bought this ring then, with this end in mind. All those months ago, he had known, been so sure. So why was I so afraid to say yes now? And I was afraid to say yes but terrified even more of saying no. I said nothing, just stared with my hand over my mouth and my eyes wet with emotion.

He came to me, placing his arms around me. "Do not say no. Say nothing, but do not say no."

"I won't say no, Aedan. I'm just afraid to say yes, too."

He kissed me, wrapping me tightly in his arms so that I melted into him. After the kiss had weakened my knees, he pulled away, taking my hand. He slipped the ring over the fourth digit on my left hand. I could do nothing but stare at it. Then I met his eyes and saw the depth of emotion flowing from them.

"I love you, Aedan." I offered him a small smile, letting my own emotions flow through our bond and show on my face.

"And I love you." He took my hand and walked me through the construction and back into the warm spring sun. We held hands and crossed the distance to my house. Our house. Our other house.

He drove back to the city to work, and I went inside to ready the clinic.

I kept the ring on.

My thoughts were interrupted by the flow of magic. It rippled and shimmered in the air, and I readied my power, only to drop it when the Goddess stepped into view.

"Daughter mine," she said, smiling at me. "Give me your hand."

I did.

"He is praying that you will say yes to him as we speak," she said, fingering the ruby in the ring. "He forgets that he prays to his mother while he prays to his Goddess," she chuckled softly. "I feel your uncertainty and your fear, but I also feel your love. I came to offer you an alternative."

"Alternative to what?" I asked.

"An alternative to forever," she said, stepping back from me, letting go of my hand. "Bind with him in the way of our people- in the old way and not the new. Give him a year and a day of your life. Live as one during that time and then decide if it should be forever. I know you love him, and he loves you more than is reasonable. Give him just a small amount of time and see where that leads." She gave me a soft smile, her eyes begging me. She loved her son so very much. It showed in every expression that moved across her face.

"A handfasting?" I asked, surprised.

"Yes. A handfasting. A year and a day that is all. Take a chance on forever. You have the freedom to decide in the end." She pulled me to her, hugging me before she disappeared in a glimmer of magic.

I saw patients the rest of the day, going through the motions and not much else. The clinic wasn't busy, which was a good thing. My mind was occupied elsewhere.

Noah called and asked for ten VID vaccines. I drew my own blood and placed it in syringes the same way I did for Alex and his friends. I didn't ask any questions, and neither did he.

When he came right before dark to pick them up, I was closing the doors and planning my night. He looked drawn. Exhausted.

"What can I do?" I asked, handing him the biohazard bag with my syringes in them.

"Nothing. It's okay. The rumblings are deeper than when the vampires came out and much deeper than when you did. I mean, we are animals, truly. Humans are scared that the stray pitbull in their neighborhood is a Shifter. They get that we don't bother them; we've been around forever. Big Foot has more supposed sightings than one of us ever has, but they are scared too. I understand. I just wish it were different. People I've known for years won't talk to me, and I'm losing my position at the hospital." He sighed, scrubbing his hand through his hair.

"I'm sorry, Noah." I pulled him to me in a quick hug. "If you need anything, let me know."

"Just these," he said, waving the bag. "I think we are getting closer to mass production of an actual vaccine, but the clinic downtown has some folks that are on the edge and need it now. Baltimore is ground zero for this thing. It's spreading, but much more slowly, thanks to your help."

"It's nothing; let me know if you need more."

"I will. Fangs being closed right now is helping slow it down. Aiyana didn't have many safety guidelines in place for feedings," he said, walking to his car.

"Grania will be different. Fangs will be better. It may always need to provide that service, but she has already talked about testing and safety requirements." I lingered at his car, resting my hand on his open door.

"I know it will be better. You did an amazing job with her. She's been much more involved in the supernatural community since Aedan's return, and she is quickly becoming a strong leader. You did that. You set her free." He patted my arm and pulled the door closed.

I watched him drive away, knowing Operation BFF was complete. I had done what I set out to do.

Back in the city, I drove to the Four Seasons, thinking about my next move. I couldn't let fear hold me back anymore. In the years since Kyle died, I told myself I was a strong independent woman. That all the men I slept with were my choice, and I was just a woman playing a man's game.

I told myself a lot of things, but the bottom line is I lived my life in fear all those years and wasn't free at all. Fear dictated my every action. Fear of love and intimacy. Fear of commitment and all that it entailed. Fear of actually living beyond one moment. Fear had paralyzed me.

I had freed my best friend, and now it was time to free myself. It's said that what you fear the most will meet you halfway. It was time to walk away from it altogether.

I found Aedan in his office, sitting at the desk, working hard on something. I went to him, going to my knees between his thighs. I pulled him close to me and buried my face in his chest. I inhaled the scent of blood, honey, and fall leaves that was all him, holding it in my lungs and in my mind. I let it out.

"A year and a day, Aedan," I said, pulling away to meet his eyes. "A wise woman suggested we do this the old, old-fashioned way. I would be honored to have you as a husband and to be your wife. I will give you everything I have and all that I am for a year and a day, and then we decide if we can do forever. That's all I can swear to you right now, but if you accept that, then my answer is yes.

He wrapped me up in his arms, burying his nose in my hair. "Thank you," he said. Taking in my scent. We stayed like that until a knock at the front door pulled us apart.

Grania came in and updated us on the Fae as well as some issues that Aedan's new vampires needed to be handled. When she noticed the ring flashing on my hand, she hugged me tightly. The smile on her face said it all. She hugged Aedan too, then left us alone.

We spent that night in each other's arms. Again.

Chapter 30

My parents came home a few days later. They looked amazing. Their skin was sun-kissed, and they moved with a languid grace that conveyed just how good it was for them to be together. They looked peaceful and in love. All of them. It made me happy to see them like that.

There were hugs and long talks between us. My mom cried when she saw my engagement ring, and my dads shot Aedan glares even as they did the bro hug, back-patting thing that men do.

We made plans.

My mother wanted a big wedding, but I did not. The thought was terrifying and not at all what I was after. I've always had an issue with weddings. People plan this one day and put so much money and effort into it, but don't think about the day after. Or the day after that. Marriage isn't one perfect day; it's thousands of days strung together. Some bad, some good. I didn't want to plan one day; I wanted to plan the three hundred and sixty-six that came after. She agreed to consider my request for a small ceremony, and I agreed not to consider anything else.

There were no fireballs, but it was a near thing.

We met with the Fae refugees and made plans with them too. Plans for war and plans for the peace that they prayed would follow. My parents stayed at the house in Westminster, and I stayed in the city with Aedan. We got together every day, enjoying the spring and each other.

I checked the status of Keelin and Finley's pregnancies and found them healthy. Arlie and Aileen became pregnant within a week of being out of Talamh na Sithe, and the pressure to take back their homeland grew heavier. It seemed that Faerie was coming alive again, and these parents wanted their children born in their homeland.

Aramea did not come back, and for that, I was grateful.

Life lulled into a state of waiting.

Aedan came to me after a long day spent with national leaders and my fathers. I knew from the look on his face that something was up. Seriously up.

"When the time comes for war, I plan on fighting against Aramea," he said without preamble.

"So, do I," I said, solidifying the decision in my mind.

"No," he said, running his hand through his hair.

"No? Really?"

"It is not safe for you," he said, gripping his hands to mine.

"War isn't safe for anyone. I'm going. If I can't fight, I'll Heal those who do." I met his fierce eyes with my own.

"It is not your fight, Anamcara," he said, begging me to see it his way.

"It's as much my fight as it is yours, Aedan. You know that. I'm going. Enough said. Do you seriously think Dani gave me a warhorse for a Guardian if she didn't intend for it to go this way? She knew. I know. You know. I may not be a sword fighter, but I am a fighter. I am a True Healer. Our People need me," I said, curling into his body. He held me stiffly, not wanting to admit I was right.

"I need you, too." His body softened, and I knew the fight was over. "You may not be a fighter, but you are a warrior and the strongest, most powerful one that I know."

There's a moment between the thought and the follow through, the option and the decision. Just one. At that moment, choices span before you like a flock of birds in flight, or better yet, branches on a tree, seemingly endless and full of promise, a life in constant flux and flow.

With each choice you make and each path you walk, the tree narrows. Starting at the top of the tree and working your way to the trunk, your route becomes more defined and certain as you go for better or worse.

I was at that crossroads now. The choice was war and fighting one branch of my family with another or sitting it out and waiting for the outcome to be delivered to me in the hands of others and my own path possibly taken from me.

One way led to the possibility of immediate danger, pain, loss, and personal sacrifice, for all of us, not just me. The other, while possibly safer, in the beginning, had a higher risk of failing and was not the path I would choose. Was I afraid of Aramea? Yes, I was.

The depth and horror of Aedan's punishment was not lost on me, and she had promised I would suffer the same fate. A Fae is nothing if not bound to keep a promise, even her. But where Aedan was one strong Fae against many, we were many strong Fae against one. Victory was not guaranteed, but we would fight together.

When the time to fight was upon us, we would do our best to free Talamh na Sithe from the tyrant who condemned the land to death all those years ago.

We met in the restaurant of the hotel, Fae and vampire alike. We ate and drank, laughing together at the stories passed around the table. Food and wine were served by the truckload. Over a hundred strong, we danced and passed around bottles of alcohol.

The women wore dresses, some old-fashioned and some new. Men wore swords in plain sight, and laughter reigned. It was like being taken back in both time and place. It was a case of tonight we drink, for tomorrow we die.

Only tomorrow brought hope. Babies grew in the wombs of once barren women. Vampires and Fae talked and mingled as one race. Never before had a room been filled with so much hope. So much understanding. So much tolerance.

Two hours before dawn, Lann picked my mother up and slung her over his shoulder like a suit jacket, carrying her through the lobby to the elevators beyond. The others followed behind with greedy eyes and clasping hands.

A half an hour later, Paul and Grania gripped hands and snuck out the side door, their eyes only for each other. I wondered about them. Paul had decisions to make. He had aged more since his brush with VID, and Grania had not aged and never would. I wondered which path they would take.

Not long after they left, I felt the fire start in my center and burn brighter by the second until it was so hot, I thought I would die from it. I saw Aedan across the room, and our eyes met; I left the conversation I was in without explanation and walked to him. Seeing only him. Wanting only him. Power leaked out of me and spread through the room like ripples on a lake after a stone has been thrown in. The room settled into silence as I stalked toward my prey. I gave him a half-grin and excused him from whatever conversation he was having with whomever he was having it with. I took his hand in mine, pulling him behind me. I needed him. Now.

I had his clothes off in our private elevator, cameras be damned. My hands, my mouth, my arms wrapped around him on the short ride to our suite. Our lips crashed against each other, fighting for dominance with each press of our tongues. He did not seem to mind.

We fell through the doors, and they closed softly behind us. We made it to the glass wall overlooking the Inner Harbor, where he pinned my naked ass against the glass and entered me fiercely. He slowed, his lips softening on mine, bringing a pained moan from me and a soft glow to my skin. He stopped moving, kissing down the line of my throat and to the hollow of my neck, the place he loved most.

My heartbeat pounded in my ears, and I was left wanting while he touched every part of me. He could reach with his mouth, his own body hard and still inside mine. He did not drink, even though I begged him to; pleaded with him and clawed his back. He teased himself to the brink, and when he moved again, there was nothing gentle about it.

I prayed the glass was shatterproof. We had already broken all the furniture in the bedroom. More than once. I didn't want to end up in the pool below our window, still tangled in his embrace. The smell of wine mingled with his natural scent, and I wondered how many bottles he had downed. I could feel his intoxication.

He dragged my head back by my hair, bending my neck at an uncomfortable angle, but it heightened my senses, and I came hard against him, dragging him down with me.

Afterward, we lay on the carpet in front of the fireplace and waited for dawn to come. He had not fed from me, and he didn't need to; I was the one who had wanted it so badly. We watched the sunrise through the floor to ceiling windows, and I wondered when the last time was that he watched the sunrise. Our bond had made him that much stronger.

Where once the dawn came and dragged him away. Now he chose to sleep or not. I watched him watch the horizon change colors, from gray to yellow, then pink to blue. His eyes were heavy with thoughts and emotions I could guess at but not understand. Only when the sun was completely above the water line did we walk up the stairs to our room and sleep the sleep of the fulfilled, the sleep of the sated, and the sleep of the righteous together. Always together.

Sharilyn spent most of her early years on the Grand Strand of South Carolina, annoying local police officers and probably pretty much everyone else. She graduated from the University of South Carolina and now lives on a small farm outside of Morgantown, WV, with various farm animals, her husband, and three kids who love to annoy her. (Karma is a bitch).

She writes Urban Fantasy, Fairy Tales, and Omegaverse novels. She loves showing Quarter horses, trail riding, reading, and being annoyed by her kids. If she is missing, check for her horse trailer. If it is missing, no worries, she'll be back. Probably.

Healer Series:
Cerridwen's Tears
Healer
House of Fire
The Scarlet Heron
The Flame Keeper
Goddess Bound

The Eight Series:
Airmed
Ravena
Teagan

Omegas of the New South:
The Omega Rule
The Omega Challenge
An Alpha's Grace

Follow Sharilyn on Facebook, Instagram, Twitter, Goodreads, and her plain old website.

www.sharilynskye.com